The Consequent Touch of McHenry Feathers

R. P. Poe

"If we wait for the moment when everything, absolutely everything is ready, we shall never begin."

-Ivan Turgenev

"And I, too, went on my way,
the winning and losing, or what
Is sometimes of all things the worst, the not knowing
One thing from the other, nor knowing
How the teeth in Time's jaw all snag backward"

-Robert Penn Warren, American Portrait: Old Style
Now and Then, Poems 1976-1978

For my father

One

World went dark.

His father long since gone but rarely there even before, passed into smoke and ash by alchemy of cremation, he walked the broken sidewalk a man yet a boy still, with a boy's acceptance of what is given without thought to meaning or consequence. Yet also a man, with full burden of all handed a boy in a fatherless home when he comes of age, his mother and grandmother looking to him, holding out hope he will break from the inevitable past, the circular path of once known. He strode the shadowed street alone, live oaks reaching, stretching, black in the damp air.

His father coming at him out of memory with 'lazy meskins never learn how to drive worth a damn; ought to send 'em all back' and then gone before indigo shadows again swallowed him whole, limbs arcing overhead, ancient, mute, silhouetted by the heavy morning light. Turning his eyes aside as the clay-colored form approached, thinking not laziness but robbery, sloth in alternate form, he tensed until the other passed and then he breathed again the stale air of once heard and still remembered, tattooed but unseen.

Beyond the sliding shadows buildings topped the ragged trees, the red brick bell tower among them calling out its twelve notes of quarter hour in sets of four. He quickened his pace. The tilted sidewalk, rent by wayward roots, patient, relentless, shortened as he neared the campus flats that stood just across the leaf-littered street. Then the broad trees fell away all at once, the sky opening, cloud-strewn, filled with light as he sprinted across the road and up the narrow drive, stopping before a tall, windowless warehouse, its sliding doors open and already busy with men in blue work shirts and trousers.

Sweat slid between his shoulder blades. He stopped, taking a breath and then approaching the wide

1

doorway where a man the color of plums, old but not old, hair half to gray, angular face sprinkled here and there with stubble, stood just inside the entrance, a veil of blue smoke floating about his head. The old man squinted, studied him like a cat might, unspeaking, disinterested, with a cloudy eye that revealed little of consequence. The man held his crooked arm at angle, iron-thin, muscular, tense as a drawn bow, a hand-rolled cigarette squeezed between thumb and forefinger hovering inches from his lips. The other hand rested on his bony hip. The man pulled on the misshapen cigarette, letting smoke drift from his mouth and past his eyes before asking if he was looking for anyone in particular. When the man said 'here' it sounded to him like 'he-uhn', boy like bu-oyh, but the man's voice seemed cordial enough, almost formal, and he soon left at the man's direction for the department office.

He walked the broad driveway lined with truck and flatbed, lifeless white beneath bluish lights, some old and scarred with rough use, some gleaming new, as faces all shades less white stopped talk, stopped work to watch him pass. A cackle of laughter escaping the crowd like a trap-caught crow sent the burn of blood across his face in a searing wave. He glanced left, then right, vengeance twisting his throat into bitter spasm. Split lip, bruised knuckle, bloodied nose, the mad-dog world rising up on all sides flashed in and out of his daydream until his grandmother's quavering voice silenced the blood with one word, familiar, quiet, laced with long known and often seen. No toleration for intolerance, she named his father as seen and truly was to the then-boy's face so as a man he again felt cold shame pass through his chest, showing his flaw as anger and anger as flaw.

He could see them both now, his mother at the broad window facing the back yard and his grandmother's small cabin-like home beyond, hands above the porcelain sink of soap-covered plates, drain board of just-rinsed glasses, above them a clear green vase of climbing ivy flanked by African violet and pansy. His grandmother seated nearby, reading the daily paper out loud, or Tolstoy, even Bronte if the mood was right, through rimless bifocals.

The scene faded as he stood before the dim office, breathing air laced with telltale exhaust, gasoline, paint thinner, before pushing open the office door. Behind a green metal desk left from the last war or earlier, the boulder form in white shirt not blue hunched over a pad and scribbled, horn-rimmed glasses flashing reflected light. He stood beneath the humming fluorescence, the sound of men arriving for work barely audible above the man's ragged breath. He waited as the man hunched, scribbled, then the broad head rose, eyes blinking, jerked from him, beyond to the door and back before nodding him to the chair. The man cleared his throat, spit into an unseen waste basket and turned to him, his mouth forming the first word.

I see here your name is Glenolden Spencer. What do they call you, son?

I go by Noll, Mr. Breaks.

The coloreds here call me Elgy, so I guess you can do the same unless you have an objection to it. I'd understand if you did and wanted to be treated different from them boys.

No, that'll be fine.

You're sure you want this job? It's hard physical labor every day.

I'm sure. I need this job.

I understand your father has passed and you're the man at home. So it's just you and your mother, then?

My grandmother lives out back of us, me and my mother, in a little house of her own.

Well then, you'll be working with Feathers.

What will I do with them?

What?

What will I do with the feathers?

Feathers is a colored feller, and a no-good lazy one at that.

I'll be working with a black man?

Call him what you want.

My father would've called him worse.

Sounds like I would've gotten on with your father but we've got to watch what we say around these boys. If they get stirred up, they can be trouble.

So, I'll be working with a black guy name of Feathers?

You need to understand something, son. You'll be the only white man in the department except for me and you won't see much of me. You still want the job?

Yes sir, my mother lost her job so I'm in need of work, even if it's working for a black man.

You'll be working alongside him. You'll keep an eye on him and let me know what he's up to. You can do that, can't you?

You're the boss and I'll do what you say.

These colored boys are as bad as the bean-eaters when it comes to getting out of work. You know what I mean, don't you son? Sure you do. Feathers is a bad influence on them all. He's got some fool idea he's better than me and you. He claims he has a whole house full of books but I don't believe it. Speak of the devil, here he comes now. Don't you let on what I told you.

-The door opened and the man who earlier had given him directions ambled in.

Feathers, this is the new worker I told you about. He goes by Noll and he'll need you to show him the ropes around here. He's got the license and can drive a double-axel truck. Now take him along and get right on setting up for the big shindig at the President's house. I'm going to go make sure them other boys have cleared out the vines by the reflecting pool.

- Elgy walked out the door.

Do I call you Feathers?

4

My name is McHenry Feathers. I go by Hen.

Hen Feathers? You're joshing me.

Looky here son, I put up a hay bale of trouble over that name. Don't you start off wrong with me now.

Alright.

No sir, you show me some respect and call me by my right name.

I will. I mean, I didn't mean any disrespect... Hen.

Alright then, sit down so I can learn you. I won't work with a man until I learnt him.

Learn me? Why do you want to do that?

You're a white man. I'm a black man and I got to work alongside you. Now I'm not happy about it but if I'm going to be working with you I have to learn you. Otherwise, we might have trouble.

I'm no trouble, long as I'm treated right.

That's right. A man can treat another man with respect if he learns him.

How do you learn someone, then?

Well, we have ourselves a sit-down talk. Sit and tell me your name again.

I'm Noll Spencer.

I knew a man once named Spencer, served with him in the war but he wasn't from here so I don't suppose you'd know him.

Probably not.

Tell me about you, Noll Spencer.

What do you want to know?

Everybody got a mama and a daddy. Tell me about them.

I live not far from here. My grandmother lives with us in a cabin behind the house. She came there after my grandfather died. The cabin is old and was built for servants. That's about it.

You're not much of a talker, Noll.

Well, my mother taught high school until she lost her job.

5

Uh-huh, I could tell your daddy was gone.

What?

Your daddy's not gone?

He is.

See what I say? I could tell.

You guessed. You couldn't tell.

Sure I could. Looky here, I know something about growing up without a daddy. My own daddy ran away soon as I was born.

My father didn't run away, he died. I'll bet you didn't know that, did you?

Still gone. How do you all pay the bills with no man about the house?

How'd you get so nosy?

We're just talking here, Noll.

I don't know if I want to tell all this to a...

Looky here, don't you start throwing names around or you won't last. We all got to work together so you better learn to get along with men not like you.

My grandmother tutors college students.

Things must be tight.

We're getting by.

But your mother's a teacher and your grandmother too?

My grandmother is seventy-eight and still tutors college algebra.

Uh-huh, I could tell you come from teachers.

How could you tell? I just told you is all.

No sir, you got that learnt look about you and in your words but you don't act uppity. Some folks do. My aunt was a teacher but she never acted like she was better than other folks. World needs more teachers, that's a fact.

It seems like all I've ever done is go to school.

Why are you here when you should be in college your own self?

I have to work.

Not in a place like this you don't. You got to get that college degree. You don't want to get stuck here. Listen to me son. Now, I'm not a believer myself but my granny used to say God helps them that help themselves.

I don't need anybody's help or anybody's advice either.

Ha! Was I preaching again? I get to going and don't know when to stop. But your education is important. You can't just let yourself...

You don't believe in God?

That's right. The meanness of this life cured me of that.

I feel like I've spent half my life at church. My grandfather even has a room there named after him.

Oh, I was raised in the church too. My granny would take it no other way. She used to say there's no word except for the word of God. But what I saw in the war and what I saw after that, the way we were treated all those years and still are, cured me of the church. I decided a man's word was what mattered and God would have to be one mean son of a...

- A young man rushed through the door.

What are you doing here, boy?

Where's that Elgy, Hen?

He's gone over to check on work at the reflecting pool, where you ought to be right now. Why are you here instead of there? You're going to get yourself fired.

Already done that.

What are you telling me, Ranse?

Elgy pushed me too far yesterday so I got right up in his face. He turned white as a ghost but he didn't say a thing, just left.

So, why you think you're fired?

I came in early to talk to him but he sent his man Lio out to the street, tell me I'm fired and can't even come on the property.

7

You're looking for trouble, Ranse. I can see it in your face.

Naw.

Why are you here then?

I got my reasons.

You got your reasons. Well then, tell me what you got your jacket on for. It's already hot out there. Old Hen's got to wonder why you keep your hand in your pocket. What you got in there, boy?

I got nothing.

Go on now, show me what you got.

You mean this knife here? It's just from my kitchen is all. I forgot I had it.

You forgot, huh? What're you up to, boy?

I got to go.

That's right. You go on home and stay there, you hear? I'll see you when I get off from work. I'll be doing my own talking to that Elgy.

This is my business, old man.

Don't you backtalk me. You get on home now.

It's my business but I'll go.

- He walked out the door.

Young man always looking for trouble where he don't need to. That Ranse is too hot-tempered for his own good. When he gets mad he stops using his head and he just acts. A man's got to use his head in this world, especially if he's a black man.

What was he going to do?

I hate to think what he might do with that temper of his.

My father had a temper. He's been gone a long time but I remember that.

He knock you around, son?

My mother too.

And leave you to remember him that way.

I'd just as soon forget him.

Think on that, son. Not too many men are all bad, even ones with a temper. You might can take some good · away from him if you look for…

What's that yelling?

Lordy, it sounds like Ranse. Come with me, son.

-They rushed through the door.

Hen's round head jerked side to side, rocking, hitching birdlike with every other step as Noll let go the door and hurried to follow, metal blinds clattering behind like frightened geese. Hen's thin hair flashed bits of silver beneath the humming lights. Beyond, Ranse stood facing a short blue-shirted man a yard outside the yawning door, red-clay skin of one thin against the gunmetal other. Glints of knife blade skittered across the smooth floor like gunshots.

Noll moved up beside Hen as they came upon the two men and he looked from one to the other, his circular past sliding up under consciousness, dim cognition, unacknowledged thought, coming to him again as sure as planets move about the sun. Like animals, he mused, with no regard for civil due, law, expectation but mere base instinct surging under brown skin and black. Go ahead and cut, kill, he muttered under his breath, the loss of mindless beast no loss at all.

He stood by as Hen surveyed the standoff, cat-like, his cloudy eye jumping here, there, emotionless, silent but for his ragged breath. He coughed long, hard, guttural so that the two men turned looking as he spat and wiped his mouth with the bony back of a hand, mumbling to himself, before they again faced each other. The square clay-colored man shrank before the rangy bulk of Ranse. Hen's voice then calm, emotionless, oddly deep for one so thin yet firm and without hesitation, sounded against the metal walls. Talking reason, deliberation, he sidled up to Ranse, a gnarled hand up as if to halt movement, suspend the moment.

Ranse cocked his head, hearing the voice, turning to Hen, Noll just behind. His eyes red, dilated, wild with threat, locked onto Noll. Hen looked from one to the other, the slightest shake of his head toward Noll nearly imperceptible. Ranse turned back to the little man. No contest there, Noll thought. The man stood arms out, ready for flight, sweat staining the blue shirt, the dark spreading across his lean chest. Noll could see he wanted no trouble but had found it as Elgy's messenger. Noll started to turn and leave them to it but stopped, instead taking a step toward the three men, hearing his own voice before realizing he had spoken.

Leave him.
-Two words enough but the third out before even the sound reached his ears.
Boy.
-Ranse turned back to him, eyes narrow, knuckles stretched against the knife handle, moving toward him in heavy bulk. Noll had seen the look, the intent to harm, make right all humiliation, all defeat, trade one's own pain for the pain of another. His father's eyes flashed before him, dangerous, violent, determined, and he readied himself. Then Hen stepped into the space between them, hand to Ranse's chest, just a touch and then held there. Angle iron thin, all bone and sinew yet unbending he held his hand still and with the other reached for the knife, palm up as he spoke, calm, level.

Boy meant nothing by it, Ranse. Word slipped from him like a dropped glass, regretted before the sound of his voice even gone from this place. Give me the knife, son. Give me the knife and go on home.

What do I do, then? My mother and aunt and sister, they count on this paycheck. What do I tell them? What I did was wrong but that Elgy, he deserved worse. I'll talk to him and get back my job. He'll give it back to me and if he won't...

No, Ranse. There'll be no harm to nobody today, you hear?

It's not right.

I know that, son. There's no fairness to it but Rogelio and Noll aren't Elgy. Lio only did what Elgy told him to. You know he didn't like it but he did it because he had to. You expect him to get his own self fired too when he has kids to feed? You have only yourself.

My mother and sister, aunt too.

They stopped being children long ago, Ranse. They'll be alright.

They count on me, Hen.

Sure they do, boy. So, you get yourself on home and we'll work it out when I get there.

-Ranse's eyes flashed once at Noll, then he took the knife blade in his fingers, put the handle in Hen's palm and walked out the door, disappearing down the tree-lined sidewalk. Lio turned and vanished around the corner without a word. Noll turned to where Hen stood, squinting at him.

Why'd you go and aggravate that boy? I nearly lost my touch with him.

It's not my fault he's a dumb jungle...

There you go again with your racist talk.

I'm not a racist.

Sound like a racist to me.

You're the racist, accusing me like that. It's not your place to...

Maybe you'd like me to call you a bigot instead.

You can't talk to me like that, you black...

You learnt that from your daddy, I bet. You're bound to turn out just like him the way you're going.

How would you know?

Seen it before.

I won't ever be like him, not ever. You have no right to say that. You don't know me.

11

You're right about that, boy. I don't know a thing about you and you don't know a thing about me. So we got to wait and see. That make sense to you?

I guess it does.

We won't get anywhere working against each other. We already got enough working against us in this place. What you just saw ought to tell you. You understand what I'm saying?

I think so.

You got to leave all you heard outside of here, make up your own mind about people. What I do know of you, I believe you can do that.

I didn't mean to say what I did.

I could see that, son. I'm not a man to lie.

It seemed wrong, Ranse against such a small man. I didn't want to see him get hurt.

You think I was trying to keep Lio from getting hurt?

I didn't like the unfairness of it is all.

You got it wrong, boy. I was protecting Ranse. He's big, I can see that for myself but he's just a kid. Lio grew up on the streets and knows how to fight. He wouldn't hurt Ranse if he could help it but when there's a knife you never can tell. You and Ranse is another story.

Well, I could see you stepped in for me and I'm sorry you had to. I just heard the word said that way too many times.

You mean your daddy?

That's the way he was. He died a long time ago but it's like he's still here.

How long has it been?

Over a year.

Son, don't you know a year or two is no time at all when you lose someone?

It seems a long time and then it doesn't.

Noll, the past follows you just like it does me and Ranse and Lio. What happened is part of you no care if you

12

like it or not. What matters is whether you let the past be who you *are* or who you *were*. You can decide that for yourself.

I'm not sure I know how.

Treat a man with respect. Take him at his word and you'll make a start at it.

What will happen with Ranse?

Don't know but that boy, he's all twisted up. I have me a bad feeling about it, a real bad feeling. Now, we better get on to work. We got ourselves a hot one today.

Two

Gray clouds, their edges ragged, fraying, skimmed treetops, buildings beyond, as he walked toward home, his legs heavy after moving furniture all afternoon from storage to a newly-built building on the edge of campus. He turned the corner and crossed the empty street to the broken sidewalk beyond, now lost in shade. Houses fronting the road stared back through darkened windows, unresponsive, vacant, their deep porches gaping, death-like, as if caught in permanent surprise. He turned his eyes, thinking of his father.

In the weeks since he had started work Elgy had badgered him on a daily basis for anything that might incriminate Hen, an extended lunch break, a job poorly done, a negative word. A month before he would have been glad to oblige but Elgy's expectations had become oppressive, more so with each day. As much as he tried not to Noll had found that he admired Hen, his integrity, his candor, even liked him, an opinion that had grown in direct proportion to his dislike of Elgy. His expected role as snitch weighed on him but he put it out of mind as he reached the walkway to his house. He knew he could never let on to his mother that there was a problem. He steeled himself as he climbed the porch stairs.

The moment he stepped through the door he sensed the change, dark, oppressive, the air inert, overfilled with quiet stillness. His grandmother sat in one corner, a book in her lap, a single lamp above her head, looking at him with a finger to her lips. He knew the routine. He stopped, bent and untied his work boots, steeping onto the wood floor in his dingy socks. His grandmother stood and walked to where he waited, placing an arthritic hand on his chest and patting his cheek. She nodded toward the kitchen and he followed her across the room and through the entrance without a word, closing the door behind them. She sat and faced him.

14

You look tired, Noll.

I'm alright. She's having one of her spells again, isn't she?

Yes, it's the worst I've ever seen her. She wouldn't get out of bed this morning no matter what I tried and, believe me, I tried everything.

I'd rather see her talking nonstop and buying everything in sight than this.

Don't say that, Noll. You know she nearly burned down the house the last time she was like that, staying up all night and cooking at all hours.

She decided she was going to be a chef. What's wrong with that?

She could never cook worth a hoot, that's what. They call it a delusion and it goes with the territory. Anyway, she's at the other extreme now. I'm not sure which is worse. Either way she worries me.

Did something happen to set her off?

Good Lord, Noll, don't you know your father's birthday was yesterday?

I guess I forgot. How could I do that? Maybe if I'd said something to her…

Listen to your Gannie, Noll. This has been brewing for a good while and that day coming along as it did just set her off, as you say. Neither of us could protect her from that.

Should we call a doctor?

She refuses to see one. You'd better go see her. I'll fix you something to eat after you're back.

I'm not hungry.

I'll find something you'll like.

-He ambled through the doorway and down the dark hallway, yellowed photos of faces he never knew askew along one wall, unsmiling, stiffly posed, a plantation home in Mississippi looming behind them. Hardwood planks creaked beneath his feet, familiar, somehow

15

comforting as he pushed open the door to his mother's room. He could see her form in the dim light stretched beneath the bedspread, rigid, corpse-like. He stopped and stared at her, for an instant fearing she was dead, unable to catch his breath before she stirred, finally turning to face him. He breathed again and stepped toward her.

Ben, is that you?

Mom it's me, Noll.

What? Who? Noll, are you there?

I'm here.

Oh Noll, for a second I thought your father had come home. How could I think that, Noll?

It must have been a dream.

Yes, I must have been dreaming. But I almost thought I could see him standing right where you are. He was wearing the pink shirt I loved so much. I wish you had a shirt that color, Noll. You'd look just like him.

A pink shirt? Are you serious? My friends would think I'm gay.

You're not gay are you Noll? You could tell me if you were. I mean, I understand how nice it is to kiss a man.

Mom, that's disgusting. I don't want to kiss any men.

Your father was a good kisser. I miss him so much, Noll.

I know.

I think I'm going to cry. I'm sorry, Noll. I know it's hard for you too. Let me look at you.

I'm alright, mom. Come have some dinner. I'll fix whatever you like.

I think I'll stay here for now. Anyway, I have no appetite.

You need to eat.

I'll eat later.

I'll bring you something, then.

Do you know how much you look like him?

Like who?

16

Like your father, of course. Noll, you can be so slow sometimes I have to wonder how you ever made it through school.

So, I look like him?

When I first met him, he was only a few years older than you are now. He had that thick hair and those deep-set eyes. His eyes were blue, not green like yours but you have his strong jaw and that lovely nose. He was so sweet to me then.

That's hard to imagine.

Why would you say that, honey?

You know how he could be. Remember what he did to that lamp, the one your grandmother gave you? We kept finding pieces of it for months after.

Oh Noll, he wasn't always like that. He had a hard life growing up in Mississippi, losing his mother so early like he did. He didn't have the sweet family I had. Mother and father never had a cross word between them, and they provided for us girls in every way. Your father had to go to work before he turned twelve, and without a woman to soften him, his father became mean as a snake.

Sounds like an excuse to me.

He could be very tender.

Yeah, and he could be mean as a snake too.

Noll, don't talk about him like that. He was your father and now he's gone from us. Can't you say something good about him?

Do you want me to lie?

Oh, now you've got me crying again and you won't want to have a thing to do with me.

I'm sorry, mom. Forget what I said.

I don't mean to keep crying like this, Noll. I don't know what's wrong with me.

Maybe you should see a doctor.

A doctor? No, I think not. Why would you say that? You can be so unkind, Noll.

Maybe it would help.

17

He'll just want me to take that terrible medication again. I just need to rest, is all. I'm so tired all the time, Noll.

Then I'd better go.

Oh, I almost forgot. This envelope is for you.

Where did it come from?

Ginger dropped it off. Noll, she's so beautiful and so very polite. You really should spend more time together. You're still a couple, aren't you?

Uh, well sure, I guess so. Listen, you rest now and I'll check on you later.

Aren't you going to open the letter?

What? Oh no, I'd better go so you can rest.

Yes, I am so tired. Just a little nap and I'll be fine.

-He walked back into the kitchen and stood, fingering the envelope and then stuffing it in his pocket.

You do look worn out, Noll. I fixed you garlic toast with parmesan cheese just the way you like it. Sit down and tell me about your work.

It's just a job, Gannie. There's nothing much else to say about it.

Tell me about the men you work with. Do they treat you well?

They treat me alright, no different than anyone else that I can tell. That might seem surprising since there aren't any white people in the department except for me and the boss, but I don't think much about it. One guy has been to prison yet he's the friendliest one of all. One of the smartest can't read or write. His last name is Ordaz and he signs his name with a big circle.

Sounds like an interesting bunch of characters.

Don't laugh but I work with a man named Hen Feathers. His real name is McHenry but he goes by Hen.

McHenry Feathers? Is he a black man, Noll?

He is.

Where is he from?

18

I don't know, around here I guess. Why are you asking?

That's such an unusual name. Wait here, I have something to show you.

-She left the room, returning a moment later carrying a frayed photo album. She opened the book and thumbed through it before holding it up to the light.

See this man? Now, he died many years ago but his name is McHenry Feathers.

Where is this?

This is Glenolden, the family farm near Vicksburg. My father was named after the place, as you were. It was quite a large plantation. Mr. Feathers was the foreman of a crew that worked the cotton and rice fields.

They were slaves?

Lord no, they were hired hands. The farm was much too large for the family to work by themselves. The workers had their own farms that they leased from the family but to be honest the conditions weren't much better than when there were slaves.

Didn't most plantations have slaves?

Glenolden did have slaves before the war.

Our family really owned slaves?

Your mother considers it impolite to talk about that part of the family's past. There's even a rumor that my great grandfather was Mr. Feathers' father.

So, if Hen is a descendent of Mr. Feathers then we could be related?

Great God Almighty, Noll, don't let your imagination run away with you.

But you can't say for sure we're not, can you?

For goodness sakes Noll, don't ever say that to your mother. The mere thought would send her right over the edge. Speaking of your mother, how did she seem to you?

You were right, Gannie. She's worse than before.

Any chance of getting her up and out of there?

19

I don't see how. I had no luck when I brought up seeing a doctor.

Did she tell you the doctors are trying to poison her?

She didn't go that far.

She was convinced of it the last time.

I was hoping she would get better for good.

You can never tell about these things but such difficulties do run in the family.

What do you mean?

Did your mother never tell you about her aunt Eugenia?

Aunt Eugenia?

Well, I'm not surprised she didn't mention it, the way your mother avoids unpleasant subjects. Eugenia is what you might call the crazy aunt. She's older than me but still living. She's an accomplished artist and has a house down near the coast, where the river meets the Gulf. You went there with me when you were a little one but I guess you don't remember. It's a beautiful spot and Eugie is not quite as crazy as your mother thinks, mostly just eccentric and as independent as they come.

I do remember a big white house on a bay.

It's a shame your mother never took you to see her, Noll. She's a bit of a hermit and can be ornery but I'd bet Eugenia would welcome you once she got used to the idea of having a visitor. Good or bad, she's a part of your family and your mother was wrong to keep her from you.

Mom thought I was dad when I first went in to see her. She went on about what a good man he was.

He was my son-in-law and I loved him in spite of his ways but good is not the word I'd choose to describe him. That's how your mother gets when she's like this, crying over the past as if she wants it back the way it was, angry rages and all. Deep down, she knows that sort of thinking is nonsense but she can't help herself.

Wasn't there anything good about him, Gannie?

20

Sure there was, Noll. He worked and took care of you and your mother even when times were lean. He was a determined man. There were people he genuinely cared about and they will tell you what a sweet man he could be. But that temper of his got in the way.

I heard people at the funeral talk about how kind he was and I didn't know what to make of it.

He could put on the charm, say he'd be nicer and you'd believe it too, even carry on intelligent conversations with no fireworks for weeks at a time. But that anger, that meanness would always return.

Do I remind you of him, Gannie?

No and you get that idea right out of your head.

Not at all?

You're handsome like he was, and as smart but other than that you're nothing alike.

Sometimes I think I am, like I still carry part of him around whether I want to or not.

You are your own person, Noll. You have to believe me. You're not him.

But people change, Gannie. What if I change?

We're all a work in progress Noll, even people as old as me. And there are no guarantees. But you have control over where you go from here. Now, a little of your father's determination could prove helpful when times get tough and one thing you can count on is that they will sooner or later. In fact, I'm afraid we're heading into one of those times right now.

What will we do, Gannie?

I don't know, Noll. I suppose we'll try to get through it as best we can.

Three

Morning lay thick beneath the reaching oaks, their limbs blackened, muscular, the air clinging to his skin like oil as he climbed out of the truck and followed Hen through the glass doors of a red brick building, a blast of cool air rushing past his already sweat-stained shirt before the doors swung back into place. The smell of book covers and old paper replaced the exhaust-laced air that had followed them in. Already waiting outside the massive double doors of the president's office, the other men waited, milling about, their faces all shades save white, tense, distracted, uncomfortable with the formality, the implied power, the extravagance of the entryway. They hugged the wall, their voices a low murmur.

One of the crew, a man younger than the rest, glared at Noll as he approached the group. He had yet to meet the man but knew he'd been hired as Ranse's replacement. Noll frowned back into his sand-colored face, making no effort to hide his dislike, seeing not a man but his lesser, alien, an intruder from outside his realm. His father's voice came at him again, prodding, goading, 'they come here, take our jobs, foul our neighborhoods; don't take any disrespect, Noll; stand up for yourself or they'll take over'. He stepped toward the man, the anger rising in him, forceful, heedless. The man sneered, looking at the men on either side before he spoke.

You're sort of pale to be on this crew, huh home-boy?

You're sort of brown to be talking to me like that, huh new-boy?

You act big for a little man.

I back up what I say.

You're dreaming, homey.

We'll see.

-Noll felt a hand on his shoulder and he turned, meeting Hen's eyes for an instant before looking away, his teeth clenched, face burning. Hen whispered as he led him to the other side of the room.

You got to undo your fists, son. You don't want to go this way, I know you don't. I've been working round you every day for nearly a month now and this is not what I've seen. I hear somebody else's words from your mouth. I know you don't want this.

He can't talk to me like that.

He's new and he's scared, that's all. You got to forget about it.

-The door swished open behind Noll and the men stepped back toward the wall, facing the floor as they milled about. Elgy approached Hen, looking from him to the men and back.

We got trouble here, Hen. What is it? Don't lie to me.

We had ourselves a little misunderstanding but no trouble, Elgy. There's no need to worry yourself about it now.

-Elgy grabbed Noll by the shoulder, pulling him to the corner.

I saw you through the window faced off with the new man.

It was nothing.

Didn't look like nothing to me.

I don't like his attitude is all.

We have so many wetbacks now they think they own the place. The coloreds think so too. I don't need another problem like Ranse. You think the new man is going to be trouble?

I wouldn't know, Elgy.

Are any of the other men in on it? They giving you trouble?

No, they treat me alright.

23

I warned you about being the only white man on the crew. Those boys always stick with their own kind. I can get rid of that new man without cause if I need to.

Elgy, it was just a misunderstanding like Hen said.

No, I have a feeling about this one. I don't like those gang tattoos. I think I'd better let him go.

But they'll think it's my fault, Elgy. If the men start thinking that way I *will* have trouble.

No, I think I'd better...

-The big double doors flew open and two men and a woman in dark suits hurried toward the exit, talking rapidly, giving the men they passed through no more notice than the furniture. A small man wearing a white shirt and red tie followed them out, squinting into the sunlight and running a hand across his bald head. He stopped at the threshold, surveying the room as if seeing it for the first time, nodding toward the men as they eyed him with furtive glances. As he turned, his eyes fell on Hen.

Hen, I'm glad to see you again.

Hello, Dr. Wooten.

I've been wanting to speak to you.

-The man turned toward Elgy.

Elgy, we don't need this many men to install bookshelves.

The office didn't specify the job but said you'd need the whole crew.

No, I believe two will do. I'd like Hen and another. Who would you like with you, Hen?

Noll here has been working with me this week. He'll do.

Then the rest of you men come with me. We have a broken pipe down near the fountains that'll take the rest of the day.

-The men followed Elgy out the door. Hen motioned Noll through the double doors and into a walnut paneled office filled with a long table surrounded by leather chairs. In one corner, a wooden desk sat facing a

24

broad window overlooking the tree-shaded commons. A stack of shelving sat at the base of a bare wall, its photos and paintings now scattered across the floor. The president turned to face them, a puzzled look on his face.

You have an unusual name Noll, not one I'm likely to forget.

It's short for Glenolden.

And your last name is Spencer if I remember right. You were in my history class for a short time.

You have a good memory.

I remember you because you weren't afraid to ask questions, good questions too. I'm one of the few college presidents that still choose to teach an undergraduate course so I take notice when I see a promising student. I also notice when someone drops my class. Was I that bad?

No, the Civil War is a special interest of mine. I liked your focus on the events leading to the war rather than the war itself.

The last time Hen was over here we talked for over an hour about that period in history. I believe he's read more on the subject than I have but I suppose you already know that.

No, I didn't. You like history, Hen?

I like books Noll, all kinds of books, some of them history books. Fact is I been meaning to come pay a visit, Dr. Wooten. I finished that book of yours.

And what do you think?

I never knew the Confederacy used the black man as a tool of war, building fortresses, hauling off wounded and the like. And that when the blacks got free they helped the Union, not as soldiers but like those men that drew a map for the captain at Fort Sumter showing the locations of Rebel troops.

Help like that was a key to holding the fort for so long.

And Abe Lincoln was a wily fox when it came to the start of the war, sending a boatload of food to the starving men at the fort so the South would have to make the first move and attack.

That strategy gave him the moral high ground to wage war as a defense of the union rather than an attack on the southern lifestyle, as some called slavery.

I'm disappointed that I missed that part, Dr. Wooten.

Why did you drop the class, Noll?

My mother got sick and I had to go to work.

I'm sorry to hear it. You'll come back, won't you? I meant it when I said you show promise.

I'm not sure if I'm cut out for college.

Noll, listen to me. It's too soon for you to know. Give school another try before you give up on it.

Looky here, Noll. Didn't I tell you the same thing? You got to listen to him now.

Noll, can I loan you a book while you're not in school and have some time to read? You can drop by my office and tell me what you think of it. Will you do that?

Alright, I'll do it.

Now, I have another mind-numbing finance committee meeting to attend. I'd much rather stay here and talk with you. Thanks to you both for installing the shelves.

Noll cradled the book in one hand as he crossed the street bordering the campus, hopping the curb and joining the sidewalk close to where it passed between two massive oaks, their trunks blocking the houses beyond. Though the bell tower called out half past five, the shade still vibrated with heat, the air around him heavy, still. A dull silence followed the bells. As he picked through the broken walkway, movement ahead caught his eye. He looked up to see Ranse's broad form step from behind a tree, glancing, furtive. Noll stopped as Ranse held up a hand.

I'm not here for you. I need to talk to Hen.

He doesn't come this way.

I've been watching and I know he's still at the shop.

Go talk to him then.

You know I can't go over there. I'll get myself arrested.

I heard Lio tell Hen he wouldn't say anything about what happened.

I'm not worried about Lio. Elgy's the one.

That's just talk.

You don't know Elgy. He's got friends in the police. He wants to put me in jail.

But you didn't do anything except stand up to him. They can't arrest you for that.

They can if I go on that campus. Now will you get Hen for me or not?

I've got to get home. I'm already late as it is.

I knew you wouldn't help a black man, white as you are. You're no different from Elgy.

You're wrong, Ranse. I'm nothing like him.

Then get Hen for me.

-Noll looked back across the street to the windowless building, hoping Hen would step through the doors and solve his problem. He turned to Ranse, his mind racing with possible excuses, reasons to decline, but found little as his shame crowded in. His grandmother's voice again came to him and he knew what he would do. He stood for a moment, studying Ranse's gunmetal face and broad nose, his black eyes holding a simple request. I could be the one asking, he thought and what would I do? He nodded and turned back to the street.

Minutes later Noll again hopped the curb, this time followed by Hen. Ranse still stood beneath the two trees as if trapped within the shadows, looking dejected, somehow smaller. He glanced to either side before approaching. Hen eyed him and held up a gnarled finger, stopping him where he stood. Ranse started to speak and Hen silenced him with a wave of his hand.

Looky here, Ranse I can see for myself you're up to no good. Don't hand me more of your excuses, boy. What trouble you get yourself into now?

I got no trouble, at least not so far.

Why are you here then?

I just need a loan, Hen. I take care of some bills past due and I got no more problem.

What criminal you get yourself in debt to?

It's not like that, Hen. I got no job. How am I supposed to pay bills when Elgy fired me?

You know better than to owe when you can't pay.

But I could pay when I had work. What do I do now?

You tell them you'll pay soon as you find yourself a new job.

These debts aren't like that, Hen. You got to pay them.

See what I say, Noll?

Leave him out of this, Hen. You think this is easy for me? You think I want him to hear it, embarrassing as it is? Why are you still here, anyhow?

Stay where you are, Noll. Ranse got himself so mixed up with gangsters and hoodlums he forgot to thank you for coming to get me.

They're businessmen not gangsters, Hen.

Call them what you want, Ranse. I loan you money and before I know it you'll be back for more.

I have a plan, soon as I pay off what I owe.

What plan you got?

I can't say but it's a good one.

You can't tell me your plan?

They said I got to keep it secret so they stay ahead of the competition.

Sounds like a scam to me.

I can make good money and quick too. You'll see.

28

Ranse, how're you ever going to keep yourself out of trouble?

This is different. Will you help me, Hen?

Go ahead on home, Noll. Ranse and me, we won't bother you with our problem anymore today.

-Hen turned, waving Ranse to follow. Noll watched as they ambled down the sidewalk between pools of shade, Hen's head tilting to one side, bobbing as he gestured toward Ranse with a bony hand, the rumble of his voice fading then disappearing beneath the traffic hum. Noll hesitated, their words still fresh in his mind, the words of two black men, and then he turned towards home wondering what his father would say if he were still alive.

Four

He crossed the street between shafts of light, molten, steam-laden in the breathless air, keeping to unmarked paths cast in deep pools of shade, sweat staining dark the brown leather of his belt, the crease below his neckline. Mockingbirds sat perched on blackened branches, wall-eyed, listless, caught like trapped flies in the honeyed stillness of noontime. The bell tower chimed its familiar twelve notes but he altered his pace little, the red brick buildings appearing again above the treetops, aloof, judgmental, finding his inadequacies obvious, grotesque, no longer amenable to change. The structures exhaled cool fragrance of book binding and paper as he passed, reminding him of all he had left unfinished, unaccomplished in those lecture halls. He turned his gaze toward what was now real to him and found Elgy standing just inside the yawning doors, waiting, expectant.

The voice of his father again returned, this time telling him to rely on no man. What did he owe Hen? Nothing. Elgy expected him to provide information, something to incriminate Hen but he had given him little. What could he give him? Sure, sometimes breaks stretched on a bit but the men also worked through their break when a job needed finishing.

There *was* something. Hen had a habit of covering for men when they showed up late or had problems at home if he felt it justified. Lately he had been covering for one worker in particular, an older man named Nando who had been late for work once or twice after visiting his son in jail. What would it hurt to tell that? Elgy would likely see it only as a minor misstep but it might be enough to get him off Noll's back. Still, he wanted to avoid saying anything if he could manage it. As he walked through the doors and into the shade, Elgy leaned forward, whispering.

You have yourself a good lunch, Noll?

It was alright.

Well, that's good.

Do you need something, Elgy?

As a matter of fact, I do. I'm disappointed in you, Noll. I know them coloreds and them wetbacks are up to no good but you haven't given me one lick of the evidence I asked for. How is it you're right there with them day in and day out but you haven't seen a damn thing? I know they have it out for me so I have to wonder if you're in on it too. Well, are you?

Am I what?

Are you in on their little secret?

What secret?

Don't forget you're the only whitey in the whole department. If you're thinking you can join up with them you can't, not now, not never. They may act friendly if it suits their purpose but the fact is you're a white man and someone not to be trusted.

I'm just trying to do my job, Elgy.

Then tell me what they're up to or you may be doing your job somewhere else.

You'd fire me for not being your snitch?

No, but I can find something if I need to. You heard how I handled that no-good Ranse didn't you?

I heard.

So, give me something.

I haven't seen much of anything.

You're bound to have seen or heard something being around them boys all day long.

There is one thing. I heard Hen has been covering for Nando when he comes in late.

Didn't I tell you them boys are lazy?

It's not like that, Elgy. Nando's son is in jail and they only allow visitors early in the day so sometimes it makes him a little late for work.

31

Late is late, no matter the reason. That's not much but it's enough, it's a start. You get on to work now and find me something better on old Hen. I know he's behind it all.

Noll spent the rest of the afternoon driving a truckload of used desks to the university satellite location ten miles south of the main campus. On his way back, he got a call from Elgy to stop by the chemistry building and help a crew put up a scaffold. Within minutes, he had set the brake and was climbing out of the truck when he heard Elgy's voice echoing between the buildings, the words unclear but the tone angry, hostile. He rounded a corner to find several men standing well back of a metal scaffold that stretched several stories into the air, their arms folded across their chests, their faces brooding, defiant. Hen stood just in front. Elgy turned as Noll approached, waving him over with a meaty hand.

Noll, get over here. I need your help. I'm trying to explain to these boys that this scaffold is safe.

What can I do, Elgy? I'm no expert on scaffolds.

You heard him say it, Elgy. He's no expert either. This scaffold is no bueno. The damn ground is soft. We've had too much rain.

You stay out of this, Lio. You're our leader here but if you can't get your men to work then I have to.

Looky here, Elgy. If Nando was with us he'd tell you it's no good. He's our scaffold man. But since you've gone and sent him home, we'll need to listen to Lio.

Are you questioning my authority, Hen?

I'm reminding you of the one man we rely on when it comes to scaffolds. After owning his own painting business for twenty years, he knows what's what. He could tell us if it's safe or not but he's at home, not here where he should be.

I had good reason to send him home. He was showing up late for work and I won't tolerate tardiness.

Do you have proof Nando showed up late even once?

If I did I would have fired him so I sent him home to think about it instead. I can't see what business it is of yours since you're not his supervisor. I'd bet my paycheck you were covering for him.

We all help each other out where we can. But I believe this here situation is my business, our business, because we got ourselves a problem and Nando isn't here to help us find some answer, if there is one to be found.

Of course there is, Hen. The solution is for one of you to climb up there and finish the scaffold so we can fix that crack. The building already has damage because of it.

The men think the scaffold is unsafe, Elgy. I can't say as I blame them. It takes a fool to put his life on the line for a damn job.

I don't care what the men think, Hen. If you men can't decide who goes up there, I'll decide for you.

The men won't risk it if the scaffold might fail.

Alright Hen, then you can be the fool. Grab that bucket and trowel and get to work. These others will pass up mortar as you need it.

No sir. I'm in agreement with the men. This scaffolding here is unsafe.

Are you defying my directive, Hen?

I'm saying the scaffolding is unsafe, Elgy.

I can fire you for insubordination.

You'll get no insubordination from me.

Goddamn it, I'll go up. Noll, haul that bucket up with the pulley once I get to the top.

Lio, I told Hen to do it.

I'm younger than him, Elgy so I should be the one to go. It makes no difference so long as it gets done.

-Elgy stepped back as Lio grabbed the thick bars of the scaffold and began to climb, the metal pins creaking like rusty bedsprings beneath his weight. Muscles rippled across his lean arms, bulging, sinuous, a large tattoo flexing across his forearm as he picked his way along one corner. The sky beyond shone an indifferent blue, flat, insubstantial, pale against his clay-colored skin. His hand had just clutched the lower rung of the third level when a slow wrenching began low in the frame, becoming louder with each second. Noll took a breath, feeling time slow, incremental, molasses-like, his every muscle tensing. An instant later, the crack of breaking pins brought him out of his trance. The scaffold seemed to pause, suspended, and then Lio released his grip, leaping from the metal bar and flying like a circus cat, acrobatic, graceful, until he tumbled onto the lawn in a blur. The men dove in all directions as the scaffold crashed to the ground, metal groaning, boards snapping. Hen rushed to Lio, who was already standing, stomping his feet and cursing every other word in Spanish. Elgy turned and began walking toward his truck, calling over his shoulder.

Get this mess cleaned up. If you boys had any sense you would have come over the roof with ropes and tackle in the first place.

-Lio started after him but Hen grabbed him by the shoulders, holding him in place. Noll stood nearby.

That bastard nearly got us all killed, Hen.

Won't do any good to tell him that now, Lio. You know that. Just let him go.

We're nothing to him, less than damn cockroaches.

You didn't just now figure that out, did you?

Hell no, Hen but it makes me feel better saying it.

I got to believe Elgy will get his due one of these days.

I hope I'm there when it happens.

How you doing, Lio? Can you make sure the men clean up without anyone getting hurt?

Long as we don't have to climb no scaffold, we'll be alright.

34

I mean to talk to Noll straight away. Elgy, he's up to something but I have me an idea how we can beat him at his own game.

-Hen pulled Noll aside.

What is it, Hen?

Listen here, Noll. Elgy's got him a man in the department feeding him information.

How do you know?

It's the only way he could've known about Nando. He has to have someone.

Hen listen, there's something I need to tell you.

It'll have to wait, Noll. We got to get on this, else someone will get let go instead of just sent home. Elgy wants to put one over on us but I figure we can get around him by giving him what we decide instead of what he wants.

How are we going to do that?

He'll listen to a white man before one of us so I figure we can have you give him a little of this, a little of that and he'll believe every word. He won't be listening to no inside man after that. I don't mean to turn you against your own but can you do it?

I don't like Elgy anymore than you do, Hen. I guess I can do it if you need me to.

I need you to, Noll. That Elgy, he's up to no good and I've got me a bad feeling about it.

Five

He walked through light the color of honey, dense, immobile, scattered beneath sprawling oak, time-fissured bark, pool of shadow. Buildings of steel and glass rose just beyond, his own reflection thrashing before him like a grounded fish. He stopped and stood still, his mother's voice coming to him above the hum of traffic, asking, cajoling him to enter where he last saw his father's ashen face, that final image escaping memory smoke-like, ethereal, leaving only a faint smell of alcohol in its place. The voice now firmer, urging, weighed with conviction, 'he's young like you, Noll and he needs someone, someone his own age, someone to talk to when he might never walk out of that room again' and then silent, leaving no space for denial, no chance for argument. On toward sliding doors and through, chill air rent by death, impersonal, antiseptic, he lowered his gaze, afraid to see his father's eyes pass in the face of a stranger.

Next to him a woman stood mute beneath yellow elevator light, squatting in threadbare turquoise, ochre, bags of food bulging in tea-colored hands, smelling of tortillas, chilies, black eyes casting to floor. Seeing her, judging, descending into habit he placed her without thought, less than he was now, far less than someday. Breath held he stepped away and through waiting doors, exhaling stale prejudice, cursing himself for acquiescing to his mother. Then her voice sounded once more, familiar, pleading, shaming his casual self-concern.

He peered down the too-familiar corridor one way then the other, bluish light cast against shining wall and floor, leaving ghost-like hues adrift in shadowed corners, open doorways. Behind the counter opposite him a broad-faced woman sat under bleached hair, pastel-patterned smock greenish in laptop glow, discolored lipstick moving as she mouthed each typed word. He cleared his throat and her eyes drifted from the screen, dull, preoccupied, off-putting, bouncing from him to screen and back until she finally spoke.

Well, what is it?
I'm Noll Spencer.
And?
I'm here to see a guy.
Any guy in particular?
I thought you would know who.
Well, we have a few to choose from. Do you want me to pick one for you? Picking out a man sounds real good to me. A woman dreams of picking out a man. You know what I mean? Although when I think about it, I don't know that want to I'd pick any of these if I had my druthers.
I'm supposed to see a particular guy. I don't remember the name.
That could make it difficult.
He's a young guy. I've never met him but I know his room is up here somewhere.
You're here to volunteer?
I'm supposed to talk to him.
Mostly we get the usual volunteers in here, the ones with the white hair. You know what I mean? We also get those snotty sorority girls arrested for public intoxication that are doing their community service here, but never a guy. Are you in trouble with the law? We don't need any young criminals wandering the halls.
You don't have to worry about me.
Hold on now, do I know you?
I don't think so.
You look familiar. Have you been here before?
It was a long time ago, over a year. My father, he got shot.
He died?
After about a week.

That's a hard way to lose someone. Did they ever find who did it?

No.

What did you say your name was?

Noll Spencer.

Of course, I remember. You're older now, all grown and handsome. You seemed so young then. It must have been a tough time for you, huh, darlin'?

Can you tell me who he is? My mother knows about him, the guy. He's young like me. She talked me into coming here to see him.

I just realized your mother was one of our volunteers, although I haven't seen her in a quite a while. She started after y'all spent so much time here, didn't she? Why didn't you say something, hon'? You must be here to see Feliciano Cruz. He goes by Felix.

I guess so. Cruz sounds Mexican. Is he a Mexican?

I believe you should say Hispanic or Latino, hon'. You know what I mean?

Alright then, is he?

He's that and much more. Is that going to be a problem? You're not a bigot are you, darlin'?

I just didn't know is all.

Prejudice is an unsightly quality in a person. You don't want something to turn that handsome face ugly, do you? Besides, I won't tolerate any mistreatment of Felix on my watch.

What's he like?

Felix is one of a kind. You won't find a more sensitive soul. He knows what it's like to be mistreated so he's tolerant of people's short-comings, even those with certain prejudices. You know what I mean? He's in the room at the end of the hall with the ribbons around the door. He did that himself. He's always sprucing up and making things pretty like that.

Why's he in the hospital?

You really don't know anything about him, hon'?

38

My mother said it'd be better if he told me himself.

Well, that's likely true. He's getting a round of chemotherapy but I'll let him tell you about it.

That'll be fine. We'll probably need something to talk about. I'm not much good at making conversation.

If he's not feeling too poorly, Felix can do the talking for the both of you without even trying. He's a talker if there ever was one.

Lucky for me then.

Do you know how it works here, darlin'?

Not really.

Well, you just check in here at the front desk and make sure it's okay to visit. The chemo can make them too sick to see visitors.

The treatment makes them sick?

Strange, isn't it? The chemo makes them sicker so they can get better. The treatments temporarily kill their immune system, so they can die of a cold that you'd hardly notice. That doesn't happen too often, thank goodness.

So, what do I do now?

Go on over and introduce yourself, darlin'. Like I said, Felix likes to talk.

- The hallway stretched before him tunnel-like, dim, featureless as he stepped forward, the chill air slipping from his mouth before he could find a decent breath. His eyes, loose in their sockets, unwilling to focus, found the corridor pitching, listing to one side and then the other as he ventured from the front desk glow, his father's face slipping in and out of memory, translucent, ephemeral. Soon, ribbons of fuchsia, lime and aquamarine danced before him, bringing back solid reality as they drifted through an open door, tangling, loosening, intertwining beneath an air vent like fleeing fish. A voice came from beyond the doorway.

Who's come to see me? What's taking you so long? Quit teasing and get your body in here right now, whoever you are. Is that you, Noll Spencer? Your mama

39

said you'd come today and I know she's too sweet to ever fib to anybody, especially someone special like yours truly, Felix Cruz. There, I can see your reflection on the floor. So, you *must* come in now because we've already met in a certain sort of way, don't you think?

-Noll stepped through the doorway.

Hello, Noll Spencer. You are him, aren't you?

That's right. You must be Felix.

What a good guess, Noll. How did you manage it?

My mother thought you might like to have someone to talk to.

Oh Lord, are you kidding? I'm going crazy in here. A person can play games on his computer for only so long, you know, before he goes psychotic. I don't even like games but nobody uses email anymore and I can't text anyone when there isn't any decent cell phone reception up here. It's like I'm stuck in purgatory. Heaven lies outside that window and hell is in these tubes.

Do you feel good enough to have company or should I leave?

Noll, do *not* leave. I'm just peachy. I love it the way you say 'company' instead of 'visitor'. It's so Southern.

Alright then, what do you want to talk about?

You, let's talk about you.

Uh, well, what do you want to know?

You're not at all what I imagined.

I'm not? What did you imagine?

Oh, I don't know, someone short, with thick glasses that likes to talk about chemistry or physics or something equally boring. You don't want to talk about chemistry, do you?

I don't know enough about chemistry to talk about it and make any sense.

Oh good, but you do seem smart. I don't mean like a smartass. I mean intelligent, not to mention nice. Where do you go to school? You are in school, aren't you?

40

I was taking classes at the university but I had to get a job to help out at home.

Oh, that's terrible, Noll. Do you miss it?

I was one of the few people I know that actually liked college. Maybe it's because I was paying my own way. I just like learning about things.

What were you majoring in?

Everything and nothing. That was the problem. I liked my classes but had no idea what I wanted to do with my life. It's probably best that I'm not in school right now.

You even like physics and chemistry?

Well sure, but not enough to major in them. What about you?

Call me Felix so I can feel like we're friends.

Alright. Are you in college, Felix?

It's difficult when you have tubes going everywhere but I'm trying to keep up via the internet. I've been at Holy Cross for the last year and my professors are working with me on making up work. I've gone to Catholic schools my whole life. My parents aren't rich but they believe a good Catholic should go to a good Catholic school. Not that I'm close to good in any way whatever. God forbid. How boring would that be?

What are you studying?

Socializing, if I'm going to be honest about it. That's why I hate being here. Cancer is bad enough but feeling like I'm stuck on a desert island is worse. No one will come see me.

Why not?

They're afraid. Cancer intimidates people that way. The idea of dying scares them. Coming here reminds them that I might die or that they might. Just the thought of it keeps them from coming. But you're here, Noll the Brave. You're not scared.

I wouldn't say I'm brave.

But that just shows how brave you are, Noll. People that brag about being brave are the ones that run at the first chance.

You have a funny way of looking at things, Felix.

That's because I'm not like most people you know.

What do you mean?

That's what I like about you, Noll. You're so innocent. Ask me something else.

What's it like having cancer?

Terrifying at first but after a while it turns into boring, everyday life. A person just can't stay terrified all the time. Mostly, it's a pain because it becomes who you are. That's what I'm trying to fight and you're helping me.

I don't feel like I'm doing much. How am I helping?

Just by being here.

What did you mean about not being like other people?

Why, do you feel that way too?

Sometimes I do.

-A young woman walked into the room.

Maya, Maya, you're finally here. Look at me, dancing with joy.

Calm down Felix, you'll hurt yourself.

I can be glad to see my sister, can't I? Maya, stop where you are and let me get a look at you. Where'd you get that hideous dress? What do you call that color, something like olive drab, heavy emphasis on drab? You look like yesterday's pea soup. I think I'm going to be sick.

I can always tell when you're jealous, Felix. And no, you can't borrow it for one of your wild costume parties.

It's not a party if it isn't wild, Maya. Isn't that right, Noll? Oh, where are my manners? Noll Spencer, this is my sister, Maya. Noll is my new friend. Isn't that right, Noll?

Why is he here, Felix?

Maya, don't be rude.

Why is a white guy in your room? I thought your little pale friends were too afraid to come up here. Why are you here? What's your name? Noll, is it?

That's right.

Maya, stop it!

It's alright, Felix. I was asked to come here. Maya, is it?

Why? Is this take pity on a Mexican week?

Noll, don't listen to her. Maya, he's here to volunteer not party. We just met and you're ruining it.

Okay, I'll stop. I just don't want anyone taking advantage of you. You need to rest.

Noll is here to keep me company for a little while, that's all. I won't overdo.

You're a brave man, Noll.

That's what I've been trying to tell Noll the Brave but he doesn't believe me. Isn't his dark, curly hair something, Maya?

You just say that because you don't have any.

Baldness can be sexy, Maya.

So, why are you really here? Are you a Latino wannabe?

Ignore her, Noll. She thinks all white people are racists. She took too many sociology classes and it warped her brain.

What's wrong with sociology, Felix?

Noll, please tell me you're not one of those activist types. I can stand only so much preaching about people's rights and Latino pride.

I don't preach, Felix.

I'd rather make friends than fight with people. I'm not so sure about you, Maya.

At least I stand up for what I believe.

Maya, do you really think all white people are racists?

Noll, don't ask that! Once she gets started on her Latino rant she never stops. It's like an avalanche of words. After a few minutes, you'll wish a real avalanche would come along and put you out of your misery.

I don't think all white people are racist, just most of them.

It's a miracle, Noll. She answered in only thirteen words. How did you do it?

But Maya, isn't it racist to say most white people are bigots?

Not if it's the truth, Noll.

You two stop bickering, someone's coming. Noll, what time is it?

It's right at five o'clock.

Damn, it must be time for my radiation treatment. Quick, hide me in the bathroom and tell them I've escaped.

Don't you need the treatments?

Noll, I think you want me to get better. Don't you think so, Maya? That's so sweet.

Isn't that what you want?

Yes but I want to know what you want. Do you want me to get better, Noll?

Of course.

Then you'll be my friend and come back to see me?

I'll try.

I'll try, Felix.

Okay, I'll try, Felix.

When, Noll the Brave? When will you return? Can you come on Saturday?

I'm not sure.

Say you will, Noll, say you will.

Wisps of hair, ghost-like, spectral, feathered above Felix's shining head, his red-rimmed eyes dilated, glassy, trapping Noll in the doorway before the wheelchair turned and moved down the hall between pools of light. The hard

44

rubber tires sounded as it moved, bird-pitched, in metronome, marking time and then fading, soon disappearing altogether. Noll stared down the corridor as his thoughts ricocheted off one another, careening away yet leading nowhere.

He stood still, his father's face appearing again, seeming almost to smile from another time, a time before failure, self-loathing left it twisted, bent to anger's form. The image remained for a moment then altered to what most remained intact, an essence, unchangeable, ineffable. Unable to admit his own failures, vengeful of weakness, scornful of difference, his father had passed on his self-made poison unseen, unacknowledged. Noll wondered how a woman he would have seen as lesser, insignificant only minutes before he now found mesmerizing.

Maya stood with her back to him, her scent drifting past in waves, the heat of her bare skin burning his face, her silken hair cascading, smelling of jasmine, clear-water streams. He leaned forward, inhaled, feeling in his breath the dark strands spilling over her shoulder, her back, the clean curve of her neck. Then he pulled back as she turned toward him, her lips rose-like, hint of smile in check, untrusting, hesitating before she finally spoke.

Why are you here? What do you really want?

I don't want anything.

Are you really a volunteer, Noll?

My mother is a volunteer, or she was. She asked me to come speak with Felix. She said he'd like talking to someone his age.

Are you gay?

What? Why would you ask that?

Well, are you?

I don't get you, Maya. First, you tell me I'm racist, then you ask if I'm gay. What next?

It's just that Felix is too trusting. I worry someone will take advantage of him.

I'm not gay and I'm not taking advantage of anyone. Felix is friendly, that's all.

He just seems that way because he likes you. He can be cruel to someone he doesn't like.

It makes sense you'd want to protect him, seeing how he's sick and all but I'd bet he can fend for himself.

Maybe. I didn't want to admit it but I could see talking to you did him good.

So, I'm not a racist anymore?

I shouldn't have said what I did. I don't even know you. You could be an axe murderer for all I know.

I think I'll settle for racist.

Let's talk about something else.

Alright. What do you do when you're not up here with Felix? Are you taking classes at Holy Cross too?

No, the church and I don't get along. I'm at the university.

So am I, in a way. I started working there a few weeks back.

Really? My father works there.

What does he teach?

Ha! If you knew him you'd think that's funny. He's about as far from a professor as you can get. He drives a truck.

I drive a truck too.

Maybe you've met him. If you did you wouldn't forget. His name is Rogelio Cruz.

Wait, your father is Lio Cruz? I can't believe that. We work in the same department.

Good luck working alongside him. He's not the easiest person to get along with. He was a sergeant in the Marines, you know.

He doesn't have much in the way of patience but you always know where you stand with Lio. That's the way I like it.

You *are* a surprise, Noll Spencer.

Now I'm a surprise, not a racist. I'm moving up in the world.

Listen, I need to go. On Thursday afternoons I deliver meals to old people. Would you like to help me?

You want me to come with you?

Are you afraid to go somewhere with a Latina?

Sure I am but I still have to prove I'm no axe murderer, don't I?

Six

Dusk flooded the narrow street, draping the small frame houses that moved past his open window in gold, platinum, their tattered rooflines sagging, listing to one side or other, their tiny yards cluttered with late-season cabbage, onion, garlic, their grass-covered curbs lined with faded car, rusted truck. Hints of jasmine, gardenia, honeysuckle swirled through the window and into Maya's tousled hair, silken, cloud-like as it hovered about her face in the shifting breeze. He looked her way and again was taken with her line of nose, curve of lip, eyes dark, gleaming. He turned back to the houses, afraid she would notice his stare. Porches deep in shade held weathered dining room chairs, end tables, cast-off couches their ripped seats white, scar-like. Old women in flowered skirts bent over tilled rows of dirt as if blessing freshly-dug graves.

Maya pulled to the curb in front of a home set beneath towering pecan trees, the once white shiplap siding now gray, streaked. She cut the engine and reached into the back seat without a word, pulling a foil-covered tray from an insulated box and stepping out of the car. Noll followed her to a metal gate set midway along a fence line where she handed him the tray and stood facing the front door fifty feet beyond. The area before them was a dense patch of fruit trees, vegetables and vines just beginning to lose their leaves, well-tended, immaculate. A pair of hens strutted between the rows.

A moment later, the door opened and a woman stepped out, stooped, shuffling, making her way down the porch steps in pauses. A flowered scarf framed her weathered face, her eyes nearly lost beneath drooping eyelids. She stopped to pull a large clove of garlic, the green top still attached, from the edge of the path, shaking the dirt from the bulging end as she walked toward them. A grizzled mutt crawled from beneath the house and crept behind her, gray muzzle swinging back and forth inches above the ground. Maya turned to Noll, her eyes shining.

This is my favorite part of the week. The old people in this neighborhood originally came from Poland and Slovakia. They call it the Cabbage Patch.

I've seen plenty of cabbage.

Here she comes, Noll. She's an amazing woman.

What should I say?

Just hand her the tray and let her do the talking. She doesn't have many visitors.

Hello Berta, how are you today?

Maya, where you been this last week? I missed you.

Do you remember me telling you about my sister that lives down on the border? I went to see her.

Ah yes, she is one who is so afraid of the Mexican gangs? She is okay, Maya?

I don't know, Berta. The border can be dangerous.

She must be a worry for you.

Yes Berta, she is.

Who is this handsome man you bring to my garden, then?

Berta, I'd like you to meet Noll Spencer.

-Noll reached out to shake her hand, nearly dropping the tray.

I am so glad to meet a friend of Maya's. She is a treasure, I think. Noll, you must see a crazy old woman standing in front of you, dirty as I am. You see these hands all covered with soil of that old earth? The good Lord above, he give me this little bit of his world for my own. I been gardening here since the wolves they roamed this fence trying to get my chickens.

You had wolves here?

An old legend says in ancient times two wolves chased the sun and moon until they caught them and ate them, so the old world ended but the spirit of the wolves

49

survived. I've seen them, Noll and I tell you they are truly spirits.

I'd like to get a glimpse of one but I guess that's not likely anymore.

The last time I saw a wolf was the night a big male stopped right where you are standing. He looked at me for a long time as if he knew me, and I decided he was the ghost of my old grandfather come back to see me so I didn't shoot him. I still keep my shotgun up there on the porch in case a wolf shows up but I think they are all gone back to the earth now, just as Berta will soon. I dig in that dirt every day, Noll. You can smell the earth of my garden? I find comfort in that smell. Isn't that strange? But I am old woman so I say what I wish and no one cares one bit.

I do like the smell. My grandmother keeps a garden at home. I till it for her every spring and help her stake up beans and tomatoes.

Maya, you find a good man here. You better keep him.

Oh Berta, Noll is just helping me deliver the meals today. We go see Mr. Kasmirez next.

Ah Maya, I worry about Mr. Kasmirez every day. He is not so well, you know, and his house it leaks terrible when it rains. You go to him now and see. You help him, Maya.

Yes, we'd better go.

You take him this garlic for me. It will help him get better. But you come back to see me next time and you bring Noll with you. Old woman like me never get to meet a handsome man too much, you know.

-As they turned to leave a speeding car rounded the corner, screeching to a halt in front of the house before a young man jumped out.

Carlos, what are you doing here?

Come with me, Maya. We need to talk.

No, we do not need to talk. You need to leave.

What is that white guy doing here?

That's none of your business, Carlos. Stop following me around.

Are you coming with me or am I going to have to walk over there and drag you away.

-As he moved around the rear of the car Noll stepped in front of Maya.

Move out of the way, Noll. I can take care of this myself.

So Homer, you think you can steal my girlfriend?

There's no Homer around here, Cisco. My name is Noll.

I don't give a damn what your name is as long as you leave, now.

-Maya shoved Noll to the side.

Turn around and go, Carlos. You have no right to be here.

You're my woman and you'll do what I say.

-Time seemed caught between shadow and light, suspended, hovering, still as a breath held. Then in a flash of movement, Carlos grabbed Maya by her hair, turning toward his car and pulling her after him. She bent forward, screaming. Noll stood rooted in place, his mind unable to make sense of what was happening. He watched as Maya reared back, kicking Carlos on the side of his knee and freeing herself for an instant before he again grabbed her, this time by both arms. Noll emerged from his stupor, lunging at Carlos just as a deafening blast echoed between the houses and down the street. Noll careened into the road, unable to keep from falling onto the rough asphalt. Not ten feet away, he watched as Carlos slammed into the hood of his idling car and tumbled to the ground. Maya, grimacing but still standing, held both hands to her ears as a cloud of gun smoke drifted past her head ghost-like, spectral. The high-pitched howl filling Noll's ears soon eased, finally broken by Berta's voice, calm, determined.

I got this one barrel left for that car there, if only I can cock back this big old hammer.

-Carlos jumped up, scrambling behind the steering wheel and disappearing in a haze of blue exhaust even before Noll could get to his feet. Maya walked a small circle, shaking her head as Berta cracked open the shotgun and removed the spent shell.

The sheriff said he'd come get me if I shot my gun again. I put in the rock salt instead of the buckshot so nobody gets hurt.

-An old woman leaned out the front door of the house across the street and cupped her hands around her mouth.

You shoot a wolf again with that big gun, Berta?

A big one on two legs, Kazia.

Dobry. Good riddance.

I only use the rock salt this time but it scared him good.

Too bad. For a man, you should use the buckshot.

The sheriff won't let me, but the gun is still loud.

It's a damn cannon, Berta. I can barely hear myself talk.

I'm sorry, Maya but I never let that boy treat you bad that way. I better put this old gun in the house before the sheriff, he comes for a visit and finds it.

Noll, are you okay? Why are you sitting behind that tree?

I'm making sure the fireworks are over.

Are you hurt?

I did a swan dive into the street but I'll live. I'm not sure if it was you or your boyfriend that sent me flying.

He's not my boyfriend.

Could've fooled me.

Well, he was once and thinks he still is even though I tried to tell him we're just friends.

Some friend.

I know but that was before he started acting so crazy. I'm done with him.

Sounds like a good idea.

52

Noll, I know you were trying to help me. Are you sorry you did?

I'm just embarrassed I ended up flat on my back in the middle of the street.

You tried and that's what counts.

Yeah, well, thanks Maya.

I'm the one to do the thanking, Noll. I think Berta has gone inside so let's go deliver the rest of these meals before they get cold.

-They climbed back into the car and Maya pulled away from the curb.

How'd you get into doing this, delivering the meals?

A friend that volunteers at the local community center told me about it.

But why do this when you could be drinking coffee with friends or heading to the beach?

I like the beach as much as anyone but take a look around, Noll. These old people have nothing. They barely make it day to day. Remember Mr. Contreras, the old man with the broken down porch? He has cancer and Berta told me this meal is the only real food he gets most days. He's so thin it makes me want to cry. How can I lie on the beach and do nothing when I've seen that?

But there are so many problems out there, Maya. It's overwhelming, like nothing a person does will make any difference.

I know it's not much but I do what I can. I have to. We all have to.

You sound like my grandmother.

Don't get the wrong idea, Noll. I know how to have fun too.

I don't know. I heard what Felix said about you and your lectures.

Don't pay any attention to him. He just hates it when someone gets in more talking time than him. I can be fun and I'll prove it to you.

How?

Buy me a beer sometime and you'll see.

Shadows fell long in the fading light, crimson, broken, cutting across ragged gables, crumbled chimneys, melding with each other and into the coming dusk. The last of the meals delivered, Maya drove the narrow streets past weed-covered lots, funeral homes, storefront churches, frame houses weathered but immaculate. People chatted across fence lines and loitered beneath street lights yet to switch on in the lingering glow, incandescent, golden, still holding the night in check.

Noll struggled to sort out his emotions. On the one hand he was undeniably attracted to Maya, on the other he never could have imagined being drawn to such a woman before today. He felt as if he had entered an unimagined world that now somehow seemed more real, more tangible than his own home and neighborhood. He again turned to Maya, seeing a tough determination in her face, her set jaw, her dark eyes, passion for fairness just beneath. He turned away with difficulty.

Just ahead a figure walked before them in halting steps, hitching, rocking to one side, head tilted, arm at angle. Noll sat up in his seat. He watched the form nearing them in the half-light and held up a hand, palm out, still, as if to quiet a restless crowd. Maya glanced at him, slowing the car. The silhouette of an old man emerged from deep shadow and slowed, listing, head cocked before turning toward the car, his lined face just visible. Noll released his seatbelt and leaned out the window.

Hen, what are you doing here?

Lordy, Noll, you gave me a start. I live around here but where on earth did you come from?

I'm helping a friend. This is Maya.

I know Maya.

You do?

You were some younger when we met. I work with your father.

Oh, I remember. You and my dad go fishing together.

Looky here, I don't mean to be unfriendly but I got to keep moving.

What's wrong, Hen?

Got a call from Ranse's mother. He's gotten himself into some kind of trouble Noll, bad trouble. I hope I'm not too late.

Why aren't you in your truck?

She said it'd be best if I came on foot.

What are you going to do?

Don't know exactly but I mean to keep that boy safe if I can. You go on with Maya.

It sounds like you could use some help.

No, son, I'll be alright. I can see you're busy.

-Maya pulled on Noll's sleeve and he turned to her.

What is it, Maya?

We can help him.

You mean the both of us? You're sure?

I'm sure.

We're coming with you, Hen.

I don't know, son there could be trouble.

Climb in, we'll get there quicker.

Seven

Hen directed Maya through fractured pools of light and beneath trees lost in the waning dusk, mute, ghost-like. Behind them nightfall swallowed the darkening street, leaving past and future nonexistent, the present moment the whole of the world. Vacant lots humming with movement, restless, unseen, sat next to bright storefronts sliced by metal bars, oddly empty of life. They passed between twin stone posts framing the road, a rusted sign overhead that read 'Elysian Fields' connecting them. Hen motioned Maya to the curb before a low-slung house of pink stucco, the wide porch bright with light. He climbed out even before the car had stopped moving, surveyed the yard and then turned to where the car sat.

You two stand aside and let them get a good look at me first. It could be trouble if they see three people they don't recognize walk into their yard. These here are good folks but they're afraid right now and they don't scare easy.

We'll wait for you here, Hen.

Noll, are you sure about this? You and Ranse got a history between you.

Don't worry about me. I offered to help and that's what I mean to do if I can.

I believe you just want to impress this young lady, but call it what you want.

Don't you need to get on to ringing the doorbell or something, Hen?

Well Noll, now that I see there's no police or gunfire, I don't feel in such a hurry. I'll just call to them from here in case they got a shotgun leaning by the door. Lavonia, Princella, you in there?

-A hand pulled aside the curtain of a porch window and after a moment the door swung open, a stern-looking woman the color of cinnamon standing just inside, stout, defiant.

Who's that with you, Hen?

Two young people I know.

Where'd you find them?

I work with Noll here, and this is his friend Maya. They gave me a ride in that car there.

You can trust them, Hen?

Sure I can, Princella.

You bring anybody else?

You're being awful careful, Princella.

Can't be too careful when there's evil about, and God himself knows evil is walking these streets this very moment.

What are you talking on about, Princella?

Ranse stirred up the devil, that's what he did. We tried to raise him right but he forgot Jesus and look what it brought him. Look what it brought us.

Where is Ranse?

Lavonia's got him hidden away inside the house.

Can we come inside, Princella? I feel like a salesman talking to you over this fence.

You sure you know these people?

I know them well enough.

Well, come on up then but beware God's wrath. That's what Ranse has brought down on us. Lord only knows how it will end.

What's this all about, Princella?

Ranse got himself mixed up with some man selling drugs or some such devilry. Lavonia, Hen is here. We're coming in now.

-They stepped through the door and into an open room with a large sofa where Ranse slouched, his face half covered in bandages. He sat up, looking from Hen to Noll.

What's that white man doing here?

Never you mind that. Your mama called me and now I'm here to help.

I don't need any help, especially from him.

Look at yourself in the mirror, Ranse. Look what you brought into this house. I had to take your sister to live with her cousins because of this.

You didn't have to send Juanita away, mama.

Yes, I did. I will not have her around violence. She's seen enough in her young life. Now, you let your mother do what she thinks best. Hen, please introduce me to your friends.

Hello, Lavonia. This here is Noll and Maya. They're lending me a hand.

I'm pleased to meet you. Thank you for offering to help.

No one can help me, mama. You're wasting your time, Hen.

What have you gotten yourself into, Ranse?

I was just trying to make some money for the family, Hen. You know I got no job since that Elgy let me go.

Just tell me what happened.

It was a mistake, Hen. I was supposed to take this one bag and trade it for this other bag and then I get paid. I did it two or three times and the money is good.

You working for some gang?

It's the devil's work, that's what it is.

Princella, let Hen do the talking. Please continue, Hen. Ranse, you speak up.

Alright, mama.

Is it gang work, Ranse?

I don't know who it is, Hen and I don't ask.

So, what happened?

I took the bag where the man told me to, me and two other boys. Before we got to the spot we were jumped and I was hit from behind. When I woke up the bag was gone. Hen, I think one of those boys got shot. There was blood everywhere.

You see a doctor?

58

No, I'm alright but I'm afraid they're going to say I owe them for that bag and make me pay up. Hen, where am I going to get that kind of money? If I had that much money I wouldn't be working for them.

Have you heard from anyone?

That's why mama and Aunt Princella called you. A man came to the door asking for me, a white man.

He had the eyes of a snake, a snake that will kill you and never even blink.

Princella, you're not helping.

Well Lavonia, I answered the door and looked right into the eyes of Beelzebub.

When was that?

It was mid-afternoon, Hen.

Could he have been with the police, Lavonia?

No, he said he was a businessman and wanted to talk over a deal with Ranse. He had an accent I don't know from where. I told him Ranse was out and that he should come back at seven o'clock.

You told him to come back here?

I will not live in my community, my house, afraid of what might come through the door. I will face it head on, with the help of my friends, of course.

It's nearly seven now.

So you're right on time, Hen.

Ranse, I don't want you moving from that couch, you hear? Lavonia, Princella, will you wait in here with Maya?

I'm waiting right here with Jesus and old Levi to keep me company, just in case we have trouble.

Princella put that rifle away before you hurt someone.

Hush, Lavonia. Don't forget that I'm your older sister. Old Levi was good company for our daddy and he's good company for me.

You don't even know how to shoot that thing.

Hush up, Lavonia. I can call on old Levi if I need to.

Just don't shoot me, Princella.

Hen sugar, if I wanted to shoot you I'd have done it a long time ago.

Noll, you and me, we're going to wait on the porch for our visitor.

Noll followed Hen through the door and onto the wide porch, the plank flooring below his shoes worn to a dull shine, sagging. He stood staring into the heavy air of early evening, dark, impenetrable. Hen found a weathered rocking chair and began rolling a cigarette, humming to himself as if he had not a solitary care. A pair of bats, erratic, beyond prediction, sped through the halo of yellow light that spilled from the porch before disappearing into the featureless shadow beyond. A siren sounded somewhere in the distance, mournful, plaintive, causing him to wonder what violence might lurk beyond the present moment. Hen reached over his head with one hand and flipped off the light switch, leaving them blind, vulnerable until they grew accustomed to the dim glow of the city rising above the horizon. Hen's voice came out of the darkness, gravel-like, phlegmatic.

That Ranse, he's still mad at everyone, especially you.

Where's his father, Hen?

He's been gone a long time.

What happened to him?

He got shot and killed right here in this house sixteen years ago almost to the day.

Who killed him?

I did.

You killed Ranse's father? But here they are calling you for help. I don't understand.

I'm not sure I ever have understood that night or what came after. You see, me and him we were friends, Lavonia and Princella too, all friends.

How'd it happen?

His name was Reece. He was a good man until he lost his job and didn't know what to do with himself, all that time on his hands, no new job to be found no matter how much he looked.

Pretty soon he got himself arrested, not that he did what they say he did. But he was spending his time at the wrong place with the wrong people and it caught up with him.

When he got out of jail, work was even harder to come by and he went to drinking and staying away from home. He would get angry too, real angry. Ranse was just boy, barely three. I would come by and help Lavonia around the house and we got to be close, too close. It happened slow, so slow neither of us saw it and then there it was big as life. We never had relations but I wouldn't have cared for her any more if we had.

Reece came home one evening after drinking all day and it happened I was still there. He got mad because there was no supper waiting for him and he slapped Lavonia so hard she fell to the floor. I held back for a minute but when he went for her again I had to step in even though we had been friends my whole life. Reece had started carrying a pistol after he got out of jail and he pulled it from his belt. The next thing I remember, we were on the floor, the pistol between us. We wrestled and somehow that gun went off. I don't know to this day if his finger was on the trigger or if it was me that fired the gun. All I know is that pistol fired and then he was dead.

Did they arrest you, Hen?

I was sent down for eight years but got out in three for good behavior.

They didn't see it as self-defense?

A man dies and someone's got to pay. They said it was manslaughter even though I was trying to protect

Lavonia. I don't know that maybe it was. I would have done whatever it took to keep her from getting hurt. Funny thing is, she changed after that. We both did. We were still friends but not like before. I always felt that I owed her, Juanita and Ranse for what I did. I couldn't be a man for her when I owed her that way.

Does Ranse know?

Lavonia said what good would it be for the boy to know? She never would tell him or let me tell him so I have to live with that too. I've tried to make amends in my way but it's never enough. It never will be enough.

-A car door slammed in the distance and they sat still, waiting, saying nothing. Then the sound of hard sole shoes on gravel, like teeth grinding, drifted from up the street. The steps paused and then started again, passing through the creaking gate. A man's form emerged from dense shadow, pale, hard-cheeked, eyes cast deep in sockets, and stood as a predator might, watching, waiting for its prey to bolt. Hen flipped the switch and the man raised his hand to block the light. Still seated, Hen studied him in the way Noll recalled, cat-like, disinterested, revealing little. Hen stood and moved to the rail before speaking.

What do you think, Noll, this man here got himself some business in this house or just trying to sell us something we don't want? Which is it?

-The man squinted up at them, an unlit cigar clamped between his teeth, eyes the color of night, reptilian, without expression. He looked to either side before stepping closer.

I am looking for a man by the name of Ranse Jenkins.

What do you want with him?

I have business to discuss.

He works for me so you tell me whatever you need to say.

He works for you?

62

That's right.

That is very interesting to know. Why can't I talk to him directly?

You got yourself a name?

My apologies. You surprised me and I forgot my manners. Allow me to start again, if you will. Good evening, gentlemen.

Evenin' to you.

I have important business to discuss with Mr. Ranse Jenkins.

You already told us that.

Uh, well, and my name is Vaditch.

You must be Polish, then.

Don't insult me. I'm Russian. I told you I need to see Ranse.

Looky here Radish, you're at my house, on my property. You don't tell me how it is, I tell you. If you go and get disrespectful then you have to leave.

The name is Vaditch.

Isn't that what I said, Noll?

That's what you said, Hen.

I believe this man here is trying to insult me.

It sure is starting to sound that way, Hen.

You're Noll Spencer.

That's right. How did you know?

I know people.

You know people?

I knew your father.

My father? I don't believe you.

Then don't believe me.

How did you know him?

Your father got around.

What are you telling me?

I just knew him, that's all.

Looky here, mister what you call yourself, I've had enough of your smart mouth. Either you leave now or you say what you have to say. Go on now and talk or get off my property.

     -Vaditch stepped toward the porch and Hen moved to the stairs to face him, Noll just behind. Vaditch stepped back.

     You take risks, gentlemen.

     Do we take risks, Hen?

     I don't believe we do, Noll. We like a sure thing. That's why Princella's got that big gun pointed this way right now.

     That's right, Hen. We'll go for a sure thing every time.

     Now is this mister what's his name going to tell us what he needs or is he going to insult us again? What do you think, Noll?

     Alright. I get the picture, gentlemen. Tell Mr. Jenkins the package he lost was recovered, so he was very lucky… this time. If he ever misplaces important merchandise again he will not be so fortunate.

     I believe I can remember that. What about you, Noll?

     I have an excellent memory Hen, especially when it comes to faces.

     Be very careful, Noll. You know little of what you take so lightly.

     Is that right, Radish? Well, I take it any way I can get it, don't I Noll?

     You do, Hen.

     You won't be so bold if we meet again, gentlemen.

     There you go insulting us again. Close that gate on your way out.

     The man vanished into the shadows and Hen sat, head cocked, listening to the footsteps disappearing into the distance. Noll leaned against the porch rail and started to speak but Hen held up a gnarled hand to silence him. After a moment, a car engine turned somewhere in the darkness. Hen pointed Noll toward the door and they stepped inside without a word. Ranse, his mother and aunt looked to Hen in expectation while Maya stood to one side, waiting for someone to speak. Noll glanced at her, catching the hint of a smile on her lips.

Out with it, Hen. What did that devil tell you?

Give him a chance to talk, Princella.

He can talk just fine, Lavonia. That Hen, he just wants one of us to ask so me, I'm doing the asking. You'll see. He'll do the talking.

Not if you don't give him a chance. You never do have an ounce patience for any little thing. You were just born that way, I suppose.

How do you know how I was born? You were not born yourself, sister.

I know what I've seen my whole life.

Our Lord has no patience when the devil is at the door.

The only devil I know is the one that has your tongue, Princella.

You two ladies want to hear what Hen has to say or you just want to stand there and argue?

Go ahead on then, Hen. See Lavonia, he knows how to get a word in when he wants to.

I don't know how but go on Hen, tell us what happened.

Alright, Lavonia. Ranse, it looks like you're off the hook. The man says you were lucky this time but not again.

They're not going to make me pay?

He said you don't owe them nothing. But Ranse, you got to leave all that behind you now. And you got to watch your back for awhile too. The man has a bad look about him.

I said he's a devil and you know it's true, Hen. Didn't I say it?

Let him talk, Princella.

65

Alright sister, I'll let him.

I don't know about the devil but he's a man to stay clear of, Ranse. You leave that work behind you now, you hear?

But I need to work, Hen. What am I going to do?

Jobs are hard to come by these days, it's true. But you got to stay away from that business.

A man's got to work, Hen.

I hear you, son.

A man's got to do what he has to do.

A job's not worth diddly-squat to a dead man.

Princella, don't say such a thing.

I saw his devil eyes, Lavonia and they burned right through me.

Lord above, am I the only sane person in this family? Tell my son he can't go back to that work, Hen.

I've said what I can, Lavonia. The boy knows what I mean.

It's what he doesn't know that worries me.

Eight

A lime-green glow of late afternoon filled the kitchen walls, viscous, fluid, as if the room lay beneath the surface of a shaded pond, dappled waves of sunlight rippling along the window panes in random lines. Noll sat at the table, across from his mother, finishing a bowl of cereal. He glanced at the clock and then at her, out of bed for the first time in a week, sallow, pale, sunken into the chair as if the simple act of sitting was an effort. She took a breath and leaned toward him.

Noll, you're the only person I know who eats cereal for supper.

I don't have time for anything else.

Have you been to see that young man at the hospital lately?

I've been busy, mom.

You have to keep going to see him, Noll. I'd go if I could but I'm just so tired I don't think I can manage it. Will you go soon?

Sure, I'll try to get over there.

Go today, Noll.

What?

Don't put it off, Noll. Go see him today.

Why today?

What if he's had a bad time of it? He might need someone to cheer him up.

But I have a party to go to.

Will Ginger be there? She's so pretty Noll, and polite. You could do worse, you know.

She invited me. That's why I can't go by the hospital.

You can go on your way.

I'm already late.

Please go see him, Noll. It would mean a lot to me. I think if it was you lying there feeling bad you'd want someone to talk to.

Alright, I'll stop in to see Felix but I'll have to make it short.

His name is Felix?

Felix Cruz.

Is he Mexican?

No mom, he's from here. Why would you say that?

I didn't know who it was you went to visit. Now I understand why you haven't been going. I didn't mean for you to have to…I didn't know it was a charity case that you'd…if I'd known he was Mexican, I would…

The term is Latino not Mexican, mom and he's not a charity case. His father works at the university and his mother is a teacher. And I haven't been avoiding him. I've just been busy. I've got to go now.

Don't be angry with me, Noll. I'm just so tired I can't think. I know I disappoint you but please don't be angry with me.

It's okay, mom. You're not going to cry are you?

I'll try not to, honey.

You're right, it's time I went to see Felix. I'm already late so I'd better go.

-As he passed into the living room Gannie stood in the hall doorway, waiting for him.

Are you on your way out, Noll?

I have a party to go to.

Well, that's good. I'm glad you're going to spend some time with people your own age. I worry about you having to take on so much with your mother the way she is. It's good to hear you're going to have some fun.

I don't know if I'll make it in time. She wants me to go by the hospital.

Oh Noll, do you really have to go? Aren't you over there often enough?

The truth is I haven't been in quite awhile. I don't know why.

Don't you get along with the young man?

Sure, we get along fine. I guess I've just been busy. That sounds like an excuse, doesn't it?

Being around the ill can wear on you, Noll. Your mother's not in the hospital but don't forget she's far from well herself and caring for her takes a toll.

The last time I saw Felix he stayed under the covers, head and all, the entire time I was there. The chemotherapy was making him sick. He shook so bad at times he could barely speak.

It's not easy to see someone that ill, especially someone you like.

I can't imagine how it must be for him.

You go on now but don't stay so long you miss your party. You need to take care of yourself too.

He entered the darkened hallway, walking past the empty nurse's station and on toward Felix's room, the polished floor reflecting fluorescent light in waves, as if a restless ocean rolled beneath his feet, insubstantial, mercurial. As he neared the door, he could see no sign of the colorful ribbons that somehow managed to capture Felix's spirit, at least on his good days.

He stopped short of Felix's room just as two nurses walked out the door, neither of whom he had seen before. One of the women turned at the doorway, quickly pulling Felix's nameplate from the entrance before hurrying to join her colleague. Noll stood for a moment, head cocked, listening for any sound but hearing nothing save the hiss of air vents. He took a step forward, leaning into the room, his hand still holding the doorframe. The room stood empty, the tables bare, the bed stripped of sheets, no trace of Felix ever having been there.

Noll's heart raced as he backed out of the doorway, his mind reeling at the thought of Felix dead. A wave of shame rose in his throat and he glanced down the hall, anxious to avoid being seen by anyone who might recognize him. He ducked into the stairwell across the hall, hurrying down a flight of steps before stopping and starting up again, thinking he should at least ask someone about him. As he reached the door leading back into the hallway he paused and stood still, his shame keeping him from turning the handle. After a moment he turned and hurried back down the steps, pushing through the exit and onto the street, nearly stepping in front of a car as it sped past. Jumping back to the curb he again felt the shame of his own self-concern rise in his throat, bitter, choking. He paced the sidewalk struggling to corral his thoughts, the image of a shivering Felix flashing before him like a silent movie. He took a breath and turned to leave.

The pulsating sound of dance music floated above the treetops as he walked through a garden gate and into the backyard of a looming brick house. Beyond the lawn, a pool and hot tub sat beside an open-air pavilion littered with potted palms and wrought iron chairs. Scattered groups of people dressed in an odd assortment of clothes stood in pools of shade, talking and sipping brightly colored drinks. Noll stopped to survey the scene, trying to remember the theme of the party. A voice sounded from behind him.

So, you finally decided to show up. The party is half-over.
Hello, Ginger.
Noll, you're no fun. Why didn't you dress up?
I got busy and forgot. What's the theme anyway?
You couldn't remember for me?
I'm sorry, Ginger. I have a lot on my mind.
It's that job, isn't it?
No, the job is fine.

You used to talk to me. Now I can barely get a word out of you. Is it me, Noll? Are you tired of me?

No Ginger, I just forgot, that's all.

Gays and Gals.

What?

That's the party theme. You're supposed to dress in your favorite gay or lesbian outfit.

Gay or lesbian outfit?

You know muscle shirts, tight pants and butch haircuts, the more outrageous the better.

So the party is about ridiculing people?

No, it's about having fun. A bunch of the guys are wearing tiaras and high heels. Doesn't that sound hilarious?

It might be funny if I didn't know what it was supposed to mean.

It's just a party, Noll. Why are you so grouchy?

I've had a bad day.

Do you want to talk about it?

No.

I have something that will take your mind off it. Come to the room at the end of the hall in five minutes.

-She disappeared into the house. Noll turned as a voice sounded to his left.

Are you too cool to dress for the party, Noll?

Ginger already gave me grief for forgetting, Vince. So, what are you supposed to be?

Guess.

Let's see. You're wearing a work shirt with the sleeves torn off, a dirty ball cap and greasy cut-offs. What's that beneath your cap?

It's hair. I'm supposed to have a mullet. Now, what am I?

I have no idea.

All this and you still can't tell?

No.

I'm gay trailer trash, Noll. Get with it.

Trailer trash?

I'm unemployed - too dumb to hold a job, I guess.

That sounds about right.

What?

Never mind.

Are you still working at the university? I haven't seen you driving around that big truck lately.

I'm there every day.

It must be weird coming to a party where you're the only one not in college.

Especially when I'm the only one that looks like I *am*.

Don't you feel like you're wasting your life away working a dead-end job instead of being in class?

I've learned more in that job than I ever did in class.

Are you going back to school eventually?

I don't know.

Where was Ginger off to?

Oh, right. I have to go, Vince.

He moved down the dimly lighted hall, past couples pressed into corners and doorways, hands in restless motion, speaking in whispers if speaking at all. Picking his way through them, he knocked on the door at the end, the stained panels smooth beneath his touch. Ginger's voice sounded through the thick wood. He turned the glass knob and entered a room cast in the crimson glow of a dozen burning candles. Across the room, Ginger waited in a red satin negligee, her breasts outlined by the sheer fabric, one knee resting on the corner of a four-poster bed. Noll stood before the closed door unable to speak, to move, the entire room spinning about her distant image. He had never seen her, never even imagined her in such a scene. She frowned at him.

Aren't you going to say something?

I…I…

Come here, then.

-He moved to her as if in a dream and she took his hand, tracing his fingers along her face and then sliding them down across her body. Noll shuddered and then leaned to kiss her, the heat of her mouth passing through him brandy-like, searing. He drew closer, moving his hands across her, and she moaned, pressing into him before backing onto the bed and pulling him after. Just as he stood and began to unbutton his shirt, a door slammed shut, followed by the sound of breaking glass and voices echoing down the hall. He tried to ignore the noise but one of the voices sounded familiar. He paused to listen.

Noll, come to me.

Do you hear that?

It's just the party, Noll. Look at me.

But someone is yelling. Who do you think it is?

I don't know and I don't care.

They sound familiar, at least one does.

Don't listen.

I won't listen.

Good, now come here.

They're getting louder.

They're just having fun.

Wait, I know that voice.

What?

Ginger, I have to go.

Noll, you can't just leave.

It sounds serious. What if they need help?

I need help, your help, right now.

I can't just ignore it if I know them, Ginger. They might be in trouble. I have to go see.

He rushed down the hall and out the back door, nearly tripping on an overturned table. Shattered glass and potato chips littered the patio like confetti. A still-intact ceramic bowl sat nearby in the close-cropped grass. Beyond the pool, a group of party-goers faced several figures dressed in jeans and matching red t-shirts, their voices rising and falling in argument, wavelike, full of anger. The noise rose and Noll again heard the voice that had brought him outside.

He moved to the side of the group to get a better look, spotting Maya as she lectured a man wearing a sequined t-shirt and a feathered boa, his cheeks covered with rouge. Maya waved her finger at him like a saber. As Noll walked toward them, Maya's companions came into view, stopping him cold. Pale and thin, Felix stood near her, smirking at the crowd and pointing at his shirt. Noll closed his eyes, unable to believe what he'd seen. By the time he looked again, Felix had spotted him and was waving in a sort of dance. Maya followed Felix's gaze and then frowned as her eyes fell upon Noll. She turned and hurried toward him, followed by the rest of the crowd. Felix reached him first.

Noll, I'm so glad to see you. Can you believe we're meeting out in the real world?

Felix, you're okay?

I'm better than okay, Noll. I'm wonderful. They let me out. I'm free, Noll the Brave, at least for awhile.

I went to see you but you weren't there and I thought that you...

Maya, look at how sad he looks. Oh my God, Noll you thought I had gone to that great disco bar in the sky, didn't you? Don't be sad, Noll. I'm here and I'm ready to party. Tell him, Maya.

What are you doing with these people, Noll?

I realize how it looks, Maya. But I didn't know what the party is about.

Your so-called party is just a hate-fest, Noll.

Go home, lesbo.

Shut up, Vince. I want to hear what she has to say.

What are you worried about, Noll? She can't be mad at you when you didn't even dress up. Besides, the babe obviously has the hots for you.

See what I mean, Noll? They're disgusting.

Why are *you* here, Maya?

The gay rights group on campus heard about the party and a few of us decided to come let them know how we feel.

I just came along for the ride but don't you like our t-shirts, Noll? I designed them myself. They're supposed to be about diversity and tolerance. It's not working very well, is it?

I like the design, Felix.

Get lost, gay boy.

Vince, what am I going to have to do to get you to stop?

Don't listen to him, Noll. I don't have anything to be ashamed of. After all, I'm the one preaching tolerance. Oh my God, did you hear what I just said? I said I'm preaching even though I'm always ragging on Maya for preaching at people. She'll never let me hear the end of it.

Felix, you're gay?

Noll the Brave, that's what I love about you. You're so innocent.

I'd call it clueless.

Shut up, Vince.

I was afraid to tell you at first, Noll because I didn't know you. But now I do and I know you'll like me no matter what.

Noll, are you queer?

Vince, you and the rest of the guys better get the hell out of here and leave us alone before I smash your face.

Alright, but I never would have figured you for a gay boy.

I can't believe you hang out with people like this, Noll.

Maya, I don't like what's going on here any better than you. I honestly had no idea what they had planned.

I can't believe you consider these people your friends.

I don't know what else to tell you.

Maya, lighten up. You're starting to sound like some boring crusader. I want to have some fun now that I'm free. You promised we'd go out if I'd come to this with you.

I know, Felix. It just makes me angry when ignorant people act so hateful.

You're sounding a little hateful yourself, sis.

-A woman pushed through the gate, calling out to no one in particular.

There's a skinny old black guy out front says he's looking for a Maya Cruz. He says it's urgent.

Who could that be, Noll?

Sounds like Hen.

Come with me, please?

You're sure you want me along?

-Ginger's voice called from behind them and she appeared in a thin cotton robe, her negligee visible beneath.

Noll, you're not leaving are you? Who's that you're with?

This is Maya. Ginger, I've got to go.

How can you leave me now, after what happened in the bedroom?

Oh, that sounds juicy. Tell us more.

Hush, Felix.

But, Maya…

Noll, we'd better go.

Wait, Maya. This is too good to miss.

Felix, you're not helping.

Is she why you're leaving me, Noll?

Ginger, something has happened, something urgent. I need to find out what it is. They may need my help.

If you leave, don't come back.

You don't mean that.

I do mean it, Noll.

It's not what you think.

I can see exactly what it is. I just wonder how long you've been running around on me.

I haven't been…

If you go with her, don't come back.

This isn't a movie Ginger, this is real life. You don't have to do this.

It is real life, your life and if you leave here we're through.

We're through? It's that simple to you?

You don't have to go off with your little senorita. You can stay here with me. It's that simple.

Don't talk about her like that. It isn't simple at all but I don't have time to explain. We need to go.

-They passed through the gate and on to the street, where Hen stood waiting at the curb.

Hen, what are you doing here?

I didn't expect to see you here, Noll. Lio sent me to find them two.

How did he know they were here?

Lio has his ways.

What is it, Hen?

Maya, something has happened. You and Felix need to come with me right away.

What has happened, Hen?

I can tell you on the way.

Nine

Hen drove the wide streets, immaculate, without shade, bordered by close-cropped lawn, manicured tree, bleached-white sidewalk free of clutter. Maya sat between him and Noll in the cab of Hen's rusted pickup, springs creaking with every bump, gasoline fumes and exhaust wafting through open windows. Felix sat in the space behind them. Books crowded the dust-covered dashboard, spilling onto the floor, sliding beneath their feet with every turn, their edges frayed, thumb-stained. A bust of Plato sat wedged beneath the windshield, eyebrows raised as if waiting for an answer. As they left the sun-drenched lawns, entering a narrow, shade-covered street, Hen turned to Maya.

Felix, Maya, your brother-in-law is missing.

Humberto is missing? What happened? Is Adela alright?

She's safe for now. Lio said the drug cartels are having a turf war in the town where she and Humberto live. The cartels killed some locals and ran off most of the other folks. Then they took over Adela's house. She was lucky to escape but her husband went missing. She believes they're after her now.

Why would she think that? Has she been threatened?

I'd call it more of a warning, Maya. Some woman contacted her to tell her she'd be killed if she didn't go into hiding.

Why would they go after Adela?

I can't say there's much sense in what's happening down on the border, but Lio thinks Humberto had something that belongs to the cartels and now they believe Adela has it. They want it back.

What will she do, Hen? Where can she hide?

She's at your parent's house right now but Lio says she can't stay.

But why?

He says he doesn't want to put the rest of the family in danger.

But Adela *is* family.

He says he means to protect your little brother and sister. He thinks the cartel will track Adela there with no problem. You know how your father can be, Maya.

We can't just do nothing. There has to be somewhere she can go.

You got to take that up with him. We're headed there now.

Hen pulled the truck in front of a frame house with a low-pitched roof, turquoise shutters and a door the color of raw salmon. Orange and red pots framed the porch stairs. Set in the middle of the close-cropped lawn, a twenty-foot flagpole held the Stars and Stripes and a U.S. Marines flag that appeared brand new. The driveway and sidewalk leading to the front door of the house held no toys or oil stains and had been swept to a dull white hue. The porch was equally bare of clutter. Maya stepped out of the truck, pointing to the flags.

Dad put up a new Marine flag.

Oh God, Maya, he's gone into his military mode. I think I'll go hide in my room.

Don't worry Felix, he has other things on his mind right now.

Turn and run while you still have a chance, Noll.

Don't listen to him. Dad isn't that bad if you know how to handle him. Tell him, Hen.

I don't know, Maya. I've seen how he can get. I believe I'll stay right here.

Won't anyone come with me? Noll, will you come?

79

-Noll followed Maya through the living room as the sound of voices echoed from the rear of the house. Maya moved across the room and toward a doorway spilling light onto the tile floor in a narrow quadrangle. She paused and then stepped into the kitchen, Noll close behind. Seated at a broad table before them, Lio and a young woman sat glaring at each other while an old man with a drooping mustache stirred at the far end of the table, his hand resting on the worn handle of a cane. Lio stopped talking and looked up at them.

Your sister is here.

Maya, thank God you're back. Help me talk some sense to your father.

Don't listen to her, Maya. Tell her she needs to go stay with her aunt in New Jersey.

Aunt Consie lives in New Jersey now?

Consuela has agreed to take your sister in. Tell Adela it's best for her to go up there right away.

Dad, why can't she stay here?

She's too easy to find here. She won't be safe.

But you can't just turn her away.

Besides, there's no room.

No room? I'll share my room with her.

You already share with your little sister.

We can make room.

I will not put the little ones in danger. She needs to go to Consuela.

I'm not going to leave Texas while Humberto is still lost down in Mexico, God only knows where.

Yes you are, Adela and that's final.

Who is the boy? He should not be here when you talk of family.

Abuelo, grandfather, this is my friend Noll. Be nice to him.

Only family should be here, Maya. He is not Mexican.

I'm not Mexican either. Do you want me to leave?

Noll, what are you doing here?

I was at a party, Lio and I heard Maya's voice…

You left your girlfriend in the bedroom because you heard my voice?

It's not like it…

What's this about a bedroom?

Hush, Dad.

I thought you might be in trouble, Maya and I…

Noll, I'm surprised you would…

Can we get back to where I'm going to stay? I have no money, no credit cards, nothing but what I'm wearing. The person that called told me they were coming for me so I ran for my life. Do you want me to go back where they can find me?

That is, *if* someone is really after you, Adela.

Dad, why would you say that?

It could be a hoax.

My husband is taken by gunpoint right in front of me and you say it's a hoax? How can you be so cold? This isn't the military, you know.

But it is a war.

Exactly, and now Humberto's caught in it and I'm left with nothing. What am I supposed to do?

Forget what I said. This is a problem and we need to fix it.

I'm not giving up on Humberto and running off to New Jersey. He would never leave me like that.

I will not put my family in harm's way, daughter.

Okay, fine, I'll find somewhere else to go. I'll go to the refugee center. They'll take me in.

Dad, how can you be so cold? Adela, you will not go to some homeless shelter.

Stay out of this, Maya.

I will not stay out of it, dad. This is my sister we're talking about.

I may have a solution.

What, Noll?

81

I have an idea.

What do you mean?

The white boy should not be here, Maya.

Abuelo, let him talk. What are you talking about, Noll?

My mother's aunt Eugenia has a house near the coast. We could ask if your sister can stay there until this gets sorted out. The cartel would have a hard time finding her there.

What do you think, Adela?

Well Maya, it's better than New Jersey.

Can you vouch for this aunt, Maya? Do you know her?

No dad, but I know Noll and I trust him.

Come on in, Hen.

-After a moment Hen stepped through the door, shaking his head.

Looky here Lio, how do you know where I am when I don't say a word, make a sound, hardly take a breath. I just can't figure it.

It comes from too many years crawling around the jungle with a gun in my hand. Hen, I need to stay here and make sure the family is safe until we understand the situation better. Can you do something for me?

Sure thing, Lio. What do you need?

I want you to take Adela and Maya down near the coast, a place where they'll be safe. Noll can show you the way.

I can do that.

Noll, I'm counting on you and Hen to keep my girls safe.

I don't need anyone to protect me. I can take care of myself.

Do what I say, Maya.

The same goes for me, dad.

At least you learned how to get along with a man, Adela. Maya, how are you ever going to get married when you're so independent?

Who said I want to get married? Maybe I like being single.

Are these really my daughters? I give up. They're all yours, Hen.

I know I don't want to tangle with Maya here. I'm just the driver. What about you, Noll?

I'm with you, Hen. I'll show the way and try to stay clear of these independent Cruz women.

-Felix leaned against the tailgate as they approached the truck.

Maya, did you get forty lashes or do you have latrine duty for the next month?

We're going to stay with Noll's aunt.

Noll has an aunty? Who would've guessed? If Noll the Brave is going I want to go too.

Noll the who? Looky here Felix, your daddy said to bring you home and that's what I did. Your mama has been worried sick about you running around all over creation in your condition.

I'm fine, Hen. She worries too much.

Well, I promised I'd get you home safe and now you're here. You can take it up with her.

Felix, you *are* looking awfully pale. Are you sure you feel okay?

Oh Maya, I don't know. I just want to have some fun.

You don't want to end up back in the hospital, do you?

Oh my God, are you kidding? Don't even mention that place. Now that I think about it, I guess I am feeling a little tired. Arguing with all those Neanderthals at the party must have worn me out.

You should rest up, then. I'll text you as soon as we get there and tell you all about it.

Wait. Will you text me, Noll? Will you be my eyes and ears, Sir Noll? It'll be like you're carrying me around in your pocket. How exciting is that?

Enough talk, Felix. The rest of you climb in my old truck so we can get moving. It's late enough already.

Ten

The last light of day edged the horizon as Hen drove the rattling truck past backwater creek and salt marsh, the black surface iridescent, impenetrable. A nearly full moon flitted between dense stands of oak and mesquite as they passed, lighting shards of glass, bits of metal unseen until that moment. Above the tree line, knots of cloud raced inland like ghost ships spun of silver. Noll sat behind Hen, watching Maya's profile in the blue dashboard light as she talked with her sister, her perfect line of nose, curve of lip. He tried to imagine what he would say to her if they had a moment alone but to his horror could think of nothing. At that moment she turned to him as if she could somehow read his thoughts, see his shortcomings.

Tell us about the house, Noll.

What?

Describe the house. What's it like?

What house?

Hello? Earth to Noll? You must be dreaming of something other than being stuck in a noisy old pickup with the three of us. Go ahead, admit it.

No, I...

This truck may be old but Nadine has been a better friend to me than most people I know. I expect she has a good many years left in her too, just like old Hen.

Oh Hen, I didn't mean it. I love this truck. Besides, she's not that old and neither are you.

That's what I'm talking about, Maya. Age is just a way of looking at time, and time is changeable. What seems a long time now may not seem so at another time. My great granny smoked, drank whiskey and still lived to be one hundred and seven. My mama always said I take after her, so I got another forty-seven years left long as I keep my wits about me.

Is that why you carry all the books sliding around under our feet, to keep your wits?

I hate being without a book if I find time on my hands so I buy the old ones that nobody wants and I keep them around wherever I might be. I feel better having them close by. Ideas are better than company if you're open to them.

You have plenty of ideas stashed in this truck, then.

Maya, these books would be thrown out if I didn't take them in. Think about that, a great book, a book by Hugo or Dickens, even Hemingway, going to the trash pile. It's a crime. So I give them a home until they die a natural death. But here I am rambling on after I interrupted you. You were asking Noll something.

Adela and I wanted to hear about this house we're headed to. Tell us about it, Noll.

Well, I've haven't visited since I was too young to remember much, but my grandmother says it's an old house on an inlet where the river meets the coast. My great aunt inherited it years ago. Aunt Eugenia is old but she still lives there on her own.

Are you sure it's okay for us to stay there?

My grandmother thinks so. We'll see.

The road ahead turned and narrowed, winding between Live oaks cast deep in shadow, their beard-like moss tossed before a shifting wind. Passing an abandoned post office, its doorway lighted by a single yellow bulb, the shiplap siding gray, warped, they turned into a stiff breeze tinged with the river, salt-laced, organic. The asphalt shifted to an oyster shell lane, phosphorescent in the moonlight, indigo blue in shadow, crunching beneath the tires like fresh snow, leading to a dense stand of trees before vanishing around a sharp bend.

Hen slowed the truck to a crawl as they entered deep shadow that soon gave way to a broad open area facing a shallow inlet scattered with thick stands of salt grass and mangrove. Puffs of cloud traced silver lines across a sky scattered with stars. To the right, beneath a sprawling oak a white frame house stood facing the inlet, its broad porch bathed in watery shadow, cool, oasis-like. Before them the silhouette of a distant shrimper tilted its wide net above the wind-ripped bay, pelicans and gulls swarming behind in the semi-darkness like nocturnal bees.

My great aunt owns the road we just came down from the old post office on. There's only one way in and one way out unless you travel by boat. That should make it safe enough for Adela.

What's your aunt like, Noll?

I don't know much about her except that she's an artist and she spends a lot of time in her studio. She lives out here alone and likes it that way. My grandmother said it's a beautiful place that might provide some comfort.

Adela, I'd guess you could do with some comfort. Sounds like you've had your share of troubles. My granny, she would head to the kitchen anytime there was trouble, her trouble or somebody else's, and whip up something good to eat. She'd seen enough hard times in her life and she knew how to help a person find a way through. She was just that type. She could put her tiny hand on your arm, just a light touch and you knew right then you were going be alright. You'll be alright too, Adela.

I'd like to believe that, Hen.

Don't you worry now. This'll all work itself out.

I'm so worried for Humberto. I don't know if I'll ever see him again. I can't stand it, the waiting, not knowing if he's alright.

Why would they take him, Adela?

I don't know, Maya. He had been acting funny lately, sort of quiet and secretive. I thought it was because we had to shut down the store. It wasn't his fault we had to close. It was just that so many people had left town because of the violence, the killings, we couldn't make ends meet anymore. He hoped the violence would soon pass and we could reopen.

It's hard to believe what's happening on the border, that drugs could cause such craziness.

If he got involved with the cartels, I'll never forgive him.

It's probably some kind of mistake.

Either way, I may never see him again, Maya. What if they really do come after me?

You should be safe here, Adela. Try not to worry.

-Hen parked the truck and they climbed out, heading up the porch stairs. Noll pushed through the screen door, followed by the others.

Aunt Eugie, are you here? It's Noll and I've brought the people Gannie told you about.

Who's Gannie?

Gannie is my grandmother, Maya. I called her while you were talking to your father.

Where did she get that name?

I had trouble talking when I was a kid.

You're still not much good at it.

What's that supposed to…?

Come in nice and slow and let me see if you are who you say you are.

Aunt Eugie, is that you?

In the kitchen Noll, if you really are him. Remember, nice and slow.

-Noll stepped through a doorway, followed by the others. Before them an old woman wearing a denim smock spattered with paint sat at a scarred walnut table, her white hair capped by a maroon bandana tied into a tight skullcap. An empty bottle of wine sat on the table next to a half-filled glass jar and a large revolver, the wooden handle worn to a dull shine. She eased her hand from the grip.

Why, you are Noll Spencer after all. You look just like you did the last time I saw you, only bigger.

Aunt Eugie, is everything okay?

What on earth do you mean? Oh, you mean this old gun. We've had some undesirables around here walking off with things that don't belong to them. Now, I don't have much in the way of valuables. I never much cared for them. But I won't start hiding behind a locked door just because some teenager has a yen for pot or whatever it is they go for these days. Why can't they just stick with something legal like beer or wine? They'd live longer if they did. Which one of you is Adela?

That's me. Thank you for letting me stay here.

I don't much like having visitors. They interfere with my work. But Gannie asked a favor and she's my sister-in-law besides being an old friend. I don't have many of those left, so there you have it.

I'll keep out of your way.

And is this your sister?

I'm Maya. If you knew why my sister needs a place to stay you'd see things differently.

Gannie told me all about it, missy. Makes no difference at all. Now get some glasses down from the cabinet. All I have is these fruit jars. I broke the last real glass six months ago. I'm damned clumsy for someone that works with her hands all day.

Aunt Eugie this is my friend, Hen Feathers.

Hen Feathers, is it? That's some name you got there. Now I have to ask myself what kind of man will carry two women all the way down here to be safe from the mob or whatever it is. Let me take a look at you. You have a fine face.

Ha! Now would you listen to that? Nobody ever said that to me before, nothing close. Are you sure you haven't lost your glasses?

These eyes are old but they see plenty. I know a good face when I see one and your face says a lot even if you don't say a word. I like that. Hen, you'll do me a favor if you let me paint you sometime. How about it? Will you sit for me? I'll provide the beer.

I'll tell you what I'll do, miss...

Call me Eugie. All of you call me Eugie. I don't care a hoot for formalities.

Alright Eugie, I'll sit for you. If you're good enough to take in these people, I suppose I can stand to have my ugly self painted though I can't understand why you'd want to.

It's settled then. We'll start tomorrow. Now, you men get out of our hair while I fix up something to eat. There's a cooler of beer on the porch and plenty of places to sit.

Hen leaned on the porch railing and popped open two cans of beer, handing one to Noll and talking a long pull on the other. Noll watched as he rolled a cigarette, pulling the cloth bag of tobacco closed with his teeth and striking a wooden match against the rail. The pinched cigarette flared briefly before settling to a dull glow. Moonlight steamed through the oaks, filling the porch and the open area beyond with blue light. Above the mangroves and salt marsh, flashing lights of oil rigs and crew boats dotted the horizon, their regularity broken now and then by a spotlight, the beam frantic, searching. Hen's voice broke the silence.

This here house been in your family a long time, Noll?

I don't know. My mother never talks about Aunt Eugie. She thinks she's the crazy aunt of the family.

She's a little ornery but no crazier than the rest of us that I can tell. Families, they like to have their myths and their secrets.

What do you mean?

Well now, take Eugie. Let's say as a young woman she's got her own style, her own ideas that don't match up

90

with the family, or she dresses different from other women and takes up work that the family can't understand. So, one day someone in the family decides she must be crazy. What else could it be? Then the idea gets passed around from one to the other, year after year until sooner or later everyone comes to believe it. After that the family, they want the myth a secret because they think having a crazy relative makes them look bad, hurts their pride.

But that's wrong. Being different isn't the same as being crazy.

Right or wrong, once that myth gets started it's hard to stop it.

Do you have secrets, then?

Every man has his secrets Noll, just like every family. Take a look at your family and see what you find.

I'm not sure I want to know.

You got to understand where you come from, Noll.

Where are your people from, Hen?

They're from around here.

Were they always from here?

You mean did my family come from somewhere else a ways back?

That's right.

They did, son. My grandfather's family comes out of Mississippi.

My grandmother's family was from Mississippi too.

Whereabouts they come from, Noll?

My mother gave me the same name as the family home there, the same name my great grandfather had.

There's a place name of Noll, Mississippi? I never heard of it.

My full name is Glenolden.

I know that name. Noll, are you telling me your family comes out of Glenolden, Mississippi?

My grandmother told me they once had a plantation there.

91

Is that right? I know the place.

The house burned to the ground when her mother was a little girl.

Yes, I seem to remember hearing something about that house.

She even has a picture of a man named McHenry Feathers.

McHenry…are you sure?

She'd have no reason to make it up and she did have the picture. I saw it myself.

Lordy Noll, that's hard to believe. Why, my grandmother's grandmother lived as a slave on that plantation and my great grandfather worked it as a freeman. I'm named for him.

There's something else, Hen. She said there's a rumor that my grandmother's great grandfather was Mr. Feathers' father.

What are you saying, son?

She said it was only a rumor but it hasn't gone away in all these years.

Now, let me get this straight. A relative of yours was the father of old McHenry Feathers?

It's still just a rumor.

Ha! Are you telling me we're related, Noll?

I can't say it isn't true and I can't say it is, so I don't know what to tell you.

It sure does set a mind to spinning. After all the trouble I've had with white people in my life I don't know that I want to be kin. On the other side, I don't know what to think of being kin to you. Might not be too bad.

You haven't met the rest of the family. You may change your mind.

You're full of surprises, boy. What else you got to tell me that I don't know?

Well, there is something I should tell you even though I don't want to.

Is it some bad news about your family?

92

In a way it is. And you may decide you don't want to claim any relation to me when you hear it.

Can't be that bad. What is it?

I…uh, well…

Out with it, boy.

I was the one that told Elgy about Nando coming in late.

You did what? Why in the hell would you do that, Noll? You and Nando get along fine.

It's not about him. I'd rather work alongside Nando than most of the other men.

Then why?

Elgy told me I'd have to provide him information on the men, especially on you. I'm ashamed to say I didn't think twice about agreeing to it when I first took the job.

I should've known the white men would stick together.

It's not like that, Hen. I don't like him any more than you.

What then?

I avoided giving him what he wanted as long as I could but then he threatened to get rid of me if I didn't give him something real. That's when I told him. I didn't want to lose my job.

Sounds like just another excuse to me.

I heard plenty of bigotry growing up but that's no reason. There are plenty of people that hear the same and end up fair-minded. I have no excuses.

Your past is a hard thing to walk away from, even if you want to. And Elgy has the power in that place. Still, it was a bad thing you did.

I'm sorry, Hen. I know it was wrong but I don't know how to make it right.

No way to make it right so you just have to live with it.

I guess I knew that.

You're young, Noll and still have a thing or two to learn about this life and the people in it. But we got ourselves a way of dealing with that Elgy now. You and me, we'll work together in figuring what to feed him and he'll lap it right up, you'll see. It'll be just like when I was a boy feeding the pigs.

Are you going to tell Nando?

I figure you'll get around to it in your time.

-Maya stepped through the door and paused, looking from Hen to Noll.

Hen, Eugie wants you in the kitchen. She told me to stay here and keep Noll company.

She's not going to start painting me, is she? I need a few more beers before I'm ready for that.

She wants you to cut up the brisket.

Did you say brisket? I'll do whatever she wants for some home-cooked brisket.

-Hen disappeared through the door.

This is a beautiful place, Noll. Why didn't you come here more often?

Gannie says my mother thinks Aunt Eugie is a little touched. She and the rest of the family wouldn't have anything to do with her.

Eugie sure is independent and crusty but she's not crazy. Why would your mother think that?

It's hard to say. My mom doesn't make much sense at times.

What do you mean?

She has trouble thinking straight. She lost her job because of it.

So that's why you're working at the university?

We even had our car repossessed.

What about your father?

He died a little over a year ago.

Oh Noll, that's terrible, first your father and then your mother. Don't you have anyone you can turn to?

I'm alright.

But it must be hard.

I don't want people feeling sorry for me.

Caring is not the same as pity. I just feel bad for you. What's wrong with that?

I don't need anyone's sympathy, especially yours. I can take care of myself.

Don't be mad. I promise I won't feel sorry for you.

Good.

I do like it when you talk to me.

I don't know why. I never know what to say.

Just say what's on your mind, Noll. Tell me you want.

I don't know what I want.

Sure you do. Everyone dreams. What's your dream, Noll? Where do you want your life to go?

I wish I knew. I feel like everyone, everything is passing me by. I look around and see other people getting on with their lives but I'm in some kind of limbo and can't seem to get out. No matter what I try, nothing works.

That must be frustrating.

It is. I can't figure out what to do about it.

You'll find a way. I know you will.

How do you know?

I can see it in you, Noll. You have a determination those other people don't have.

You see that?

Tell me what else you think about. Do you ever think about me?

Do I think about you? Well, I...

Just tell me what's on your mind. It can't be that hard, Noll. And be honest. I can take it.

I'd like to tell you, Maya. I think about what I want to say all the time, but...

But what, Noll?

-Maya moved closer to him.

Sometimes I look at you and you look so...I mean, I see you and I want...

What? Tell me.

I want to…

-The door swung open and Adela leaned out, looking from Maya to Noll and back.

Oh, did I interrupt something?

No, Adela. We're just talking.

Really Maya, is that all? It seems like more than just talk to me. And you have that guilty look I know so well.

What do you want, big sister?

Eugie says dinner is ready.

Okay.

Are you coming? Or do you two need more time alone?

We're coming, Adela.

In that case, Eugie said for Noll to bring the ice chest with him. I'll hold the door.

How thoughtful of you, Adelita.

Always glad to help, little sister.

Eleven

Sunlight drifted before the morning breeze, dappling the thick grass, skittering across the lawn in waves, restless, alive as Noll strained to lift a roll of canvas into the back of Hen's truck. The wind, tinged with salt, acrid, organic, swirled about his head, mussing his hair as his mother's hand might and pulling at his shirt. Behind him, Adela sat on the porch swing gazing out over the mangrove and salt flats. In the distance, a heron sailed low above the marsh, silent, ghost-like. Hen lifted a stack of boards and stood upright, cocking his head, listening, breath held. A car door slammed somewhere out of sight and then a voice called over the rustling breeze. Adela moved to the porch rail as a woman rounded the hedge.

Yoo-hoo, Eugenia, are you here? Oh, good, she finally got a housekeeper. Don-day es-tay Eu-gee-nee-ah?
What?
-Adela leaned on the rail, frowning. The woman glanced at Hen as she strolled toward the house.
Oh my, she has a gardener too?
-She turned back to where Adela stood, hands on her hips.
Where could Eugenia be? Don-day es-tay Eu-gee…
How can I help you?
And she speaks English too. Eugie must really be doing well these days.
-Eugie pushed through the door, walking to the edge of the stairs.
Hello, Mary Kate. What brings you out here?
Where did you find help that speaks English, Eugenia? And you have a gardener too, or is he a handyman?
These are my guests Mary Kate, not my employees. Now what can I do for you?

Oh my, how was I supposed to know? Anyway, the Women's Club wants to know if you'll come speak to us at our meeting next Wednesday. We have a number of members who are artists, you know. You made such a fine speech to the Chamber so I thought it would be a nice entertainment for the members while they eat their chicken salad.

The Women's Club, huh? Well, Mary Kate I'm doing a series of drawings capturing the prejudice and racism that's so rampant in this country nowadays. How does that sound?

You don't want to talk about your wonderful portraits?

I could talk about how easy it is to recognize sexual frustration in a person's facial features. That's always a crowd pleaser.

Sexual frustration?

Well sure. See all those wrinkles on either side of your mouth?

I don't recall having any such wrinkles.

Sure you do, Mary Kate. I believe I can see them from here.

But what about your landscapes? You don't want to talk about those?

No, Mary Kate now that I think about it, sexual frustration is overdone. I believe I'll speak about prejudice. That's what interests me and that's all I'm willing to talk about.

Uh, well let me talk to the board and I'll let you know.

Fine, you just go do that, Mary Kate.

-The woman put her hand to her mouth, hurried to her car and left. Eugie turned to the garage, where Hen and Noll stood watching the woman's car disappear behind the tree line.

Alright Hen, I just talked to Cyrus, my Greek god and the man that builds my canvases so he's expecting you.

Don't forget to pick up a few pounds of shrimp. The market is right down the road from Cyrus' place. Noll, Hen, thanks for helping me with this. I always built my own canvases but when my arthritis flared up again it got to be too much of a pain, in the literal sense. It's hell getting old. People just live too damn long.

The rattling truck creaked in complaint as Hen drove the winding blacktop edging the ragged coastline. Lines of rust-tinged cloud roiled overhead, imposing, impossibly close, crowding the flat landscape like unwanted guests. Bursts of white dust rose up before the shifting wind, suspended then torn to nothing in an instant.

Turning into a narrow alleyway, Hen pulled up to the unpainted cedar shake building Eugie had described, setting the brake and peering through the windshield as Noll hopped out. Two wide doors at one end of the workshop rattled and then swung open and a tall, burly man with a thick beard stepped out, coughing and slapping sawdust from his apron with his cap. He seemed as broad as the workshop doors. Noll shook hands with the man, trying not to wince beneath his iron-like grip.

Please excuse the sawdust. I am carving twelve holy disciples for St. Vassilis' church. The church lost them to fire two years ago.

You must be Cyrus.

Cyrus Fotopoulos is my name. Don't laugh, it is Greek. We Greeks are proud of our names even if they make Americans to laugh.

A friend taught me I shouldn't laugh at a person's name.

You must be Eugie's nephew, Noll. You are the one with the pretty girlfriend, I think.

Girlfriend?

So, that means you are Hen.

McHenry Feathers. Pleasure to meet you, Cyrus. Call me Hen.

Hen Feathers? Oh, I see I am not the only one with such a name to make people to laugh. Welcome to my workshop.

-Cyrus lifted the boards and canvas form the bed of the truck with ease and they followed him into the building. A line of wooden sculptures in various states of completion stood atop a long workbench.

What girlfriend?

Never mind about that, Noll. So, Cyrus, tell us about your project here.

When St. Vassilis' plaster statues are burned, the church fathers go to Eugie for help. A long time ago she paints a mural for the chapel just like Michelangelo, I think. So, she tells them wood sculpture is best and sends to me.

The faces look real, like they're actual people.

Yes Noll, they are from my family back home. That is my uncle and there my grandfather and my cousin, Andrea. It is like having them here with me.

All of your family still lives back in Greece?

All of them.

Do you miss them?

Sometimes, Noll but this is my home now.

What did Eugie say about a girlfriend, Cyrus?

Not now, Noll. I can see Cyrus needs to be getting back to his work and we need to get moving too. Cyrus, can you point us to the fish market?

Of course, Hen. The red house at end of the alley is Olney market. The owner is not so friendly, I think but they have the fresh seafood.

A low-slung shiplap building painted a garish shade of red stood before Noll and Hen as they climbed out of the truck and made their way across an oyster shell parking lot, brilliant white in the full sun, and on to

Olney's Seafood Market. As they approached the entrance a man carrying a plastic bag full of shrimp stepped out the door, frowned at them and then hurried down the street.

Noll followed Hen under an orange sign swinging before the constant breeze, creaking, grating metal on metal, and into a large room scattered with live bait tanks, their white sides streaked with rust. Stacks of beer stood along one wall next to a metal ice chest filled with single cans buried in ice. The other wall held several discolored metal tables and chairs, empty except for a red-faced man in a grimy cap hunched over a can of beer. He looked up and leaned back in his chair, squinting at the two of them.

Noll turned as a toothless man behind a high counter grunted and spit before facing them, his lined face scowling, leather-like, one eye rolling in its socket as if beyond control, the other scrutinizing their every move. Noll stepped next to Hen and leaned toward him.

The guy behind the counter is giving us the eye, Hen.

Looks like he's only got one to give.

Do you think he's the owner?

Cyrus warned us about the man. Don't pay him any mind. Let's get us some shrimps. I believe I can almost taste them already.

He looks like he wants us to leave.

I'm not leaving here without some shrimps. I believe I'll have a beer while I'm at it. How about you? It's on me.

Uh, sure.

-Hen fished two beers from the ice, handing one to Noll before popping open the other. The man behind the counter jumped from his chair with the sound and called through a door directly behind the counter. A moment later, a stout young man with a pockmarked face emerged and stood behind the man. A dragon tattoo circled his neck, disappearing beneath his sweat-stained shirt. The man with the wandering eye spit again before speaking.

Them beers ain't free.

No problem, mister. We want some shrimps too, three pounds of them.

Shrimp ain't for sale.

Say again? What do you mean not for sale?

I mean just what I said. You understand plain English?

But I just saw a man carry a bag of shrimps out of here.

Them was yesterday's shrimp and he got the last of them. These are today's and they're not for sale.

These here shrimps look fine to me.

Ain't for sale.

Why not?

They ain't ripe yet.

Hey Olney, that's a good one.

Shut up and drink your beer, Horace.

We need to get a move on, so we'll just get those shrimps and be on our way.

Like I said, they ain't for sale. Are you trying to start some trouble here?

I'm just trying to buy some shrimps.

Come on, Hen. Let's get our shrimp somewhere else.

No sir, Noll, we're here and we have a right to buy what other people can buy.

You got that wrong. I'm the owner and what I say goes.

Well, these here live shrimp will do just fine.

-Hen grabbed a net, filling a large plastic bag from the bait tank and weighing it before tying off the top. He tossed the bag on the counter.

Let me see here, three pounds at $3.99 and two beers at $1.50 adds up to $15.00. With tax, sixteen and a quarter should cover it.

-Hen threw the cash down and turned for the door. The red-faced man jumped to his feet.

You heard what Olney said, boy.

I don't recall asking for any help, Horace. Sit down.

But Olney, are you going to let a colored boy talk to you like that?

Let's get on out of here, Noll.

Your money's no good in my place. You take those shrimp and you'll regret it.

Are you coming, Noll?

Just a minute, Hen.

-Noll walked to the counter, picked up the money and stuffed it in his pocket.

What are you doing, Noll?

I'm taking your money, Hen. It's mine now.

-Noll fished the bills back out of his pocket and slapped them on the counter.

There, I've paid for your shrimp with my own damn money.

It's too late for that, sonny. Them shrimp stay here.

If it were up to me old man, you wouldn't get a dime of this. You have no right to talk to my friend that way, no right at all. This is the twenty-first century in case you didn't know.

Go get those shrimp from him, Jimmy.

-The young man slipped beneath the counter, rounding the end and heading for Hen. Noll stepped in front of him and the man stopped. Horace moved up beside Jimmy.

Out of the way, boy.

We have no quarrel with you, Jimmy. Your boss is the problem.

Don't waste your time on them, Noll. We're paid up so let's get on out of here.

Let's go get those shrimp, Jimmy.

Alright, Horace, as soon as I take care of the shrimp right in front of me.

-Jimmy grabbed a handful of Noll's shirt just as steps sounded in the doorway. He looked up, then let go and took a step back.

Hello, Cyrus.

Ah, there you are, Hen. Is Noll with you? I was hoping to find you before you leave.

Noll and me were on our way out but we ran into a little problem.

What is wrong here, Olney?

Stay out of this, Cyrus. This boy is causing us trouble and we aim to take care of it.

Jimmy is causing trouble?

No, Cyrus the colored feller right in front of you is.

I got us these shrimps here, Cyrus and paid for them with cash money but Mr. Olney seems to think they still belong to him. I say they're bought and paid for, so we can be on our way.

Olney, why do you insult Mr. Feathers?

I told him they ain't for sale to the likes of him but he wouldn't listen, Cyrus.

And what do you stand there for, Jimmy? You make trouble, I think.

Uh, no Cyrus I don't want any trouble, especially from you. Olney told me to get those shrimp back.

Why the shrimp not for sale, Olney?

They just ain't Cyrus, that's all.

But I see Pinky Fellers walk by my shop just now with big bag of shrimp. He buys them from you I think.

That's right, Cyrus.

You sell shrimp to me, Olney?

Why, uh...yes, Cyrus. You know I've sold you plenty shrimp.

You sell shrimp to me now, Olney?

Uh...why sure, Cyrus.

104

Then you sell to Mr. Feathers. He is no different from me.

But Cyrus, think what you're saying.

I know what I say.

Ah hell, Cyrus. Alright, whatever your name is, take the damn shrimp and get the hell out of here, both of you.

You're going to let them get away with it just like that, Olney?

Shut up, Horace unless you want to take it up with Cyrus.

What? Oh…no I don't need to take anything up, Cyrus. I'm just going to go back to my table and drink my beer in peace. No need to give me another thought, no sir.

-Noll turned and followed Hen and Cyrus out the door, listening for the sound of footsteps behind but hearing only the high-pitched whistle of wind through screen. Noll and Cyrus waited beneath a nearby palm tree while Hen went to his truck and tossed the shrimp into an ice chest. He turned to where they stood.

Well Cyrus, I believe you just saved Noll from having to pick his self up off that nasty old fish market floor.

What? I had everything under control in there, Hen.

You might could outrun Jimmy but you wouldn't have much chance in close quarters. He had you by forty pounds, at least.

So this is the thanks I get when I stick up for you?

Looky here Noll, I appreciate the thought but the best thing you could've done for me is stop talking and get your young self out of there. Besides, we need to be thanking Cyrus here instead of arguing about it.

You're right, Hen.

Looky here Cyrus, why'd you come down here, anyway?

I forget to give you these snapshots of the sculptures Hen, the ones I finish. Eugie asks me to send them.

Fine, fine, we'll be glad to take these to Eugie but let Noll buy you a beer first.

Let me buy the beer?

Sure thing son, it's the least you can do.

I know a bar one block away. The owner is good man. He is not like Olney.

Let's go, long as the beer is cold and we can keep Noll here out of trouble.

Twelve

Cyrus led Noll and Hen to a faded blue house set on four-foot cedar posts and edging a crushed shell parking area that doubled as the local ferry landing. A short line of cars waited in the brilliant, shadow-less light for the ferry's return. Nearby, a sign reading "Last Chance Bar" vibrated before the gusting wind, its metal guy wires humming like bees. Beyond the building, a vast bay shimmered beneath the noonday sun, the emerald green shallows fading into aquamarine at the channel. Wind-whipped saltwater stretched to the horizon, featureless, razor-flat.

Cyrus pushed through the rain-stained door, walking up to a massive mahogany bar worn to a glowing reddish-brown. Between two carved columns, a salt-corroded mirror reflected the dappled bay through windows lining the far wall. Flags from countries across the globe hung overhead in rows, their bright colors rippling in the breeze. Cyrus held up his hand, grinning at Noll before bringing his thick palm down with a heavy slap.

Do we Greeks pour our own beer or do we wake up the lazy Aussie bartender?

-A stout man wearing a Scottish kilt walked out a door adjacent to the bar, a slight smirk beneath his walrus mustache. Cyrus slapped the bar again.

Cheers, Cyrus. How're you going?

Farley has a dress on. The world, it makes to end soon I think.

A dress? Cyrus my boy, if you want me to pour you a pint of the golden nectar you'll call this by its proper name.

You must mean a skirt, then.

Whoa, Cyrus don't let those big Scots from Celtic Union hear you. They'll toss you to the back of beyond and leave you there.

They are only little children, I think.

Oh yeah, and my mother was Marilyn Monroe.

Farley, all this talk has made my friends thirsty.

Well, she'll be right soon enough. You'll have a pint and my condolences if you have nothing better to do than hang around with this Greek baboon.

This is Hen and Noll.

Welcome to the Last Chance, gents. It's our little piece of Down Under on the bay.

You're a long way from home, Farley.

Well, Hen I enjoy a visit to my folks back in Oz now and again but this is my home now. I wouldn't have it anywhere else but right here. There's no place like it, even in Australia.

It's good to know you're where you belong, when you find it.

You are a wise man, Hen. I can't on my life understand what you're doing with our Cyrus here. What of you, Noll? What's your excuse?

Noll is Eugie's nephew.

Is that right, Cyrus? Our Eugie, is it? Well, my pleasure, Noll. Eugie is our biggest fan and head cheerleader, has been for years.

Fan of what?

Fan and cheerleader of the only true sport, Noll, rugby of course. Cyrus and I play for the Hunslayers, a true mongrel of a team. We have players from all over the world, good ones. Our boys are big too.

We make room for little ones like Farley, I think.

Admit it, Cyrus. The team wouldn't be the same without me.

That is true. We would be better.

I asked for that one didn't I, Noll? Speaking of rugby, I have Celtic Union on the deck waiting for wedges and another pitcher so I'll be off. They get a bit testy if their beer gets warm. The bangers even accused me of pissing in the last pitcher but they drank it anyway, of course. I was tempted to oblige them this time but I couldn't stand the thought of defiling the sacred brew. Cheers men!

-Farley disappeared behind the bar. Hen and Noll followed Cyrus to a table near the windows.

Hen, tell me what happens at Olney's place. Why does he insult you?

Well Cyrus, there will always be backward-thinking people and prejudice no matter where you go.

Do you mean the prejudice of the black man, the slavery?

Around the time of the Civil War, they called slavery the "peculiar institution" so it didn't sound as bad as it was.

That's right, Noll. This country was torn about slavery more or less from the start. Even the Constitution said a black counted as only three fifths of a man. There's nothing equal about that.

People make a big deal of emancipation but prejudice just went underground and it's still here, just under the surface. I know people who claim they aren't prejudiced but who discriminate against people almost every day, all kinds of people.

Looky here Noll, people fear what's different, whether you're black, white, brown or red. Prejudice has no care what color you are. Some of the worst is against people from across the border, even if their great grandfather was the last one to come across.

Or like the Jew in Europe. You can see it in Greece even today. I have seen it myself.

Bigotry knows no country, no border, Cyrus.

But Hen, the Civil War ended nearly a hundred and fifty years ago. Why are we still talking about this? What's wrong with people?

Civilization is a fragile thing, Noll. Progress is slow and it'll backtrack soon as you look the other way.

How can you be so calm about it, Hen?

Books did that for me, Noll. I didn't get much from school and I dropped out before I should have but I've tried to make up for it since. I've read everything I could find on slavery, the Civil War and prejudice, civil rights too. The human mind is the hope for the world, Noll and ignorance is the enemy.

Well, ignorance or not there's no excuse for the meanness and cruelty still out there. The whole thing pisses me off. I feel like going back to Olney's and kicking a little redneck butt.

Cyrus, I don't believe Noll can hold his beer. Listen to the young man talk.

This isn't the beer talking, it's me.

Looky here Noll, violence won't solve much of anything.

Maybe not but I sure liked watching the way those bigots cowered when Cyrus showed up.

There is some good in being big and playing rugby, I think. Now I must return to my workshop but you will visit again soon I hope, Hen and Noll. We still have much to discuss.

-Cyrus stood and drained his glass before disappearing through the door.

Let's have another beer, Hen. This time the round's on me.

The round was on you last time, Noll.

I know. I just like the way it sounds.

-Noll stood and turned toward the bar, scanning the room for Farley. The entire room appeared empty except for a single table tucked into the far corner, nearly lost in shadow. Noll took a step but stopped in mid-stride as something about the table caught his attention, something more sensed than seen. He could just make out a lone figure seated at the table, staring right at him. Noll stood frozen in place.

Vaditch.

What's that you say, Noll?

110

Hen, it's him. He's right there across the room, staring right at me.

You mean the man from Lavonia's, the Polish man who came after Ranse?

He's Russian and it's him, it's Vaditch.

You're seeing things, Noll.

No, I have a clear view of him now. Turn and see.

No sir, I believe I'll just sit right where I am, enjoying this view here of the ocean and the birds flying by.

But Hen, I'm not kidding. It's Vaditch.

No more beer for you, Noll. I've never known a man to have more trouble holding his liquor.

Hen, this isn't good. How did he find us?

Looky here now, step aside and let me see what you're going on about.

-Hen turned and stood, letting his eyes adjust to the dim interior. Then he shoved his chair out of the way, muttering under his breath as he began walking toward the corner. Noll followed. A moment later they stood before Vaditch, a cloud of cigar smoke drifting about his head.

Hello, gentlemen. Please sit so we can talk in a civilized manner. The furniture here is decrepit but it will do for our purposes.

We got no purpose with you, Radish.

Please Mr. Feathers, I ask you to pronounce my name correctly. My name is Nicolai Vaditch. People call me Vaditch. I have called you by your given name. I simply ask that you, as they say in this country, return the favor so we can be on friendly terms.

I'm not looking to make any friends today, Vaditch. What are you doing here?

This is a free country, is it not Mr. Feathers?

How did you find us?

I have many contacts, Noll.

You can call me Mr. Spencer.

I see you have some of your father's spirit.

111

Leave my family out of this.

Oh, but they are already in it, Noll.

What are you saying?

You have an Aunt Eugenia, do you not?

I'm not saying.

It helps nothing to feign ignorance.

What do you want with Aunt Eugie?

And your aunt has guests, I believe.

Looky here, Vaditch you best stay clear of Eugie's place. She doesn't take to strangers.

That's right, Vaditch. She's started keeping a gun close at hand. Someone prowling around is likely to get shot.

You misunderstand me, Noll. I am here to offer my assistance.

You mean the way you assisted Ranse the other day?

That was business, Mr. Feathers. I needed to convey a message to Mr. Jenkins and you were able to assist. In this instance I am the one providing the assistance.

Who says we need any help?

You have no concern about your guests? I'm surprised to hear it, Noll.

We can handle ourselves.

Why are you here, Vaditch?

As I told you, Mr. Feathers, I am here to assist Noll's aunt and her guests.

Assist them with what?

I'm simply keeping an eye on their whereabouts.

Who sent you, Vaditch?

Let's just call them a concerned party.

Looky here then, Nic. You tell your friends we take care of our own business. We don't need anybody's help. I got that right, Noll?

You got it right, Hen.

112

You don't realize who you're dealing with gentlemen but I'll pass along your comments just the same.

You best remember our comments too. I hear Eugie's a crack shot with that old pistol of hers.

Thirteen

A light breeze smelling of mud flat and saltwater drifted past palmettos fronting Eugie's porch, stirring, rattling as Hen followed Noll up the steps. The weathered stairs creaked beneath their feet. A late afternoon sun flickered through the reaching oak that filled the lawn behind them, dappling the porch slats like splattered paint. Hen paused, touching Noll's arm before he spoke.

I been thinking about that Vaditch and I believe if he wanted to hurt Adela he would've done it by now.

He could have gone after any of us at any time.

That's true, son and there's no reason he would've shown himself if he meant to do us harm. Still, I can't figure what he's up to and I don't like it.

If he *is* here to protect Adela then there must be somebody else out there looking for her.

I was thinking the same. You and me better patrol the grounds after dinner. I believe I'll just sleep out on this porch here tonight to keep an eye on things. Better not alarm Adela or Maya unless we have to.

-Noll pushed open the door and they walked through the living room and on to the kitchen. Eugie stood at the sink rinsing dishes and grumbling under her breath as she stacked them on a nearby drain board.

Aunt Eugie, don't you have a dishwasher?

These two hands of mine are the only dishwasher around here unless I can rope someone else into doing it. What about you, Noll. Washing dishes is a great skill for a young man to have. The ladies will love it. Besides, it's fun and relaxing. See how peaceful I look?

Eugie, don't you know our Noll here won't fall for your Tom Sawyer talk?

Don't listen to him, Noll. I meant every word I said. See how relaxed I am? No doubt Hen has had women

114

do his dishes for him all his life so he doesn't know a thing about it.

If I ever find myself a woman to do the dishes, I'll know I've died and gone to heaven.

Hen, you don't even go to church. How can you believe in heaven?

I never thought going to church had much to do with heaven, Noll.

So, you believe in heaven?

No, but I sure do believe in hell.

How can you believe in hell and not in heaven?

Noll has a point there, Hen. How can you?

Well Eugie, I've seen enough of hell right on this earth to know that it's real but I don't of know much that I'd call heaven.

Oh Hen, take a look around. Heaven is there if you're open to it. This place is my idea of heaven. You men stay for awhile and you'll see.

What do you mean, Aunt Eugie?

When I watch a line of pelicans coast just above the water or hear the wind rattling the palms along the porch I feel it. When I smell the inlet on a warm night all bursting with life I can't help but feel the essence of this place and the bit of heaven it occupies. The spirit of the inlet fills this house every day, sustaining me as if it was the very air I breathe. Pay attention and you'll feel it.

You're lucky to have such a place.

It's my sanctuary, Hen and I *am* lucky to have it. But the world I'm talking about is there for anyone who'll take the time to see it. There are many versions. This just happens to be mine. I don't know about the great hereafter the Bible-thumpers talk about but I know this place and it's heaven to me.

As much as I might like to spend a little time in heaven we got to keep an eye out for what hell can bring along tonight, Eugie.

What do you mean, Hen?

I don't know, exactly. We ran into a man that has dealings with the drug gangs or some such business and he more or less said he's here to help protect Adela. I don't know what to make of that so I'm going to keep a close eye out. I'll be sleeping on the porch tonight. Noll and me, we'll patrol the area after dinner.

If he found Adela, then someone else may know her whereabouts.

That's true, Eugie.

Is she safe here?

Don't know that either but this is the best we've got so we'll stick with it for the time being. Where is she now?

She's been in her room since breakfast. I believe she's grieving over her husband. And she hasn't eaten a thing all day, although I've tried to feed her. It must be hell for her not knowing what's happened to him.

Sometimes heaven can be hard to find.

That's true Hen, and you can lose it once you find it if fate is against you.

Eugie, you and me think the same. I believe we must be related somewhere deep in the past.

The world is full of such surprises. I'm going to try to get some work done before dinner. Noll, will you come to my studio and help me with something?

- An image of Maya and their interrupted conversation kept dogging Noll's thoughts while he followed Eugie out the back door and on to a cedar shake-covered studio tucked behind a grove of pear trees, it's wide barn-like doors slightly ajar. As he approached the doorway, he glimpsed Maya's form vanishing beneath a vine-covered arbor set beneath the massive oak that stretched over the front lawn. He stopped and stared at the arbor for a moment before turning and stepping into the broad room, its slat floor splattered with paint of all colors, especially crimson, two wooden easels set in the middle. Diffuse light falling from a row of high windows cast the

116

room in a bluish hue. Canvases of various sizes leaned against the far corner where Eugie stood pointing to a spot on the floor.

Noll, you see that discolored board there next to the canvas? Come over here and pull it up for me. Hurry up now. After all that dish-washing I could use a drink but I have to get this chore done first. Under the board is a trap door to my hiding place. Use the latch to open the door, then reach in and flip the light switch on your right.

-Noll lifted the board, revealing a circular metal latch. He grabbed the latch and pulled open the narrow door. A set of concrete stairs led into darkness as he reached in, finding the switch and flipping it. The narrow room below burst into view.

What's this room for, Aunt Eugie?

My father survived one of the worst tornados ever to hit this county so he built this room as a storm shelter. I use it for something else. When I said I don't have much that a thief would want, it was true mostly but I do have a few things of value. Give me a hand and we'll take a look.

-Noll took her arm and they descended the short flight of stairs leading into the small room. The walls were covered with photographs, drawings and paintings, some in gilt frames, others frameless.

These pictures are famous?

Not the kind famous you hear about on the news but I couldn't come close to affording even one of them if I wanted to buy it now.

How did you afford them in the first place?

My grandfather was a collector so that accounts for most of them. The rest I traded for when I was young, before the artist became well known. I used to come down here and spend time with them now and then. They inspire me. But getting up and down those stairs is a bit risky for an old woman who lives out here by herself. Once in a while I'll have someone I trust bring one up. I keep it

117

hidden among all the other canvasses. That's what I want your help with.

-She lifted a small painting from the wall, handing it to Noll.

That's by a Russian artist named Kandinsky. He was very spiritual and claimed he could hear the colors as he painted.

He could hear color?

He said yellow sounded like a trumpet playing a single note. They call it synesthesia.

-On a three-legged table pushed into one corner, Noll noticed a photo. He picked it up to get a better look.

That's Sergio, the great love of my life.

You were married?

No, my fiancé was killed in the war. We loved each other but we had so little time together I barely knew him. I met Sergio after the war when I was overseas on scholarship. He was an Argentinean journalist living in Rome and I was there to study. Isn't it funny the things you remember?

What do you mean, Aunt Eugie?

Noll, don't you think it's about time you started calling me Eugie?

Alright, Eugie. What do you remember about that time in Rome?

I won't bore you with all that, Noll. But if you should find a love like Serge and I had, do whatever you can to keep it.

What happened to him?

He went back to his wife and kids in Argentina.

He was married?

He finally confessed. I was angry of course but I got over it.

How did you?

I learned to appreciate Rome for the wonderful time it was. Serge was a part of that time, a big part. In a way he'll always be with me, as if he's on assignment somewhere and due back any day. Memory is funny that way.

You weren't at all resentful?

Not after a some time had passed. Serge was a good man, smart and funny and great in bed.

What?

Noll, you're blushing. Thinking of Maya, are you? I can see why. She's a beauty.

No, I, ah…

Oh Noll, you'd better enjoy life while you can. It goes by too fast. Besides, you'll have plenty of regrets by the time you're my age. No sense in adding to them if you can help it. Enough talk. Help me out of here so I can have that drink.

-Noll helped her up the stairs and then closed the door before securing the latch. After replacing the slat, he turned to where she sat in an overstuffed chair covered by a paint-splattered blanket. She nodded him to a nearby chair and pulled a bottle of cognac from under a side table, half-filling two glass jars and handing one to him. She leaned back and held up the glass.

Live long and live well, Noll Spencer.

Long and well to you too, Eugie.

It's strange the conversations you can have while standing over the kitchen sink.

What do you mean?

Do you believe in God, Noll?

I guess so, Eugie.

Well, do you or don't you? I don't any have patience for a man who won't say what he thinks.

I don't know what to believe.

Not knowing is alright. There have been plenty of great thinkers who weren't sure about God.

Why do you ask?

Do you go to church?

I haven't been in a long time. I don't know why, exactly. It's just that it stopped making sense to me. What I

119

heard there and what I saw in the real world didn't meet up. So, I stopped going.

How'd your mother take to that?

She didn't like it but she finally stopped nagging me. I guess she realized I'd have to decide for myself.

She's still devout in her church-going then?

She does enough praying for the both of us if that's what you mean. She and Gannie both do.

That's what I figured. Do you know they're the only living relatives other than you I've kept in touch with?

You never wanted children?

I never had the slightest interest in being a mother. Besides, I was too busy making art.

Are you ever lonely?

Sometimes I am but so is the whole rest of the world, kids or no kids. Loneliness is part of being human. Value those lonely times and the solitude they bring, Noll and you might learn a thing or two.

I have a feeling you're trying to tell me something, Eugie.

I had a long talk with Gannie about you.

What about?

I didn't tell her. I just asked her what kind of person you are. What I wanted to know is if you're someone I can count on.

What did she say?

She said you're as loyal and reliable as they come.

She said that about me?

I have a favor to ask of you, Noll. Like I said, you, Gannie and your mother are all the family I have left in this world and I'm old and getting older every day.

You look like you're doing alright to me.

Maybe so, but you never know what the future holds in store. I'm an independent and stubborn old woman and I've made my own decisions, called my own shots, my whole life. It's the things I can't control that haunt me now. What I mean is I don't want to end my life lying in some nursing home, kept alive when I shouldn't be, wasting away like a forgotten piece of fruit.

Nobody wants that.

I want you to be my voice, Noll. I want you to be sure they let me go when my time comes. I'm not afraid to die. I've written it all up, legal-like. Will you do it?

Shouldn't someone older, like mom, be the one to ask?

But don't you see, Noll? I can't ask her. Her religion would get in the way. She'd have to choose between me and God, and you know as well as I do who'd win that fight. Same goes for Gannie.

What would I have to do?

Just tell the doctors what I told you. Don't let them hook me up to a bunch of tubes when it'll do no good.

That's a serious request. Are you sure you trust me to do it?

Give me your word and I will.

I'll do what you ask, Eugie.

Let's drink on it and then we're done here. May the end of the line be quick and painless.

And may it not come anytime soon.

I believe I'll go check on Adela before I get back to work. In her frame of mind there's no telling what she might do.

Noll walked the winding shoreline, the inlet beyond unsettled, restless, small flocks of night herons fluttering among the mangroves like dim specters. Speckled trout broke the dark water in sharp pops as the waning moon, still nearly full, appeared between silver-edged clouds, casting the low horizon in silhouette. Salt grass lining the beach vibrated before the wind. Noll turned with a start as footsteps passed nearby. He stood, breath held, listening.

Noll, is that you?
Maya?

I'm over here in the arbor. I was hoping I'd find you. Come join me.

-As Noll walked beneath the archway, he could just make out Maya's shape on the bench. He sat beside her.

Noll, what are you doing wandering around out here?

I'm walking the place to make sure everything is alright.

Well, is it?

Is it what?

Is everything alright?

I guess so.

Isn't it better than alright now that you found me?

I believe it was you that found me.

Don't get smart. Just answer me.

Yes, it's better, Maya. I was wondering where you'd gone off to.

I've been trying to cheer up Adela. She misses Humberto.

That's what Eugie said.

She said she misses his companionship but even more not being able to reach out and touch him. Touching is important with someone you love.

Is it, Maya? I didn't know that.

Yes you do, Noll.

What sort of touching?

Stop teasing me.

Am I teasing you?

Touch me, Noll. Kiss me.

-Noll ran his fingers across her cheek and she leaned into him. Taking his free hand she guided his fingers over her body as she pressed herself into him, her breath quickening as they fell back across the narrow bench. Noll kissed her hard, running a hand through her silken hair and across her neck, down to the buttons of her blouse. As he fumbled with the third button, a light flashed across the ground beneath them. Steps soon followed and before Noll realized what had happened Hen's face appeared beneath the archway. Noll jumped to his feet, leaving Maya lying across the bench. Hen turned his back before he spoke.

Lordy Noll, I sure do hate to bust in on you like this but we've got us a problem and I need you to come with me right away. Maya, you get yourself on up to the house double quick.

What is it, Hen?

Never you mind what it is, girl. Just get yourself on up to the house.

-Noll watched in dismay as Maya disappeared into the darkness. He sighed and turned to Hen.

What's happened, Hen?

I was down by the water at the far end of the property and I found a johnboat hidden in the reeds. The boat wasn't there thirty minutes before, I'm sure about that. There were footprints in the mud too. Looks like about three of them.

Should we call the sheriff?

We got nothing to report but somebody's lost boat washed up on the property. The sheriff won't have care about that. No sense in wasting our time. I got me Eugie's big pistol here. You take it, Noll.

I don't know anything about guns, Hen.

That won't matter if they see you point that big barrel their way.

Why don't you take it? I'm likely to hurt someone.

I got this midnight special here that Lio loaned me. It's just a pop gun but it'll do the job if I need it to. Now, let's go see what we can find. I want you to head east and I'll circle west. We'll meet back here in ten minutes. If someone gives you trouble, you wave that big gun around like you know what's what.

Do you think someone's come after Adela, Hen?

That boat might belong to some kids out gigging flounder or wade-fishing the flats. It might be teenagers looking for some privacy. No way to know for sure but I got me a bad feeling about it. If they are after her it's best we take the fight to them instead of letting them have a say in what happens next.

Fourteen

Hen emerged from the darkness into a restless pool of moonlight where Noll stood waiting, one hand fingering the grip of Eugie's pistol, the other wiping sweat from his face. A furtive moon blinked through the trees overhead, casting their shadows in a cage of limbs. The inlet murmured before the hastening breeze. Hen looked up and down the shoreline twice before speaking.

No sign of no one. Sure is quiet out there, too quiet. No birds stirring, nothing. You see anything?

Not a thing, Hen. Maybe it *is* just some kids off fishing or making out, like you said.

Maybe, but we need to keep a close eye out. We'll go up to the house and let the women know what's up. No telling what Maya told them. They might have them a bad case of the nerves.

I'm feeling a little jumpy myself.

You and me, we got to stay cool, Noll.

I'll try, Hen.

You go in the front door. I'm going around back so as to be on the safe side.

-Noll pushed through the screen door and stood in the living room, listening but hearing nothing. He checked each of the bedrooms and headed for the kitchen where he found Hen standing beside the table, a broken glass at his feet. Hen held a finger to his lips and nodded toward the back door, then leaned toward Noll, speaking in a low whisper.

We got footprints outside the back door, lots of them. Where is Eugie's workshop?

It's behind the house, just beyond a row of pear trees.

I'll follow you, son.

-Noll rounded the grove of trees and pushed through the wide studio door, Hen close behind. Except for the chairs, table and easels, the room was empty. He moved across the floor, scanning the room before turning to Hen.

This is not good, Hen. Where could they have gone?

Eugie say anything to you about leaving?

No and they would've told us if they decided to go.

That broken glass in the house may mean something but there's no sign of a fight in here.

But something is different. Those chairs have been moved and a bottle of cognac is missing. Help me with this trap door, Hen.

- Hen pushed the chairs aside as Noll removed the loose slat, twisting the metal latch and lifting the door. The cellar stood below them dark and silent. After a moment, Eugie's voice sprang out of the darkness.

I've got a gun down here and I'm not afraid to use it, whoever you are. Get on out of here and maybe I won't have to shoot you.

Aunt Eugie, it's Noll and Hen up here. Come on out.

Noll, is it really you?

-An instant later Adela emerged from the darkness, leading Eugie up the stairs by her arm. Noll stepped aside as Eugie collapsed into one of the chairs and stared up at him, gasping for air.

Damn it to hell Noll, they took Maya. You've got to go find her.

They have Maya? Who took her?

I don't know. I brought Adela out here for a brandy, to try and sheer her up. We were having a drink in the cellar when we heard voices coming from the house. As soon as we reached the studio door we could see them in the kitchen, two skuzzy-looking hombres with tattoos all over their arms. They had a hold of Maya and were headed this way so we skedaddled down the stairs and closed the trap door just in time.

126

Why would they take her?

I couldn't say but she put up some kind of fight, Noll. I saw her wallop one of them but good. I sure hope he doesn't decide to return the favor.

Which way did they go?

It's hard to be sure but it sounded like they were headed for the inlet.

Come on, Noll. I know where that johnboat is hidden. Eugie, do you have a gun down there in that cellar?

No Hen, that was all bluff. The gun I gave you is all I have.

Do you have a phone out here?

My phone is in the house.

Alright then, lock those big doors when we're out and stay put until we get back.

Hen, don't leave us here.

Adela, you know we got to find your sister. Take this pistol. It's small but it'll get the job done. Just don't shoot me or Noll.

-They hurried beneath the reaching trees, through pools of shadow, scattered discs of moonlight littering the wet lawn like silver coins. Seagulls called out in the darkness overhead, their cries nearly lost in the rattling wind. Branches slapped Noll's face as he drove through the thick underbrush, a step behind Hen. Hen paused, head cocked as if listening. An instant later Maya's voice rang out, followed by three gunshots. Two more shots sounded, clearly different from the first three. Noll jumped past Hen in a rush, climbing through the dense thicket and bursting onto the shoreline itself. He looked one way and then the other, seeing nothing, hearing nothing other than Hen's approaching footsteps. The big pistol hung heavy in his hand.

Stay cool, Noll and have your wits about you. They'd be heading for their boat so that's where we'll go too. Keep that big gun ready.

We can't let them take her, Hen.

127

Be quiet and listen. Someone's coming.

-They stood near the edge of a narrow path, a wall of brush on one side, the sandy shoreline on the other, the ink-black inlet beyond. Several yards ahead, the bushes seemed to rattle and then stop, only to repeat the restless motion after a short pause. Noll raised the pistol with his shaking hands, aiming it toward the sound. Standing next to him, Hen reached over with outstretched fingers, easing the barrel toward the ground. He leaned to Noll, whispering.

There's only one of them, Noll.

There could be more. Or it could be the wind. Your imagination might be playing tricks on you.

I hear somebody coming alright. I spent too much time crawling around the jungle to forget what it sounds like. They don't move like a man either.

How can you tell that?

A man moving through brush sounds heavy, like he's fighting it. A woman will be careful and try not to break anything.

-Just then, a figure burst through the brush, falling onto the pathway with a high-pitched grunt.

Maya?

Noll? Noll, where are you?

Maya, we're over here.

-Noll rushed past Hen and knelt beside her.

Are you hurt, Maya?

I'm scratched up a little is all. I'll be alright.

What happened to your cheek?

One of those bastards slapped me.

You're okay then?

I'm so glad to see you, Noll.

Eugie said there were two men. How'd you get away from them?

I'm not sure, exactly.

Where'd they get off to, Maya? We don't want to run into them if we can help it.

128

They won't be running into anyone, Hen. They're back down the inlet, shot dead.

They shot each other?

Why would they do that, Noll?

Then what *did* happen?

There was another man waiting at the boat. They shot at him as soon as they spotted him but they weren't much good at it. Two shots was all he needed.

This man, he talk funny, like he's from another country?

How did you know, Hen?

What'd he say?

He told me to run back to the house as fast as I could.

He say what his name was?

I heard one of the other men call him something that sounded Polish or something. I'm not sure.

His name is Vaditch and he claims he's Russian. We best go see what we got before we call the sheriff. Maya you get on to the house.

I'm not going back there alone. I'm sticking with you.

Are you up to it, Maya? It could be ugly.

I'm coming along, Noll and that's that.

You keep that pistol handy, boy but don't point it at nothing or nobody unless I tell you to. Maya, you should've seen what he just about…

Let's get moving, Hen.

-Noll and Maya followed Hen through the dense underbrush and on to where he had last seen the beached johnboat. Glints of moonlight jumped among the marsh grass, mingling with reflected buoy and channel marker. A foghorn moaned somewhere on the dim horizon. Hen stopped at a break in the shoreline, kneeling onto a flattened area of reeds and tracing the ground with his gnarled fingers. He stood and surveyed the area before turning to Maya.

Those men fall in the water when they got shot?

Yes but the water is shallow. They couldn't have floated away this fast.

No, they didn't float anywhere. Old Vaditch, he's good. He took them and the boat away from here. Not a thing left for the sheriff to see.

He did what he said he'd do, Hen.

That's right Noll, he did.

What did he say he'd do?

We met up with Vaditch down by the ferry. He told us he was here to protect Adela.

But why would someone we don't know want to protect my sister, Hen?

I can't say I know the answer but I'd bet someone wanted to send a message to whoever took Adela's husband.

You mean another cartel?

What Hen is saying does make sense, Maya. One cartel will show another they can't operate in their territory. Protecting Adela could be a way for them to make it clear who's in charge.

Alright then, we better get ourselves back and check on Adela and Eugie.

Adela is safe?

She's with Eugie. Those hombres must've thought you were Adela.

What would they have done if that Russian hadn't come along, Hen?

You don't want to think about that, Maya.

Are we safe now?

Maybe, but we'd best keep an eye out. They may decide to try again.

-Noll turned as Eugie's voice rang out from beyond the brush line, calling him. An instant later she pushed through an opening in the thicket and bent over, gasping for air.

What are you doing here, Eugie?

That's a good question. I'm too old to be running around in the middle of the night.

You were supposed to stay locked in the studio.

I heard those gunshots and decided I'd had enough of cowering behind locked doors on my own property. I fished out this old bat I use to kill rats and set out to see what had happened. I'm relieved to see you found Maya safe and sound.

Looky here, I don't much like standing around in the dark when we don't know who might still be about. Let's us do our talking back at the house.

Knots of cloud, torn, blood-hued, streamed over the trees in ragged arcs as Noll sat on the porch steps, watching dawn move across the inlet, trying to piece together the previous night, a night that now seemed less than real beneath the light of morning. He shuddered to think of Maya disappearing and instead tried to focus on the scene before him, somehow feeling reassured by the wood beneath his feet, wind against his face, shafts of sunlight moving across the bay at random. He breathed in the salt-tinged air as a flock of ducks sped low over the restless water.

The door creaked open and a moment later Maya settled next to him, two cups of coffee cradled in her hands. She handed one to him without a word. He glanced at the side of her face, her sleepy eyes, uncombed hair rose-tinted in the early daylight, finding her more attractive than ever. He wanted to take her back to the arbor, begin where they had left off. He turned to her, wanting to say what he thought but hesitant, fearful that the strange night had changed her, turned her from him in some way, a way never to be explained, never understood. She looked into his eyes, waiting for him to speak. He took a deep breath.

Maya, I…

-Eugie burst through the door followed by Hen.

131

Noll, something's happened with your mother. Gannie wants you home right away. She said it's urgent.

What is it, Eugie? What's happened?

She said your mother had been talking crazy all yesterday and finally locked herself in the bathroom early this morning. She thinks she may have a kitchen knife with her.

I'd better go right away then.

Is this a surprise, Noll?

I wish I could say it is. The truth is she's been having trouble for some time now.

Gannie thinks she intends to do herself harm. She doesn't scare easy and she sounded scared to me.

Looky here Noll, you best take my truck.

I can take your truck, Hen?

You best get on then.

Noll climbed into the truck, turning to Maya, searching her face in the early morning half-light but finding no clue as to what he should say, his mind preoccupied with thoughts of his mother. Reaching through the window, she took Noll's hand in hers.

Please call me when you have a chance. I hope your mother is alright.

I wish I didn't have to leave like this, Maya. It seems we're always getting interrupted.

What a strange night, and now this. It's hard to believe all that's happened. It's like we've been in some sort of dream.

A dream or a nightmare.

You should go now. Your mother needs you. I hope she'll be alright.

At least you're safe, Maya.

Be safe yourself, Noll. I worry about you.

132

Fifteen

Noll drove beneath a cloud-strewn sky, pale sunlight halting, vanishing, reappearing between wind-tossed trees like a cryptic Morse code. Bait houses and sun-ravaged piers trailing torn flags and loose strands of lights, frayed, gap-toothed, passed through his view before fading from sight. Edging the narrow highway, tall grasses vibrated before the coursing breeze. Empty back roads soon gave way to the city bustle as he made his way home. A short time later he pulled to the curb and hurried into the house, finding Gannie in a straight-backed kitchen chair that faced the bathroom door. A dim light crept beneath the threshold.

She's in there, Gannie?

She locked herself in about four-thirty. A knife is missing from the kitchen and I think she has it. I told her I was going to call the police but she screamed that she'd kill herself if I did, so I called you instead.

What's it all about?

I haven't the slightest idea. She's been depressed lately. You know that as well as I do. But nothing happened in particular that I could tell.

-Noll moved past her and placed a hand on the bathroom door.

Mom, it's Noll. I'm here now. Why don't you open the door so we can talk?

I don't want you to see me like this, Noll. I haven't put on any make-up and my hair's all a mess.

I'm sure you look fine. What happened, mom? Why have you locked yourself in there?

I can't go on like this, Noll. My life is a mess. Nothing is ever as it should be.

What isn't as it should be, mom? Tell me and maybe we can make it right.

You can't make it right. I can't and Gannie can't. If your father was here, he could do it. I don't think anybody ever will again. I'm so unhappy, Noll. Every day I wake up and see the same terrible mess that's my life, no job, no friends. Soon, I won't have a home. I'm so ashamed.

But mom, we're doing alright. I have a job and we'll get a car soon.

It's not a car or money that's the problem, Noll. Don't you understand that?

Maybe if you opened the door then I could understand.

It's me, Noll. I'm the problem, a problem with no solution, a problem with no answer, a zero. I might as well not exist.

Don't talk that way, mom. Just open the door. I want you to look at me. Open the door and look at your son.

-The interior latch clicked. Noll reached for the knob, turned and released it, letting the door drift open. His mother sat before him with her back to the tub, her arms outstretched, the inside of each crossed with cuts from wrist to elbow. Blood trickled down her palms, staining her blue robe a dull violet. An empty prescription bottle sat next to her. She looked up at Noll.

Mom, what have you done? You have cuts all over your arms.

I wanted to feel something, Noll. I felt so empty. I couldn't stand it anymore.

There's blood everywhere.

I just wanted to feel something. Don't be angry.

Did you take this medication?

I took it all, the whole bottle. If I can't feel something then I'll feel nothing at all.

Good Lord, she's cut her wrists, Noll. She'll bleed to death.

These cuts aren't deep, Gannie but we need to get her to the hospital.

She's a god-awful mess.

Grab that medicine bottle and help me get her to the truck.

Sunlight filtered through oak leaves, casting Eugie's porch in flickering hues of green and blue. Noll sat at the top of the stairs, scanning the narrow inlet and the bay beyond, crystalline in the morning air. In the clear light of day the events of the previous night, the johnboat, the kidnappers, the gunshots, all seemed surreal and beyond belief. A blue heron floated along a thin line of marsh grass before gliding to a stop among the mangroves, schools of silver shad skittering before it like a handful of unwanted diamonds. The screen door creaked behind him and Noll turned to find Maya at his side. She gazed at him as if about to speak.

An instant later Hen's voice came out of nowhere, a confusion of words pulling Noll from his daydream. He blinked at the bright light, looking to either side of the truck and trying to clear his head before he leaned out the window. Hen stood below him, staring up at the high flatbed.

What happened to you the last few days, Noll? I've been trying to get a hold of you.

Elgy sent me across town to move the new law school dean into his office, him and his assistant and his secretary and his student aides. I never saw so much leather.

I know where you been. I sent word I was looking for you. What I mean is how come you never get back to me?

I don't know, Hen. I guess I've been busy, like I just said.

You stopped answering your phone too?

135

I don't even know where it is.

I wanted to ask after your mama. Why don't you climb on down out of that cab and tell me about her?

I don't believe I will, Hen. I like it up here.

Your mama alright, son?

She was tired of living and took a bunch of pills.

She in the hospital?

She came home last night.

What about you, Noll? How're you doing?

She didn't do herself any real harm. The doctor said he'd release her as long as I'd keep an eye on her.

She alright to go home?

She agreed to see a counselor. The doctor insisted on it and gave her some other medication, the kind that won't kill you. We'll see if she keeps that up.

It's a tough thing to see your mother out to hurt her own self, that's a fact. You taking care of yourself, Noll?

Why do people want to kill themselves, Hen? The doctors say it's because they can't see a way out of their unhappiness. I knew how unhappy she'd been lately. I should've seen it coming.

Come on down out of that cab, Noll.

It's quiet up here.

It's past quitting time. Let's you and me go get ourselves a beer.

I don't have a car to drive but I feel like I do when I'm sitting up here. Do you think that's strange?

Climb down out of there and you can drive my old truck anywhere you want.

I believe I'll sit tight, Hen.

Not for long you won't. I just spotted Maya getting out of her car and she's headed this way, not looking too happy either. I believe I'll wait for you someplace else.

Noll Spencer, what on earth is wrong with you? You can't be bothered to return your phone messages?

I've been told that once already today.

Did you hear it from your little spice girl, Pepper or Nutmeg or whatever her name is?

Her name is Ginger.

I'll bet you're back with her already.

No Maya, she left me. Remember? You heard her yourself.

Come down out of that truck and talk to me face to face.

No, I think I'll stay right here.

Why didn't you call me, Noll?

My mother…

I know. We were worried sick after you left, worried about your mother but about you too, Noll. I kept calling and calling. Eugie finally called your grandmother and she filled us in on your mom. At least she returns her calls.

I've been busy.

But it's been days, Noll.

Not long, really.

I'd have thought you would want to talk to me, see me even. All you had to do is call.

I've had a lot on my mind.

That's all you have to say?

And I've been busy.

Stop saying that!

What should I say?

If you don't know it won't do any good for me to tell you.

It won't?

So, that's it? That's all you have to say to me?

I don't even know where my phone is.

That's your excuse?

I've been trying to remember.

I guess I misunderstood you, Noll. I guess I misunderstood us. Well, maybe your spice girl will put up with being ignored but I won't.

Maybe it's in my locker.

Goodbye, Noll. Don't bother calling if you ever find it.

-Hen watched Maya drive away as he ambled back over to the truck.

Where'd she go?

Looks like you just lost yourself the favor of a good-looking woman, Noll. That ought to wake you up. You ready to come down now?

Did I say something wrong?

It's what you didn't say that's the problem. You know how hard it is for a woman to come up here and talk to you like she just did? She took a chance and you let her down hard, Noll.

I did?

Yes you did. That's a fact.

-Noll climbed out of the cab.

I don't know what's wrong with me, Hen.

We all have ourselves a bad time now and then but you been having yourself one right after the other.

I can't seem to get anything right.

Let me buy you that beer, son. I know just the place we can go. You won't run into anybody you don't want to talk to there.

That sounds good to me, Hen.

Honeyed light stretched across the late afternoon, leaving long-limbed shadows crossing narrow, curb-less streets as Hen drove past houses once new, now without paint, weathered, sagging, their yards littered with spare car parts, cast off bathtubs. A warm breeze carried the dried straw smell of early fall past Noll's window, grass gone to seed, leaves beginning to turn, the end of life also a beginning. Even as the latent heat of summer seemed to hold time in check the air carried an unmistakable sense of change, palpable, nearly solid.

Hen slowed, pulling in front of a cedar shake building, the black exterior broken only by a single door

138

painted a glossy red. In the center of the door, at eye level, a slim window made of thick glass looked out onto the street. A small sign over the door read "Queenie's Place".

Hen approached the heavy door, pushing a small button nearly hidden off to one side then stepping back as a face appeared behind the glass, levitating, floating from side to side. A moment later a buzzer sounded, releasing the lock with a metallic click. Hen pushed through the door and into the dim interior, Noll following a few steps behind.

A massive bar of mahogany and oak covering two walls of the windowless room faced them as they stepped in, its high counter crowded with men in oil-stained work shirts and coveralls. The men turned to study them for a moment, frowning, murmuring among themselves before turning back to their drinks. On the wall behind the bar, a framed .45 caliber slug lay buried in the plaster, the date and name of the shooter scribbled beneath. Mismatched tables and chairs lined the opposite wall, lighted by the crimson glow of a neon beer sign. Behind the bar, a wide-faced woman the color of walnut set down a glass before she noticed Hen.

Why, Hen Feathers how're you… what's that white man you got with you? You know this bar is only for select patrons, select *black* patrons.

Now Queenie, you just hold on and let Hen tell you how it is.

What do you got to say, then?

I say you got to know the facts before you can decide what's what. Who can say what's black and what's something else?

Say what? Are you messing with me, Hen Feathers? You know Queenie won't tolerate any disrespect in her place.

Noll here is my distant relation from our family in Glenolden, Mississippi.

What are you saying, Hen?

I'm saying Noll here and me, we come from the same family, got the same blood.

You must be talking nonsense, Hen because I don't understand a word of what you just said.

Looky here, Queenie. You know for a fact you don't have a drop of white blood or Indian blood or Spanish blood in you?

Now how can I know that, Hen? My daddy left home before I was born and I never knew his daddy, my granddaddy. I don't even know their given name. How am I going to know what blood my family has?

There you are, Queenie. You could be kin to the Queen of England for all you know.

Now you're talking nonsense again, Hen. The only queen in my family is me.

But you don't know for sure now do you? Well, I do. I know Noll is kin and my namesake, old McHenry Feathers is a part of that family. Now open us up a couple of cold beers and let us get to talking. Noll and me, we got a lot to talk over.

Hen, I don't want to cause you any trouble. Why don't we go someplace else?

No sir, you and me got a right to be here same as anybody else. Sit down and get yourself comfortable, Noll.

-They moved to a table just as Queenie appeared, setting a beer in front of Noll and then slamming the other in the middle of the table without looking at Hen. She turned to face Noll.

You pick some strange company for yourself, mister.

Yes 'mam, I mean no, I mean …thank you for the beer.

I suppose you want this on your tab, Mr. Feathers?

Yes Queenie, that'll do just fine. Did I tell you how nice you look today?

140

Don't you try to play nice with me. You better just drink your beer and not say another word.

She sounds mad.

Naw. You like fishing, Noll?

I haven't done much fishing but I like it alright.

I'm going down to Haney Creek this evening to check my trot lines. I got me a little johnboat I keep hidden at a friend's place right on the creek and I'm hoping to have a catfish or two waiting on me. Why don't you come along and see what I find?

I don't know, Hen. I should probably go check on my mother.

You've been spending a boatload of time with her, Noll. You got to make time for yourself too.

She might need something.

Your granny there at the house?

Yes, she's there.

It won't take us too long to check those lines. You'll be home by midnight or thereabouts. Your granny can take care of things at home until then, can't she?

I guess she can.

Alright then, we'll go as soon as we finish us these beers. There's no telling what you might see floating that creek at night. It'll do you a world of good, son.

Do you think Queenie is mad about me still being here? Maybe we should go.

You don't need to worry about her. You're staying right here. Wait a minute. You feel it, don't you?

Feel what?

You feel how it is to walk into a place and have people look on you as less than them, as unworthy of stepping into the place.

That's why am asking. Shouldn't we just leave?

But don't you see, Noll? That's how it is when prejudice is around. That's how it is for some people their whole lives. Black, brown, yellow, white, it makes no care what color you are. And it's not just color but where you

141

come from too. That's how it is for the people that cross the border looking for a better life. That's how it is for poor people.

I don't much like it.

But it's a gift, Noll. You get to see for yourself how prejudice feels. On top of that you get to see how black people can think just like white people, just as prejudiced, just as blinded by it.

But I don't want to cause trouble for anyone. I can leave if she's going to be mad about me being here.

Don't you worry about Queenie. She's just wants to show me who's in charge. Besides, she thinks if she lets only black folks in here she won't have trouble but that's not true. You can't tell if a man is a problem by the color of his skin any more than by the color of his hair. Most folks don't want any trouble but some just can't stay away from it.

Like my father.

I don't know about that. I was thinking about Ranse. I'm afraid he has trouble following him around just like his daddy did. But let's leave Ranse out of it for now.

What do you think Vaditch meant about knowing my dad?

I don't know what to make of Vaditch but I wouldn't trust a thing he said about your daddy. Best you do what you can for your mama and forget about what you can't change.

You're probably right.

Looky here Noll, you're a young man with his whole life ahead of him. Don't you get to thinking your life is written in stone. You got plenty of choices ahead of you and you can be whatever and whoever you want. What do you want for yourself, Noll? You want a wife and family? You want to travel the world?

I don't know, Hen. Everything is so confusing. I don't know what I want now or what I should do tomorrow or next week, so I don't do anything. I'm stuck. I wish life could be simple and clear. Maybe then I'd know what to do.

I never saw that in my time, no sir. This life here is messy and hard to figure. Like the song says, 'The future is uncertain and the end is always near'. That's as close to the truth as a man's going to get. You got to live your life anyway, son. Pick something and go after it is what I say.

It sounds easy but it's not.

You got that right, so drink up. We're going to catch us some fish. Now, that's what I call real living.

Sixteen

Crimson fingers of sunlight reached across the sky, fading, iridescent as Hen pulled into the short gravel driveway next to his compact home. Oil-streaked kerosene lanterns, turning before the steady breeze, hung at both ends of a narrow porch that stretched the length of the house. A wooden swing drifted before two broad windows, their panes rippled with age. Between them, a tattered leather harness hung on the wall next to a wreath of rusted barbed wire. Noll paused to admire a horseshoe nailed above the door before he followed Hen inside.

He surveyed the room without speaking. Shelves crammed with books occupied three walls, broken only by wide louvered windows. Here and there, piles of magazines and newspapers spilled from chairs and tables onto a large circular rug. A book-littered side table sat in one corner beneath a reading lamp and set of black and white photos in tarnished silver frames.

You weren't kidding about rescuing books, Hen.

I'm mostly satisfied as long as I have a cold beer and a good book. That's how I like to spend my time when I'm not at work. That is, except for fishing.

Have you read all these books?

Not all of them but I'm working on it. I hope I never get so old I've read all the books I want to read. That would be a sad day for old Hen but it's not likely. I'd have to live to a hundred fifty.

Where'd you get the lanterns and other antiques on the porch?

My grandfather brought all that here from Mississippi. I keep it around to remind me of my family history. I still use those kerosene lanterns.

Do you resent that your family was once held as slaves by my family.

I don't hold any hard feeling toward you, son. That past lies outside me and you. We didn't have a say so in it. Mostly, I'm sorry for the suffering of all those people. They're my people but they're your people too, if you think on it. Those were hard times, sad times. Families separated and sold off, men and women beat, lynched or worse. Prejudice was wrong then and it's still wrong but not your wrong Noll, not if you don't let it be.

I have let it. I've been prejudiced against people I didn't even know for longer than I want to admit. It doesn't make much sense when I look back on it.

You got plenty of company there but we can't change what's done. We got to get on with life. That means we got to get on to the creek before the fish all get caught by some other fool. Let me get my fishing case and we'll go pick up Felix.

Felix is coming with us?

I promised him he could come help me next time I went to the creek.

Felix doesn't seem like the fisherman type.

He never went fishing a day in his life so he wants to try it out. That's what I like about Felix. He won't shy away from something he doesn't know. He's determined to live life while he can. You could learn a thing or two from him, Noll.

Felix stood at the curb, waving as if Hen might pass him by. Spotting Noll, he ran into the street to meet them. Noll studied him as he climbed into the rear seat. He still looked pale and thin.

Noll, why didn't you tell me you were coming with us?

I just found out myself. How are you feeling?

I feel like having a party. That's why I'm here, Noll. Hen said he'd let me join his fishing party. Get it?

A fishing party, huh?

145

That's right, Noll. We're going to party with the perches.

So, that's what you think fishing is?

It is. It's one big party. We're going to conga with the catfish and tango with the trout. We may even bosa nova with a bass. This party is taking on a decided Latin feel and I like it.

It seems to be musical in any event.

Of course Noll, what's a party without music? Too bad Maya didn't come along. She loves to dance.

Did you see her this afternoon?

I did and now that I think about it, I'm glad she wasn't invited. She was in one bad mood.

Did she say what was bothering her?

No, and I didn't ask. I could see those claws would be out any minute so I stayed as far away as I could. Why are you asking, Noll?

No reason.

Looky here, I'll say it if you won't. Noll is the cause of that anger you were wise to steer clear of, Felix. He went and earned himself the wrath of a woman scorned.

Noll, what did you do?

I don't want to talk about it.

That's what he did alright. He didn't talk about it.

Alright Hen, we've done enough gabbing. Let's go fishing.

See what I mean, Felix? The man just won't talk.

A waning moon drifted high overhead behind a loose veil of cloud, trailing light, opaque, comet-like as Hen pushed the small johnboat into the current, water tapping the metal sides in regular rhythm. The electric prop hummed to life and Hen sat back humming to himself. Noll surveyed the banks on either side of the creek, dim but visible in the bluish light. Beyond the bank to his left, cattle called out from a broad pasture cleared of underbrush. On the side opposite, crowded stands of pecan,

146

cypress and sycamore towered over the creek, their lower limbs reaching out to the running water in low tunnels of leaf and branch. Mayflies dripped from the undersides of limbs as they drifted past, taking flight and floating through the spotlight like lost spirits.

Hen spotted a buoy and pointed the spotlight toward it, slowing the motor and letting the boat drift in the swift current. As they drew near the float came to life, moving one way and then the other, bobbing, almost vanishing below the surface for an instant. Hen grabbed a wooden pole from the beneath the seat and pointed it toward Felix, tapping him on the shoulder. One end of the pole carried a metal hook.

Looky here, Felix you take this pole, grab the line beneath the float and pull it to the side. Then all you have to do is lift it into the boat and that old catfish will come with it. When you get it in here Noll will put the fish in that big ice chest there.

You mean we have a fish already?

Why else you think that float is moving around like it is?

Watch me catch a fish, Noll.

Looky here now Felix, don't fall in. That current is stronger than it looks.

-Felix leaned far over the side, snagging the float on his first try and pulling it toward the boat. Within seconds he had a large catfish flopping at his feet. An instant later he was perched on top of the bench, waiting while Noll wrestled the fish into an ice chest. He lowered his feet and peered into the ice chest.

Quick, take a picture, Noll. We need a record of my first fish or my dad will never believe it. He thinks I can't do anything.

Who needs a picture when you can show him the real thing? Besides, we're just getting started. What do you imagine he'll say when you show him a whole ice chest full?

Are you kidding? He'll have a cow. Oh, I can't wait to see his face.

They worked their way up the creek, Felix checking lines one by one while Noll wrestled fish into the cooler. When they had checked the last buoy, Hen steered alongside a shallow eddy, tying the bow to an overhead branch and allowing the boat to drift in the shifting current. He pulled several beers from a small ice chest, handing one to Felix and another to Noll before popping one open for himself. After a long sip, he leaned back and switched off the spotlight. Their eyes soon adjusted to the darkness, the creek surface and shoreline emerging beneath the quarter moon, the towering mass of trees lurking on the bank opposite, impenetrable, forbidding.

Headlights flashed through the tree tops as a truck engine roared to life, followed by young men's voices and the sporadic popping of gunfire. Noll tensed as the noise drew near before fading into the distance. The remaining silence enveloped him, broken only by the sound of his own breath and the surging eddy. Moonlight played across the water, mercurial, ever-changing, rippling before half-submerged tree limbs, trailing after in thin ribbons of silver. On the far shore sycamore leaves moved before the breeze, flickering in the half-light, sounding like rain against stone. No one dared speak.

Somewhere beyond the black shoreline an owl hooted once, followed by another deep inside the dense stand of trees. A moment later another called and then another. In seconds the entire forest erupted with the caterwauling of owls, their cries sounding from all directions at once. Noll turned to Hen, almost yelling to make himself heard.

What are those owls doing, Hen? I can't believe they're so loud.

Those are gray barred owls having themselves a meeting.

There must be a dozen or more of them out there. Does it mean something when they make so much noise?

Some folks believe the sound of the owl is a bad omen, the sign of trouble to come. I believe it's a sign that we got to be moving before it gets too late for you young people.

Do we really have to leave, Hen? It's like another world out here, a magic world.

It's past time to go, Felix. Once I untie the boat, we'll drift back downstream and check the lines on the other side. I put out only a few over there because the current is mostly too strong. Felix, you're doing a fine job but be watchful of that current.

You sound like a mother hen, Hen. Get it?

-Hen motored toward the opposite bank and let the boat drift in close to shore.

Alright Felix, the next float is coming up. There's got to be a big daddy on that one the way it's jumping around. Don't lean too far, now.

-The words had scarcely left Hen's lips when the bow caught the tip of a submerged log, spinning the boat in a half-circle and tipping it to one side. In an instant, Felix disappeared over the edge, vanishing beneath the dark water. Noll sat for a moment trying to understand what he had just seen. The surreal image flashed across his vision as words making no sense crowded his consciousness. He blinked, knowing he must act. At once he stripped off his shoes, diving over the side and slipping beneath the opaque surface. The current tugged him downward as he stared into blackness, feeling his way more than seeing. Suddenly, the scene emerged in a greenish glow. Hen had turned on the spotlight.

-He spotted Felix at once. Held by the surging current, he lay prostrate, struggling against a tangle of black branches that already grabbed at Noll's feet in the swift water. Without thinking, Noll relaxed and let his body drift past the submerged tree, avoiding the larger limbs. He knew if he misjudged the timing, he would never reach Felix but at the last moment he took hold of a branch, swinging himself around to the downstream side of the tangle. Once there, he reached in and grabbed Felix by one arm, pulling him through and pushing him toward the surface with all his strength. Felix broke through the surface an instant before Noll, coughing and thrashing about as Hen pulled him aboard. Noll climbed in after him. They sat in the bottom of the boat shivering and trying to catch their breath. Felix looked at Noll and started to chuckle, within moments laughing and coughing so hard he could barely speak.

Noll, that was awesome! Can you believe what just happened? What if I'd drowned down there? Man survives cancer only to die bagging fish. How ironic would that be? No one would believe it, not even me!

-Noll looked at Hen and shrugged.

Looky here boy, get your skinny self covered up before you catch cold or worse. There's going to be hell to pay when your mama hears about this. She won't like it one bit and neither will your daddy. I don't even want to think what Lio will say, don't want to think about that at all.

Seventeen

The night air held a damp chill of early autumn as Noll stood before a modest frame home, a single flagpole planted squarely in front, light from a distant streetlamp pooling at his feet. The low gravel roof sparkled beneath the city's glow. Before him, a lone mesquite tree filled the small lawn, its palm-like leaves stirring now and then before a light breeze. U.S. and Marine flags flapped overhead. The house showed little sign of life except for a porch light partially blocked by a closely trimmed shrub and the dim glow of one window, the window Felix had said belonged to Maya and her younger sister.

Noll stared at the window, wishing Maya would somehow sense he was there and look out the blinds. He imagined her stepping through the front door and tiptoeing through the dew-covered grass to where he stood. It had been a week since she had come to see him at work and he winced now to think how he had treated her. He bent and picked several pebbles out of the street, tossing them at the window and calling Maya's name in a loud whisper. He tossed another pebble and then another before the blinds stirred as someone peered out. A moment later the front door opened and to his surprise Lio stepped out.

What are you doing here, Noll?

Lio, I thought…I expected…

When we're at work you can call me Lio but here you call me sir or Mr. Cruz.

Yes sir, I was hoping to talk to…

Do you know what time it is, Noll?

I didn't mean to wake you, Lio… I mean, sir. I was hoping to talk to Maya.

I'll ask you again. Why are you here?

I'd like to see Maya.

I'd like to see Maya, sir.

Yes sir, that's right, Mr. Cruz.

And what are your intentions, son?

My intentions? Ah, to talk to her?

A phone call would do the job.

She won't return my calls.

It sounds like she doesn't want to talk to you. Is that the case, Noll?

I don't blame her the way I acted the last time we spoke.

You're here to apologize, then?

Yes sir, I guess I am.

And what are your intentions after that?

My intentions?

You're here, aren't you? So, I have to ask myself if I want my daughter seeing someone who has dropped out of college, who seems to have no direction in his life, not to mention he's white.

Does being white matter?

Our people stick together, Noll. Someone like you upsets the usual way of doing things, the tradition. People don't like it.

People like you?

I have plenty of reasons not to like whites but I'm not so sure about you, Noll. The men at work treat you like you're just one of them. They don't notice what color you are. You do the same as far as I can tell. That's right, isn't it?

Yes sir, I think so. When I started work there, I had plenty of bias against people that didn't look like me. But the guys at work are just people, no different from anyone else. It took me a while but I learned that.

On the other hand, we're talking about my daughter, about her future. I won't have her seeing a man who has no ambition, no plan beyond where he is now.

I may go back to school.

Have you thought of joining the armed forces, Noll? The Marines gave me a purpose and made a man of me.

152

You think I should join the Marines?

Sure, son. They'll pay for your college and make you an officer. Eventually you can retire with two incomes like I did. You can see we're doing alright and I didn't even go to college. So, what about it, Noll? Do you hear what I'm saying?

Yes sir, but I'm just here to talk with Maya.

Do you mean to tell me you're asking if you can date my daughter?

Do I need to ask?

You bet you do.

-Maya stepped through the doorway.

No, you don't. Dad, leave us alone so we can talk.

Noll and I were having a man to man discussion about what he wants from life, about his future.

You brought up the Marines?

What's wrong with that?

He didn't come here to be lectured on how great the service is. He's here to see me.

We were having ourselves a good talk, weren't we Noll?

I appreciate your thoughts on my future, Mr. Cruz.

See Maya, we see eye to eye.

Oh, brother. Please give us some privacy, dad.

Alright but keep it short, daughter. You have an early class tomorrow. You don't want to be late.

I can manage my own schedule, dad. And I don't need anyone's help getting to class on time.

-Lio turned, grumbling as he disappeared into the house.

Did you come here for a reason?

I wanted to see you.

And?

Maya, I'm sorry for the way I acted last time. I don't know what was wrong with me but it doesn't matter now. I was inconsiderate and rude any way you look at it. I hope you'll be able to forgive me someday.

153

Is that all you have to say?

I want to say whatever will make it right. Just tell me what it is and I'll say it. Please Maya, I don't want to go on like this, not knowing if I've ruined everything. My life is messed up in so many ways. I need something to be right. I want that something to be you.

It hurt me Noll. For you to act like you could care less after I was so worried about you was humiliating.

I know, Maya.

But I've missed you even though I was angry. I wanted to see you but I wasn't going to take a chance on getting hurt again.

I understand and I want to make it up to you.

How?

I want to ask if you'll go somewhere with me.

Ask me then.

Eugie is having an opening for some of her portraits at a gallery in town. She wants us to join her, if you'll come.

I understand what Eugie wants but what do you want, Noll?

I want you there with me, Maya. Will you come? She's said Hen's portrait will be in the show.

Oh, that should be interesting.

Or maybe hilarious. I tried to talk him into going but I doubt he'll show up. So, will you go with me? It's tomorrow at 7:00. I can be here a little before then.

Alright, Noll I'll go. I'd better get back inside. I have a test in the morning and I haven't finished studying.

-She took his hand, squeezing it as she leaned toward him and whispered.

This house has eyes, Noll so no hanky-panky. I'll see you tomorrow.

-She kissed him lightly, turned and walked back to the house, vanishing through the door without another word.

Clouds crowded in on themselves, packing the horizon with shades of indigo and gray as Noll made his way to Maya's house the following evening. He hoped any rain would hold off until after midnight. A blue haze of exhaust trailed behind him as he bounced along in the topless, dilapidated jeep Eugie loaned him once they had finished hanging her paintings. Now and then he caught a glimpse of the road flying by through the rusted out floorboard beneath his feet.

Maya waited for him at the curb, trying to stifle a laugh as she climbed into the sunken passenger seat. She wore a tight-fitting black dress and red sandals, and had tied her hair up in a loose knot. Wisps of hair seemed to frame her face in black silk. Noll gripped the wheel and stared at her until she turned to him, smiling.

What's wrong with you, Noll? You look like you're in shock. Do I look that bad?

Are you kidding? You look amazing when you get dressed up.

This isn't dressed up. Don't forget, we're going to be around a bunch of artists and probably a beatnik or two. If I'd known we were going in this old thing I'd have borrowed dad's fatigues.

Old Sherman here belongs to Eugie. She said she'll give him to me if I take good care of him. He smokes a little but he sure beats walking. We'd better get going.

Noll followed Maya as she squeezed her way through the overflowing crowd and into the gallery, a former storefront now bright with spotlights. Small groups gathered in front of paintings, sipping champagne and trying to talk over the country and western music echoing through the open back door. As he grabbed two beers from an ice-filled tub, Noll spied Eugie in the opposite corner holding forth beside one of her portraits. He peered at the image for a moment before deciding it was someone other

155

than Hen. When he turned to hand Maya a beer she had vanished. He scanned the room for her but instead spotted Ginger a short distance away just as she saw him, frowning before hurrying to where he stood.

What are you doing here Noll, spying on me?

Nice to see you too, Ginger.

There's nothing nice about being stalked.

I'm not stalking you. Why would I do that?

You're probably lonely and wishing I'd come back to you. Why else would you be at an art opening? You understand nothing about art.

I understand enough to know what I like and what I don't. That would apply to more than just art.

What's that supposed to mean?

I get that you're still mad at me, Ginger but the reason I'm here is my Aunt Eugie is one of the artists. That's her over there in with the white hair, wearing the pink scarf.

You never said you had an aunt that's an artist.

I didn't know until recently. She painted the portraits along the far wall. One of them is of a friend of mine.

Don't bother trying to impress me, Noll.

I'm not trying to impress you.

Sure you're not. Just don't get any ideas we can get back together. I'm here with my new boyfriend. There he is over there. Oh, is that your little Mexican friend he's talking to, the one from the party?

She's from here just like you, Ginger.

Wherever she's from, I'll bet Basil has already asked her to sleep with him.

To do what?

She'll do it, too. Women can't resist Basil. He's French. See how she smiles at him? She's already decided.

What are you talking about? I thought you said he's your boyfriend.

We have an open relationship, Noll.

Didn't open relationships go out of style in the seventies?

Noll, you're so yesterday. I hope you don't mind leaving here alone.

-Noll spotted Maya talking to a tall, thin man with shoulder-length hair. She turned and made her way across the room, the man following. As Maya drew close the man moved next to her, draping his arm across her shoulder before he spoke.

Ginger, see who I found. This is the beautiful Maya.

Basil, what happened to you? I couldn't imagine where you'd gone to. Now I see. I knew you were up to something kinky.

Well, perhaps. I think I've talked Maya into a little tryst. But who is this poorly dressed person spoiling our party?

It's only Noll. Noll, this is my boyfriend, Basil.

We French prefer the term lover, Ginger. I think Maya and I fit rather well together, don't you?

Maya is here with Noll.

You don't mind sharing, do you Maya?

Well Basil, I do like French cooking, especially the herbs. But I want to know what Noll thinks.

Yes Noll, what it is that you think? Or do you have even a thought in that manly head of yours?

I've always wondered why the Brits don't much like the French. Now I'm beginning to understand.

But do you have a thought about Maya and Basil?

Maya is free to make her own decisions. I'd like to say it's been a pleasure but instead I'll go say hello to Eugie. After all, she's the reason I'm here.

Why can't you say what you want, Noll?

Maya, if you decide to go play with your little French friend I can't stop you.

157

Did I say that's what I'm going to do? Were you even listening?

You said something about cooking but I can't read your mind.

Just listen to me, Noll. Are you sure you heard his name in all this noise?

-She winked at Noll. Noll stepped back, looking at them in turn.

Wait. Your name is Basil and you're dating Ginger?

Ginger and I, we are intimate. We French don't date.

It sounds like a spicy relationship, huh Noll?

Yes it does, Maya. Makes you wonder what's cooking, doesn't it?

Could get steamy, you never know.

Bound to be saucy.

The French do like their sauces.

Maybe so, but I'd rather go find Eugie than wait around to find out. What about you?

Yeah, I've lost my appetite.

What do they say, Ginger?

Don't worry about it, Basil. You think you're so funny, Noll. You're just jealous.

No Ginger, I'm not jealous, I'm leaving. I hope *you* like French cooking.

Noll took Maya's hand, leading her through the back door and into a fenced-in courtyard, the cement patio doubling as a dance floor. The band finished a tune and launched into a rendition of *Silver Wings* as Noll pulled Maya to the middle, putting his arm around her waist and swinging her across the floor in a brisk two-step. He stared into her dark eyes as they circled to the halting rhythm, spinning through the warm air, pulling closer, any need for talk now gone, the world around them remote, suspended, the music moving from one song to the next, accepted as is, unnoticed. Time hovered out of awareness.

Finally, Maya took Noll's hand, leading him from the floor. He stood gazing across the dimly lighted yard, the gray-haired band members, the strings of colored lights, the guests' voices coming to him in waves through the gallery door, all somehow less than real. Maya squeezed his hand and pulled him out the back gate and into a night heavy with the scent of fallen leaves, grass gone to seed. The air though still warm held the chill morning beneath its stillness.

They moved through neighborhoods of frame houses, windows aglow behind drawn curtains, closed blinds, and beside the university, at that late hour still humming, alive. Across the boulevard oaks stretched over the narrow street, casting the sidewalk in deep shadow as if concealing what was to come. All at once the treetops came alive with a darting glow that seemed to jump leaf to leaf, restless, searching. A moment later a wall of smoke passed across their path in a running line.

Noll, is that smoke? Where is it coming from?

See that glow the next block over? Someone's house must be on fire.

That's terrible. Shouldn't we call someone?

Jesus, Maya, it could be my house. Mom and Gannie would be asleep. I have to go.

Wait, Noll.

I'm sorry, Maya. Make the call. I have to go.

Eighteen

Noll raced across the busy street, dodging cars and hopping the curb without thought, moving past darkened houses and toward the hastening fire, his heart pounding. The second he rounded the corner the house came into view, windows dark, driveway quiet, and he slowed, a sense of relief passing over him as he scanned the roof for fire and found nothing. For a moment, he thought the smoke must have come from somewhere else. An instant later flames burst through a side window, a window adjacent to his mother's bedroom that had been dark only moments before. He threw himself at the house.

Smoke streamed from the eaves as he slammed through the front door and fell to the living room floor, the ceiling now draped in moving blackness. Crouching to the floor, trying to see a way ahead he scrambled down the hall calling for his mother, careful to stay beneath the thick cloud, even the air near the floor acrid, choking. He crept along, checking each open door, making sure the room was empty, finally reaching the door to his mother's room and grabbing the knob, the metal warm but not hot. He pushed through.

A wall of smoke collapsed into the doorway. Feeling his way along the wall and toward the bed he plunged forward into the heat, his mother's ragged breath coming to him through the blackness. Reaching toward the sound, he found her hand still warm to the touch and he took firm hold. She sat upright, coughing and flailing about before he could grab her by both arms and pull her toward him, realizing with relief she could walk. Wrapping his arms around her, he rushed her from the room and down the hall, fingers of fire crackling beneath the doorway behind them.

The street seemed oddly quiet as they pushed through the front door and into the still night, both of them falling to the lawn, gasping. Maya appeared out of nowhere, kneeling next to Noll and taking his mother's hand in hers as sirens came to life above the treetops. Noll sat up with a start, realizing Gannie could still be somewhere inside. She had taken to sleeping in the house instead of her cabin more often than not. He jumped to his feet, racing through the rusted gate and into the backyard, calling her name. Her cabin was dark. He stopped, looking from the cabin to the house and back, not knowing what to do, fear sending his throat into spasm. He took a step toward the house but hesitated, seeing it nearly beyond entering a second time.

Praying he would find her safe inside, he started toward the house again but the sound of her voice came to him out of nowhere, rising in soft undertones, stopping him where he stood. A vision of her spirit passing above the flames came to him, raising the hair on his neck before he turned toward the sound and found her kneeling beneath the shadow of a nearby tree, eyes closed, lips moving. He stepped toward her as the house groaned, a wall of flames leaping above the rooftop and vanishing in a cloud of sparks. The wail of a siren echoed nearby and she opened her eyes, turning to him, her face calm, radiant.

I prayed for the Lord to send you to us, Noll and you came. I watched through the window as you led your mother from the house. I've been thanking God for bringing you back. Will your mother be okay?

She'll be alright. I was afraid you might be inside there too.

I was in the cabin working on a quilt and I must have fallen asleep.

Lucky for us you did. It was a close call getting mom out. I can't believe our house is gone, Gannie.

Lord Almighty, what will your mother do now that she's lost everything? She's already so frail of mind.

Let me take you to her, Gannie. She'll want to know you're safe.

161

We need a plan before we go see her, Noll. We're without a place to live and we have no car. Once she realizes the situation, she's likely to become hysterical. I have no idea what to tell her.

We'll tell her not to worry, that we're all still alive. Then we'll figure out what to do.

But how will we, Noll? The cabin is tiny, with barely enough room for one old lady. Dear God, I never in my life thought we'd end up homeless.

We won't be homeless. I have an idea what we can do.

Tell me now, before we go to your mother. I can't stand the thought of facing her without something that might give her hope.

I know where we can go and I have a way to get us there. That's all she needs to know.

Houselights flickered through the trees as the jeep bounced along the now-familiar oyster shell road, a dim cloud of dust trailing behind in the moonless night. The smell of salt marsh mingled with the acrid odor of smoldering oak leaves, filling the damp night air. Foghorns sounded beyond the trees. Noll glanced into the rear view mirror at his mother and Gannie huddled beneath a blanket, a chill wind swirling about them, and forced himself to focus on what had to be done right then, each step one after the other, no time to worry over a future set somewhere beyond sight, featureless, stripped of expectation.

He rounded the dark line of trees and the house came into view, the deep porch glowing with hazy yellow light, Eugie standing at the top of the stairs, looking in her pink scarf just as she had earlier that evening. Noll cut the engine and turned to his mother.

Where are we, Noll?

This is Aunt Eugie's house, mom. Don't you remember?

162

Well, it's so dark I don't know where I am. And I'm cold, too. Did you say Aunt Eugie? Why are we here of all places, Noll?

We need a place to live and Aunt Eugie has offered to share her house with you.

We're going to be staying with Aunt Eugie? I never imagined life would become so deprived that I'd have to go begging for help, especially from a crazy aunt. Noll, isn't there anywhere else we can go?

Mom, Eugie's not crazy, she's an artist.

There is no difference that I can see. It's just not proper work for a woman.

She's made a good living at it. Besides, you can't be picky when you have nowhere else to go. Be glad you'll have a roof over your head.

I don't see anything to be glad about.

Try to be polite, at least. Eugie is doing us a favor, although I don't know why after the way this family has treated her.

I never thought I'd fall so low as to live in the same house with a crazy relation, an artist to boot. What will people think?

-Eugie called to them from the stairs.

Are you going to sit out there all night trying to make up your mind or are you going to come on in to Eugie's home for the wayward and dispossessed? It's chilly out here and I could use a drink.

I don't need to be asked more than once, Eugie.

You always were of the practical sort, Gannie. Come on in.

-Gannie climbed out of the jeep and hurried toward the house, Noll and his mother following at a distance. They made their way up the stairs and Eugie led them through the house, ushering them to the kitchen table. She poured shots cognac and then downed the rest of her glass before refilling it. Noll's mother stared at the amber liquid.

Bottoms up, Elizabeth. I imagine you could use a drink after what you've been through.

I've always heard that artists stay up all night drinking and acting uncivilized. Now I see it's true. It must be close to two in the morning.

Actually, it's after three and this brandy represents the height of civilization in my book. Finish that glass and you'll see what I mean, Liz.

-She swallowed the brandy in one gulp and Eugie poured her another.

Eugie, you're the only person that ever called me Liz.

I admit you don't seem much like a Liz but you might get there if you spend enough time down here on the inlet.

It does seem peaceful.

You should see it in the moonlight, Liz. Then it's magical too.

I could use a little magic right now, Eugie. I just don't know what we'll do without a place to call home. What are we going to do, Gannie? Oh, now look at me.

Try not to cry, Elizabeth. We should be grateful for Eugie's hospitality. Let's try to take each day as the Lord offers it. I for one am going to get some sleep.

I think I'll join you, Gannie. Mom, you should probably try to get some sleep too.

I am tired, Noll but I believe this brandy really is the height of civilization.

Take it easy, mom. You're not used to drinking.

Oh, Noll go to bed if you like. I believe I'll get a little more civilized while I have the chance. Can I have another, Eugie?

Well sure, Liz. I believe there's hope for you yet.

The next morning Noll sat on the porch drinking coffee and watching seagulls play on the wind, their calls carrying a welcome bit of the everyday, the expected.

164

Sunlight skittered across the inlet, cascading onto the lawn and casting shadows near the house in deep indigo. A nearby palm rattled before the hastening breeze.

He heard the door behind him open and close. A moment later his mother sat beside him in a pair of canvas pants and a t-shirt, cradling a black 35 mm camera in her lap. She stared at the horizon without a word. Noll studied her for a moment, seeing a difference yet unable to put a name to it. Dark hair flew about her face in curling strands, her familiar pained expression replaced by a calm lack of concern. She turned to him and for a moment he thought she might smile.

Eugie was right, Noll. There is something special about this place. We stayed up all night talking and then I went out before sunrise and walked as far as I could in both directions. It's beautiful here but there's a peacefulness that goes beyond beauty.

They say the sea air is good for you.

Of course it is. The air here is so filled with life. Can you feel it, Noll? Can you smell it, organic and alive, crammed with the essence of life striving for something better? Can you sense the expectation, the hope just itching to burst out?

I've never heard you talk like this, mom. You seem different.

I feel different, Noll.

Are you okay? You're not going into one of those high energy periods where you think you can do anything, are you?

Don't worry, it's nothing like that.

What is it, then? There is a difference. I can see it.

It's true, something has changed. Before we got here last night I imagined I would be afraid of the future, of having no place to live, of having lost everything. And I *was* afraid. But walking out there this morning instead of fear I realized what I really felt, if I let myself, was relief.

165

Losing the house was an end to a part our life but it also was a beginning. As I walked along the inlet, I realized I had been given a gift, the gift of starting over. You've been given that gift too Noll, if you're willing to take it.

I'd like to see losing our house as something other than bad luck but that's how it looks to me.

But losing the house is a chance to leave behind all the bad luck you've ever had, to start fresh, to turn from the past to what's next.

You make it sound so easy.

There's nothing easy about change. But sometimes life offers up a chance to try something new, to become someone you've never been before, to become who you want to be. Did you know I wanted to be a professional photographer when I was your age? I had hundreds of photos stored in the attic from those days. I dreamed of traveling the world taking pictures.

Why didn't you do it?

I wasn't brought up that way. We were taught to be responsible and go for the sure thing, so I played it safe and went into teaching.

Teaching wasn't so bad, was it?

No, I loved it. But I always wondered what it would've been like to do what I dreamed of.

Your photographs were all lost in the fire, weren't they?

It's not such a bad thing, Noll. I have a chance to start fresh now. I'm determined to take that chance. Eugie gave me this old camera and I intend the use it. What do you want for yourself, Noll?

I wish I knew.

You don't have any idea?

Not really.

Oh Noll, you worry me. You've had so much to deal with in your young life.

I'll be alright, mom.

166

That's what you always say. You want everyone to think you're the strong one and you'll take care of things. But you don't always have to be, Noll. I can be strong too.

Sure you can, mom.

You don't believe me but you'll see. And do try to think about what I've said, Noll. You do worry me.

Part II

Nineteen

Noll spotted Ranse at a distance moving toward them in deliberate stride, unhurried, determined, anger caught in tilt of head, swing of arm, one hand hidden beneath his jacket, solid, bulging. Elgy stood facing the opposite direction, his back to Ranse, watching as Noll and Hen loaded a flatbed truck with broken and dilapidated furniture. He held a broken table leg in one hand, swinging it to and fro, clocklike. Noll stepped back, touching Hen on his arm without a word and nodding in Ranse's direction. Hen coughed heavily and spat before turning.

Elgy followed their gaze, spotting Ranse a half block away. He turned and walked to his truck, taking something from the glove box and stuffing it into his pocket. He slammed the door as Ranse stepped up to him and pulled a pair of work gloves from his jacket. He let the gloves drop to his side, his eyes heavy, without expression. Elgy stared into his face. Ranse lifted a flask from his coat pocket with his free hand and pulled on it, then he held up the gloves, thrusting them at Elgy.

You see these here brand new work gloves? I bought them for a job, a job I could've had. My man in the office there told me I had it. All the boss needed to do was make a few calls, check up on me, and I was in. So I bought these here gloves since I knew I would need them.

Looky here, Ranse, what're you doing here? You're bound to get yourself in trouble coming around this place.

This is my business, Hen. You stay out of it. I'm here to talk to Elgy. I got to hear what he has to say.

What do you want, Ranse?

Tell them what happened then, Elgy. Tell them what you told that boss about me.

I don't know what you're talking about.

169

You blackballed me, Elgy. I had a chance for a new start but you told him I was no good on the job, not to hire me. You told them I was lazy. Why'd you do that? I worked hard when I was here and for what? For no reason, that's what. And now I got nothing, no way to make a living, no way to pay bills. You know what that does to a man, Elgy? You know what it is to have your manhood taken from you like that, to have your self-respect taken, to be left with nothing, no pride, no hope?

You're already in trouble for coming back on campus. You best leave out of here right now instead of making things worse.

Can't get worse for me, Elgy. You made sure of that.

You brought this on yourself.

No sir, that's a lie. You brought it on all us men with your disrespect, your badmouthing, you treating a man like a dog, even worse than you'd treat some animal. That's what did it. I can't let you go on. It's got to stop here, got to stop now.

That sounds like a threat, Ranse.

-Elgy gestured with the table leg as he spoke.

Sounds like the truth to me.

You can't come in here and threaten me, boy.

There you see? That's just what I'm talking about. I'm a grown man not some boy.

You get yourself a load of trouble when you come here and threaten people.

Why do I need to make a threat when I'm right here? I'm telling you to your face.

I pegged you for uppity the first time I set eyes on you. I knew I never should've hired your young smart ass. Coloreds like you have no business telling men like me anything, especially to their face, but you get under the spell of troublemakers like Hen and they lead you straight to hell.

Nobody has to lead me when I make decisions my own self. I know what's good and what's bad, and you're as bad as they come, Elgy. You're not man enough to deal straight. You go under the table and sneak around like some coward. I know evil and evil can't go on. It has to be stopped.

Hen stepped around Elgy, putting a hand to Ranse's shoulder, just a touch, without a word. Ranse glanced at him, only for an instant but long enough for Elgy to pull a small pistol from his pocket. He pointed it toward them, his mouth twitching, hand shaking.

Ranse spotted the pistol and in an instant had jumped to one side, his eyes wide, knocking Hen backwards and into Elgy. The pistol went skittering across the pavement. Ranse moved toward Elgy and he raised the table leg, wheeling it around and slamming it into Ranse's side. He stumbled back in surprise before he turned and again lunged at Elgy, landing a glancing blow across his chin. As he stumbled past, Elgy followed, swinging the heavy club in a half circle and catching Ranse on the back of his head. Ranse fell hard. Noll stood watching, rooted in place, unable to move as Elgy raised the table leg again, bringing it down on Ranse's back with a sickening thud. Ranse groaned and turned on one side, struggling to protect himself from another blow.

Elgy stood over him for a moment, a half-smile on his lips. He raised the club again, taking aim for Ranse's head as Noll came out of his daze, realizing he must act, knowing it must be now. He lunged at Elgy, grabbing his arm and holding it in place. They stood over Ranse, frozen in place, staggering, the club hovering in air like a torch. Then Elgy freed an arm, backhanding Noll across the mouth and sending him tumbling onto the pavement. The warm taste of blood crossed his tongue. Sprawled against the ground, he turned to find Elgy facing him, the club held high once again. Noll raised an arm, waiting for what was

171

to come, hoping to shield his face from the blow. The crooked smile returned. An instant later a shot rang out, splitting the air, echoing between the building walls.

Elgy flinched and then stared at Noll, his face contorted, confused, as if he wanted to ask a question but had no idea what it might be. He swayed in place, looking to one side then the other. Noll watched as the club fell clattering to the asphalt. Elgy swayed once more, his face pale, eyes vacant before collapsing in a heap only feet from Ranse. Hen stood just beyond, holding the pistol in his palm as if it had appeared out of thin air. He dropped the gun and looked to Noll.

What have I done?

Is he dead?

I shot a white man, shot him dead. I've got to go, to leave this place right now.

But Hen, he would've killed us, me and Ranse. You had no choice.

You get Ranse to the hospital. He's bound to have a rib or two broke. It could kill him if he moves around too much.

-Sirens wailed to life in the distance. Ranse groaned as he turned onto his back, looking from Hen to Noll and back.

What's happened here?

I got to go, Ranse. I killed Elgy and I got to go.

But Hen, why do you have to leave? We'll explain it to the police. They'll see you had to do it.

A white man is lying there shot, Noll. Somebody has to pay.

I'm going with you, Hen. I go to get away from here. They'll say I did it.

No Ranse, you're hurt. You better go with Noll. He can help you.

I don't need no white man's help.

This boy saved your life, Ranse. Elgy would've finished you off if it wasn't for Noll. I got to move but he's going to take you to the hospital. You do what he tells you.

I'm not hurt that bad, Hen. Just take me with you.

I got to move fast, Ranse. Besides, I think you busted a rib or two. You go on with Noll.

Hen, I'm sorry I got you into this. I was trying to find me a honest job. I wanted Elgy to stop lying about me but I didn't want to bring you into trouble. Hen, you got to believe me.

I believe you, Ranse. Now, you go on with Noll.

-Noll stretched out his hand but Ranse waved him off.

I don't need your help. You got to take me with you, Hen. They'll put me in jail for sure.

-Ranse tried to raise himself but fell back, wincing in pain. Hen turned, disappearing between the buildings before Ranse could say another word. Noll bent down, taking Ranse under his arms and helping him to his feet.

Where will he go?

He's going to lay low, find himself someplace to hide. He's a hunted man now. I got to get out of here, get myself taped up but you can find him, help him hide out. You go on and find him.

What can I do? I don't know anything about hiding out.

You got yourself a car?

My aunt gave me her old army jeep.

Take him someplace away from here, someplace the police won't ever look.

But isn't that against the law? Shouldn't he talk to the police?

Won't do him any good. You have to help him. He saved your life.

I didn't ask him to kill someone.

Not just someone, a white man. Don't you get it, boy? They got to put him in jail or me in jail or the both of us. You go on and find him.

I've never broken the law before.

I got to go find myself a place to hide too. You do what you got to do. I'll do what I do.

Twenty

Noll approached his car, the jeep Eugie had given him, thinking over all he had told the police about Elgy's assault on the three of them, about Hen saving his life and Ranse's as well. He had done his best to defend Hen but could see it had little effect. The authorities knew of Hen's past and had drawn their own conclusions. He knew it would not go well for him.

Darkness moved between oval pools of lamplight as he reached for the car door and then hesitated, sensing a presence, something more than light and dark, something solid beyond the blackness. He waited, close to deciding it was only the wind when footsteps sounded from beyond the light. A moment later Lavonia appeared, looking in both directions before motioning him to where she stood just beyond the shadow of a sprawling Live oak. He hesitated, trying to reason out why she was there. She waved him over again, the frustration obvious in her expression even in the dim light.

Lavonia, what are you doing...?

Noll Spencer, hush up and come over here. Do you want everyone to know I've come to find you?

-He followed her into the darkness.

I don't understand.

You just listen to me and you'll understand all you need to. I want you to take Hen out of here, the sooner the better. You got to hide him away for awhile.

Where is he?

Let me talk and I'll tell you.

But why does he need to hide? If it wasn't for him I'd be lying in a morgue somewhere right now.

Now you listen to me, young man. You may think you understand the way of this mean old world but you don't.

It wasn't him that was in the wrong. I'll convince the judge Hen had to shoot Elgy and it was lucky for me that he did. I can explain it so he'll understand, I know I can.

Lord help me, you do have the unfounded certainty of the young. But there's plenty you don't know and plenty you don't need to know, especially when it comes to a man like Hen, a man in his condition.

What condition?

That's none of your concern.

Do you mean that he's been to prison? I know all about that.

You just listen up and do what I say. Hen needs your help and the way I see it, you owe him.

But what about...

No more questions. Will you help him or not?

But I'd be harboring a fugitive. That's what the police just warned me about.

Well, you know Hen can't go to my house. The police already came by looking for Ranse.

Did they find him?

No, he's made himself scarce.

Where has he gone?

I don't know and I don't want to know. I've done what I can for Ranse so I've given it to the Lord to decide. Now, will you help Hen or not?

Like I told Ranse, I don't know how to hide someone from the law.

That doesn't make no never mind. Are you willing to help is what I'm asking?

You're asking me to break the law?

Lord God Almighty, what will become of us? I should've known you wouldn't be willing to help. Why should you? He's not your people. He's not even your color. If he was white I'll bet you'd see it different.

Are you saying I'm racist?

I'm saying you'd help Hen if he was one of your own.

I wouldn't have to.

There it is right in your own words. You see yourself and people like you different from me and Hen. We're the ones that break the law, shoot people, even people about to stave your head in with a table leg.

I didn't mean it that way. I can see you and Hen aren't like that, not at all.

What did you mean, then?

I don't know but I'm not a racist. At least, I don't think I am. I know I don't want to be. That should count for something.

Are you sure about that, son? Can you honestly say the fact he's a black man is not on your mind?

Listen to me, Lavonia. I know Hen better that I knew my own father. I understand him better than I understand my own mother. I've seen the sort of man he is day in and day out. I know he's black and I'm white but the difference between us is the difference between two people, one older, one younger, growing up different but still just two people.

You think it's that easy but it's not. You can't ever understand what it's like for Hen or Ranse, much less for a black woman like me.

And you think you can understand what it's like for me?

No, neither of us understands the other.

That's how it is, then? You'll never understand me and I'll never understand you? Well, I know I can take Hen at his word. Whatever you say, I have no doubt about that.

Alright then, will you help him?

Tell me what to do, Lavonia.

Hen has some people in mind that might be willing to hide him. He'll tell you how to find them.

So, where is he?

There's something else you should know. These people I'm talking about, these people Hen knows, they are from his past. They're the sort that lives outside the law. I don't know how they'll take to someone like you, someone that looks like you.

I don't care about that.

What I'm saying is these people can be dangerous. Helping Hen could be trouble for you. Are you still willing to help him?

I said I will, so I will. I just need to know where to find him.

He's hiding in that old burnt out house you and your mama used to call home.

But I'm staying in my grandmother's house out back. Won't the police look for him there?

He figures they won't look too close at a house that's mostly burned down. You just got to be careful. He said to meet him in the alley out back.

I'd better go then.

I have one more thing to say to you, Noll Spencer.

What is it?

Thank you for what you did for my boy, Ranse.

He told you?

Ranse is too proud to admit any such thing. Hen told me what happened.

What I did wouldn't have mattered if Hen hadn't been there.

Well, only the Lord above knows all the good that happens in this world but I'm grateful he included you in his work today.

Noll pulled into the alleyway behind Gannie's cabin, creeping along as he peered through the windshield looking for some sign of Hen. A mangy tomcat passed through the headlights, his fight-scarred ears flat against his head as he slipped along the fence line before disappearing between two broken slats. At the far end of the alley near a cross street a white car sat close to a broken down single-car garage. Noll thought he could see the glow of a cigarette through the windshield.

He braked to get a better look at the car and as he did the jeep rocked to one side for an instant and then righted itself. He froze, waiting for the blow that might follow. An image of Elgy falling to the ground, his eyes dark, glassy invaded his thoughts. An instant later, heavy breathing snapped him out of his daze. The breathing slowed followed by a rustle of canvas. He strained to peer into the rearview mirror without seeming to but found only blackness. Then a hand grabbed his elbow.

They got to be watching your every move, son. Don't let on you know old Hen is back here. I got myself covered up with this canvas top here so we can go on but you got to stay relaxed. Think like you got somewhere important to be and you got to get there soon. If you hear what I said just move your head a little, but only a little. You know they got to be watching close.

-Noll gave a slight nod and eased down the alleyway. He avoided turning to look at the white car as they passed. Once past the car, he turned onto the side street and then onto the main thoroughfare, trying his best to check his mirrors without being obvious about it. After he had followed the road for several minutes, he again felt Hen's bony hand take hold of his arm.

Noll, we got any cars following us?

I've been watching and I haven't seen any sign we're being followed.

Alright then, I'm coming up front. I can't stay down here like some rat in a hole anymore. My old bones are likely to get stuck this way and I won't ever get out.

-Hen groaned as he emerged from beneath the canvas and climbed into the passenger seat.

Looky here Noll, you remember how to get to Queenie's? Turn right up here and then left. You'll recognize the place.

You're going for a drink? I thought you needed to hide out.

There's a man there that can hide people good, so I'm going to see what he can do for us.

For *us*? I don't need to hide from anyone.

Sure you do. You got me in this car here and if they find me they're sure to arrest you too.

I guess I knew that, but won't they be watching Queenie's?

Maybe. We got to wait a little and then I can go up and see her.

-The familiar dark cedar shake house with the red door glowed under a string of yellow lights as Noll pulled to the curb and cut the engine. They sat for a moment before Hen climbed over the door without opening it.

The door works Hen. You don't have to climb out.

I know that. I just don't want to attract any notice if I don't have to. Now you wait here while I go talk to Queenie and find out what I need to.

I'm not going to sit here like some chauffer. If I'm going to help you I need to be in on what's said.

What do you think Queenie'll do when she spots that pale face?

I'll stay where she can't see me. I've done this before. I know how it works.

Alright then but you stay out of sight, you hear?

Who are you going to talk to?

Man by the name of Shaky Shackleford. He's got a bar of his own but he stays away mostly and let's his ex-wife run it. He's a gambler and got himself into owing money to one and everybody so he tries to keep himself out of sight. That's why he's good at hiding people. He's been dodging folks so long he knows all there is to know about it.

-Noll kept to one side as they approached the heavy red door with the small window in the center. Hen pressed the buzzer and stepped back. A moment later the door opened and Queenie's stout form and broad walnut-hued face filled the space.

You get out of here, Hen Feathers. I don't want the police coming round here now or ever.

But Queenie, aren't you going to let me come inside where I won't be seen.

Didn't you hear what I just said?

But I got to find someplace to hide.

Well go hide then, just don't make it here or anywhere close to here. I got enough problems of my own without you bringing more down on me. You hear what I'm saying to you, Hen?

I just need to talk to Shaky. Let me come in, Queenie. He's bound to be inside there.

Well you know wrong because I ran Shaky out of here two days ago. He was up to no good, bringing some undesirables around and causing trouble, and you know I don't need none of that.

Where is he now?

I don't know and good riddance is what I say. You and him bring trouble with you wherever you go. Now get on out of here before a put Cleodis on you.

-She turned without another word and slammed the door.

Noll peered into the darkness as the headlights jumped along the gravel road before them, its surface like an oversized washboard. He had never seen a place as dark. Trees choked with underbrush seemed to rise up around them on all sides, wall-like, sucking in every ray of light the jeep could throw off. Hen sat slumped in the seat next to him mumbling to himself and sucking on one cigarette after the other.

The road ahead took on a reddish glow that soon spread to the treetops and the thick air beyond. Pools of fog hovered above the ground like crimson-hued specters. Noll slowed as Hen sat up, stubbing out his cigarette and stretching a bony finger toward the windshield. A clearing appeared to their right, the far end occupied by a tarpapered house set on piers and draped with lights, all red. A hand-painted sign next to the door read "Shaky's Country Cobra Lounge". Hen coughed into his free hand deep and long before he spoke.

That there is Shaky's place. I sure do hope he's around. I was betting on finding him at Queenie's. He's not much to count on but he's all I got.

That's a strange name for a bar.

Shaky got bit by a big king cobra when we were together in 'Nam. He made it through alright but had the shakes ever since.

That's how he got his name?

He was born Marvin Shakleford but no one except me remembers that now.

Will there be any problem if I go in there?

Too poor out here to turn people away, no matter who.

-They climbed stairs made of warped planks set on bricks. Hen pushed through a black metal door and they stepped into a single room scattered with castoff tables and chairs. In one corner a makeshift bar of plywood sheets set on empty oil drums stood beneath a six-foot long stuffed cobra decorated with multicolored holiday lights and Mardi Gras beads. A man the color of weak tea leaned both hands against the bar and glared at them. Even from across the room, Noll could see the rhythmic movement of his bald head. He reached beneath the counter, pulled out a baseball bat and set it on the counter, patting it with the palm of his hand.

I got me a big black pistol in a holster bolted to this oil can here and I know how to use it too.

Shaky, what's gone wrong with you? I never saw you so jumpy.

-With that Shaky's head jerked back and a tremor shook his entire frame before he righted himself and leaned forward. He peered across the dim room as if Hen was somewhere far in the distance.

Hen Feathers is that you?

Last time I looked in the mirror it was still me, Shaky. What's got into you?

My eyes aren't too good anymore. I see a white man walk through that door and I think the liquor control come to shut me down.

Well, it's just me.

Worse, then.

What?

You can't come in here, Hen. I heard what you did and I don't want you bringing any part of that here. I got trouble enough following me around these days. The sheriff sees us together he'll think I had something to do with a white man getting shot. I can't go back to prison, Hen. I'm too old.

I just need a place to hide, Shaky.

Can't hide here.

I don't want to hide here. I want you to find me someplace.

No sir, too risky. You go find somebody else can help you hide out.

I don't know somebody else.

You got to leave out of here, Hen. You're too hot.

But Shaky, we served together. That doesn't count for a thing?

I got troubles of my own, more than I can handle. You get on out of here, Hen. Don't make me pull out my pistol.

You wouldn't shoot your old friend, would you Shaky?

Friend or no friend, I do what I have to. Your white partner better get you out of here before something happens, something bad.

-The instant Shaky bent to reach beneath the counter Noll grabbed Hen by the arm, pulling him down the steps and out into the parking lot without a word while Shaky's voice echoed through the open door. They climbed into the jeep and Noll pulled back into the heavy blackness. The dense forest stood beyond, airless, still, as if waiting for what was to come.

Twenty-one

Hen slumped in his seat, staring into the darkness and saying nothing, his only movement the circular press of thumb on forefinger, rotating in clockwise spirals, out and in, counterclockwise, in and out. The jeep jumped the washboard gravel in a rhythmic rattle of sheet metal, nut and bolt while Noll peered past the headlight glow, searching his thoughts for a next move, an answer to Hen's unspoken question. A moment later the tree line opened, giving way to flat pastureland dotted with cattle barely visible under a gibbous moon. The rich odor of sea salt and marsh enveloped him like an unseen cloud.

He glanced at Hen, struggling to imagine his thoughts, the curving path of his life, the lonely isolation of a man without options. Hen could be brusque, even rude in his grumpy frankness, but nothing about him came close to cruel, much less criminal. He was as good a man as Noll had known in his life, better than most, better than his own father. A wave of shame broke over him at the thought and he waited for it to pass, wanting to know the truth where it stood, not where it was said to be.

Trying to match word and thought, he turned to Hen a second time but only for an instant and when he faced the road again a Charolais bull stood directly ahead, perpendicular, massive, covering the road from side to side. Noll slammed the brakes, sliding sideways as the jeep veered onto the shoulder, bounding past the staring bull and over a shallow ditch before rattling to a stop thirty yards beyond. Hen sat unmoving, still staring into the distance while a cloud of red dust drifted over the jeep, swirling though the headlights and disappearing into the darkness beyond. Noll gripped the steering wheel unable to move. After a moment, Hen's voice sounded above the hiss of the engine.

Looky here Noll, I got something to ask, something that needs asking. I need you to listen.

We almost got killed and you want to talk?

I got to know.

Alright, I'm listening.

What do you do when your own people turn you away? What do you do? People I know most of my life, Queenie, Shaky, they tell me to leave like I was some stranger off the street, like I'm some old stray dog come around begging for scraps. How does that happen?

I don't know, Hen.

Not just them either because word got around too fast. Must be everybody I know, more or less. A man thinks he has friends he can count on and then he finds out different. Nobody willing to lend a hand, help find a place to hide, nobody but Lavonia and she can't help when she's got Ranse to protect.

We'll figure out something.

It's hard for a man to ask for help, damn hard. Don't they know that? I never ask for a thing but when I do this is what I get. I can't figure it.

It's hard to understand, Hen.

I know people get selfish. I know they think of themselves first. But you got to believe your friends will be different, treat you different. I don't know what I did but it must've been bad.

It's not you, Hen. They're scared of what'll happen if they get caught. They're protecting themselves. We'll find someplace to go. Just give me a minute to think.

-Hen slapped his bony knee and doubled over, laughing to himself in hoarse cough-like guffaws. His lips held a bitter smile.

I never would've thought it. No, I never would've.

What? What didn't you think?

That a man I've known only these few months would be the one to help me, a black man, and the only one to help too. On top of that he's white.

186

It's not black and white. It's just me and you, Hen.

You're right about that. I'm black and you're white but we didn't choose either way. It's just how it is. People are people, some good some bad, most in the middle and none but you willing to help out.

Not exactly. You said Lavonia would help if she could. What about Lio?

Now there's a good man and he's not black or white. But his house is one of the first places the police would look. He said he'd hide me down in Mexico but I can't go there.

Why not?

I don't have that kind of time.

What do you mean?

Never you mind about that now. We got to find us someplace to light before it gets too late. Besides, if we sit here too long that big bull might pay us a visit.

Eugie's place can't be too far from here. I can smell salt water. It's too risky to stay there for long but tonight should be alright and she may have some ideas where we can go next.

Uh-huh, I could tell you were about to find us a plan.

How could you tell when I didn't know myself?

I could see it there right on your face, waiting for you to find it.

You couldn't see anything.

Sure I could. All this time and you still don't believe old Hen? You should know better by now.

I know the bull has arrived, that's for sure. We might as well get moving.

In spite of the late hour, lights still blazed throughout the house as Noll rang Eugie's doorbell. He knew her penchant for painting into the early morning hours was usually confined to her studio, so he puzzled over the light spilling onto the porch like a yellow stain as footsteps sounded from beyond the doorway. When the door finally opened, Maya stood before him. Noll took a step back, blinking. As tired as he felt, he wondered if it was really her or just a cruel trick of his imagination. Her hair glistened beneath the warm light, a physical darkness, satin-like and the thought struck him that he had never before that moment appreciated the extent of her beauty. Her image filled his mind, leaving no room for thought or word. Hen's voice brought him back to his senses.

Noll, you forget how to talk or you already asleep?
No, I…
Noll, what are you doing here?
I should be asking you that, Maya.
I came to see Adela.
Adela's here too?
If you weren't so busy doing who knows what you might know that. She and Humberto are staying here until they find a place of their own.
Her husband is back?
The Border Patrol found him dumped on some back road near the border, not far from Roma. His abductors told him he'd been mistaken for someone else. They let him go but warned him he can never return home.
And they came here?
He got a job at that bar down near the ferry. He always dreamed of being a chef and he figures this is a chance to start. He and Adela are using Eugie's studio as an apartment.
But why are you here so late?
Noll, it's not even midnight. Basil and I were out and thought we'd drop in.
Basil, the French guy?
We came here together.
I thought he was with Ginger.
He's with me now.
But Maya, why him of all people?

188

Don't frown at me like that. At least he knows I exist. At least he has time for me. So, now it's my turn. Why are you here?

Something bad has happened and we need a place to stay tonight. I was hoping Eugie could help us out.

Noll, we can find us someplace else. Sounds like Eugie's got herself a house full of people.

-Eugie appeared in the doorway.

Why, I thought I heard the voice of Hen Feathers. I believe we've got ourselves a regular party now. Maya, find us a bottle and bring it out to the porch. Tell the others to leave us alone. Hen and I have some catching up to do.

Eugie, something's happened and we need...

Let me do the asking, Noll. Eugie, I'm asking for your help. I killed a man today, a white man.

Now there's some news. Did he need killing, Hen?

I wouldn't be here now if Hen hadn't shot him, Eugie.

It's a fact he was about to stove Noll's head in with a club, so I shot him.

Then you did what needed doing, Hen.

Maybe so, Eugie but the police won't see it that way. I need to lay low for awhile. That's why Noll brought me here. I need a place to hide and none of my old friends will help me. Noll says they're too afraid to help but I got to find a place, and soon.

Why not hide out here?

It's not safe, Eugie. Hen needs a place with no connections to either of us, a place the police would never think to look.

You mean you need to get as far out of the mainstream as possible? There's one person that comes to mind right away. His name is Nip Nepplelipper.

There's a real person by the name of Nip Nepplelipper?

There is, Noll and believe it or not he has the biggest bottom lip I ever saw on a human being. When I

189

was a little girl, I used to sneak up on the horses when they were dozing. Once I got close enough, I'd give that bottom lip a good strum with my finger and they'd nearly jump out of their skins. Nip makes me want to do the same every time I see him.

Does he live near here?

He lives on the water and I mean literally on the water. The road there is awful but old Sherman can make it. The good news is that he's about as far out of the mainstream as you'll find in this life. You can go see him in the morning. If you went now he'd probably shoot you.

-Maya pushed through the door carrying a large bottle of cognac and four glasses. She faced Noll as she spoke.

Eugie, the others have gone off to the studio. Do you mind if I join you?

Well, I'll put it to you like this, Maya. Pour a glass for Noll and one for yourself, and then hand me the bottle. Hen and I are going down to the water were we can catch up without getting bothered. I can't imagine how a grumpy old hermit like myself ended up with a house full of people but there it is.

-Hen's deep cough filled the night as he and Eugie climbed down the stairs and disappeared into the darkness. Noll turned to where Maya sat cradling a half-full glass in her lap.

Gannie and mom must already be asleep, although I don't know how with all this talk going on.

They're not here. Eugie said they left this morning.

They didn't tell me they were going anywhere.

They're off to the national park for an outdoor photography workshop.

My mother is in west Texas? She doesn't even like leaving the house.

People can change, Noll.

We'll see.

190

You don't believe a person can change for the better?

Things aren't always as they seem, Maya.

What's happened to you, Noll?

I don't know.

Why did you stop calling? Was it something I did, something I said?

No, nothing like that.

Then why?

I didn't decide to, it just happened.

You couldn't just pick up the phone?

I meant to call, I wanted to but I couldn't seem to get around to it. I know it doesn't make any sense. I just felt stuck. All I could do was to get through each day.

I hope you can get unstuck someday, Noll. I've missed you.

I'm here now. Can't we take up where we left off?

A lot has changed since I saw you last.

You mean the French guy? You can't be serious about him.

Why not? He is good-looking, after all.

I wouldn't know about that. I'm sorry I didn't call, Maya. I just needed time to figure things out.

What did you figure out?

I want to start over, Maya, the two of us. A lot happened and I needed to sort it all out but I'm past that. You'll see. It'll be different now.

Noll, you don't understand.

I do understand. You're right about people changing.

But, Noll...

I can change, Maya. I'll prove it to you. Just give me a chance.

Noll, Basil has asked me to marry him.

He what? Maya, you don't want to marry him. Remember what he was like at the gallery?

Oh, he was just playing.

I find that hard to believe.

He's not like you think he is, Noll. He's a gentleman.

A ladies' man is more like it.

Think what you like. I should get back to him. I came here to see Adela but I didn't think I'd run into you.

So that's how it is?

Noll, you've been though a lot. Don't give up on yourself. Don't give up on whatever it is you want.

I hope you know what you're doing.

I have to go. Besides, there's someone here to see you.

-Maya disappeared through the door as Felix stepped out.

Felix, you're here too?

Noll, I heard about the fight and Hen shooting some man. I'm so sorry. Are you alright? It must have been horrible.

I still can't believe it happened.

Do you want to talk about it?

Not really.

That's a relief. Just the thought of blood makes me nauseous.

What are you doing here, Felix?

I came to see Adela. I finally talked Maya into bringing me. She's gotten so difficult since she met that obnoxious Frenchman. I had to beg, Noll. It was humiliating.

You don't like him either?

Well, Basil is handsome and he really knows how to dress. But that's just the problem. He thinks he's too good for the rest of us.

Maya doesn't think so.

Oh, I don't know what's wrong with her, Noll. She'll get over it sooner or later. I just hope I survive until then. But speaking of clothes, you could learn a thing or two from our obnoxious French friend.

192

What are you talking about, Felix?

Noll, you have to get with the times. Add some pizzazz to your wardrobe.

What's wrong with the way I dress?

What's wrong is all that drab color. You look like you just stepped out of a 1960 Sears catalogue. I might have to start calling you Noll the Boring. Oh, that was mean, wasn't it? I'm sorry, Noll. I can get that way when it comes to fashion.

Do I really look that bad?

No, you're as handsome as ever but you need to spice things up. Get some bright colors and shirts that won't wrinkle. And try wearing pants other than jeans once in a while. What looks good on you?

I've never given it much thought, Felix. Are you sure about this?

Noll, remember that bar I took you to, the one where I told everyone we were a couple?

How could I forget?

I only said it so no one would bother you.

That was thoughtful of you.

Trust me. I know some of those people all too well.

They were a friendly group and I had a great time.

That's because you're so likeable when you let yourself be.

What's that supposed to mean?

It means when you let yourself live a little and have some fun. But Noll, you stuck out like a sore thumb in those shabby clothes of yours.

I look shabby?

Sorry, the words just spill out before I know it. Fashion talk just does that to me.

Maybe you could give me a hand in figuring out what sorts of clothes to try.

Noll, would you really let me go shopping with you?

I hate shopping so I could use the help.

193

I could be your fashion consultant?

Let's not go overboard, Felix.

I'll take care of you, Noll. Lord knows you need it.

What?

Oops, I did it again. But all this talk of clothes must seem unimportant after what you've been through.

I'm glad to get my mind off it. I like talking to you, Felix.

Do you really, Noll? That's such a nice thing to say. It's just that I'm worried about you, Noll. I'm worried about what will happen next. What are you going to do?

We'll hide and hope we don't get found.

Twenty-two

Hen peered at the vanishing road through fog the color of weak tea, wall-like, impenetrable, as if the earth itself had changed form from solid to gas. Dense mist surrounded the jeep as it entered a narrow path lined with salt grass, the leaves beaded, dripping. Hen waved the jeep forward with gnarled fingers. Damp air captured the turn of wheel on gravel even before it sounded, leaving in its place a muted cousin, thin and without substance, the world around them an apparition, approximate, uncertain. Silhouette of gull and heron passed before the dim light of sunrise like specters, there but not there, disappearing onto a blank canvas.

Noll slowed as the road turned to sand. Tufts of grass crowded twin tracks that narrowed into trails and then seemed to vanish altogether, a matt of fallen stems the only sign of direction. They followed as best they could. A rose-colored rectangle formed before them, differing from the surrounding air only by hue, edge, the growing shape somehow solid in the shifting light.

Hen held up a hand and Noll came to a stop. They squinted through the windshield, the popping sound of a hammer coming to them above the engine hum. Noll turned the key and the jeep shuddered and fell silent, the hammering suddenly louder as the sky lightened and then cleared in a rush of salt-laced wind. Before them stood a house set on piers, its crimson walls trimmed in lavender and green, a man leaning from a ladder, staring at them. Noll turned to Hen, his mouth open but without sound. Hen chuckled and shook his head.

Eugie didn't say she was sending us to a brothel.
It's someone's house Hen, not a brothel.

Might as well be, the way it's painted. I thought we were supposed to hiding out, not advertising where we are. I bet you could see this place from outer space.

Well, that's the only way the police will find it. I don't know where we are but it's a long way from anyplace else so stop your griping.

That there must be the man we're looking for.

He doesn't look too happy to see us.

I wouldn't be too happy either if I had to tell everyone I met my name is Nip Nepplelipper.

He's climbing down the ladder. Let me do the talking, Hen.

I can speak for myself, boy.

Eugie's my aunt so I'd better be the one to deal with this guy.

-The man stepped off the ladder and began moving toward them in a shuffling slant, crab-like, arms out from his sides, legs bowed, his ruddy face a near match of the reddish house. As he neared the man slowed, eyeing them each in turn, his mouth half-open, his hanging lip impossible to miss. Noll peered at the size of it.

Are you men lost?

We're looking for Lip…uh, I mean Nip. Are you him?

Maybe I am, maybe I'm not.

I'm Noll and this is Hen. I believe my Aunt Eugie called about us Mr. Lipplenipper.

The name's Nepplelipper. You got some kind of speech problem?

No, I, uh…

How do I know you're who you say you are?

Well, would I know Eugie called if I wasn't?

Maybe you would, maybe you wouldn't.

I'll give you my word that Eugie's my aunt and that's how I know she called you, if you really are Lip..uh, I mean Nip.

You trying to be funny?

196

No, why do you say that?

You can't get my name right or maybe you won't. I've come across wiseacres from the city before. They don't fare too well around here.

-Noll stared at the man's flapping lip.

I didn't mean anything by it.

What are you staring at, then?

What? Staring? I...uh...nothing...I'm just trying to find...mister...uh, him...you.

-Hen took a step toward the man.

It's me the reason he's here, the reason Eugie called. I'm in trouble with the law and need a place to hide out for a while. Eugie thought this would be the place to come.

Nobody said nothing about a black man.

Is that a problem?

Maybe it is and maybe it isn't. What did you say your name was?

McHenry Feathers is my name but I go by Hen.

-The man leaned forward, eying Hen from head to toe.

Hen Feathers. That's some name you got for yourself.

You going to tell us to leave now?

No sir, I don't mind having a feller with a name like that around here, not at all. I'm not so sure about your partner.

He's just young is all. He'll be alright.

Maybe he will, maybe he won't. You sure he's not some wisecracker?

His mouth goes off before he knows what he wants to say but he means nothing by it. Looky here Nip, you hear from Eugie or not?

I got word from Eugie alright but I don't know any particulars. I got no phone so she called the One-armed Jacks and they brought word.

The One-armed Jacks?

197

Bert and Dill Jacks. They're twin brothers that have a fishing guide business around the west end of the inlet. Everyone calls them the One-armed Jacks because you never see one without the other right close by.

What does the one-armed part mean?

You're going to have to tell me your name again, son. Ever since I got struck by lightning I can't remember much of anything.

I'm Noll Spencer, Eugie's nephew.

Well Noll Spencer, when they were teenagers the brothers were out sailing their catamaran and a squall popped up out of nowhere. They thought they could outrun it and nearly did but in their hurry to get the boat to shore they didn't see that a power line had come down in the big wind. They both had one hand on the mast when it touched the line. The force blew them right into the water. It's a miracle they didn't drown.

They each lost an arm?

One lost his left and the other his right. They'll tell you that between the two of them they can handle just about anything but I've known them for years and I can tell you there's not much either one can't do on his own. They're always out fishing, hunting or playing golf when they have the time.

I've never seen one-armed twin brothers.

Well, Noll you're about to. They'll be over here soon. See those boards lined up on that table over there? I collect old planks that wash up along the shore, cut them to the likeness of a fish and paint them up real bright, and then the brothers sell them to the well-off types they take out fishing. Odd the things a man can do to make a living, huh?

I guess it is. So, are you saying we can hide out here for a while?

Maybe I am, maybe I'm not. It all depends.

We'll pay you for it.

Nope, it won't depend on the likes of money.

Then what *will* it depend on?

You can read, I reckon?

Well sure I can read, can't everyone?

Not when they've been struck by a bolt of lightning.

Were you really struck by lightning?

I was trying to land a big redfish right over there by those mangroves when it happened.

You can't read because of that?

The fool doctors said the jolt crossed some wires in my head. Hell, I knew that already. I can't read or write a lick anymore. Words and letters jump around on the page like a herd of fleas.

So, you want us to read to you?

And write a letter or two.

Hen is the book expert. He has a house full of them. I imagine he's a better reader than I'll ever be but I can write up whatever you need.

You like a good book, Hen?

You got to know a book's better company than most people, Nip.

You'll feel right at home, then. I collected books for years until I ran out of space. I keep them in my workshop over there. That's where you and Noll can bed down.

You're a book collector that can't read?

Strange, isn't it Noll? Now there's a cruel fate that takes from a man the one thing he values most and for good measure leaves him with a paralyzed lip.

The lightning paralyzed your lip too?

That's why it droops like it does.

I hadn't noticed.

Don't lie to me son, even if you mean to spare me the embarrassment. I mean to take the truth head on, whatever it is.

The truth is a hard master, Nip.

Maybe it is and maybe it isn't, Hen but it's the only way for me. Now let's go take a look at your new home.

-Noll gazed down the gradual slope, past the workshop and toward the stretching shoreline and the shallow inlet beyond, bright in the honeyed light. Marsh grass lining the edge vibrated before a steady wind. Dense stands of mangrove framed the narrow point of land, the darker green of deep water a hundred yards offshore. To one side a ramshackle pier jutted into the water, its warped planks stained by the lapping waves. A heron appeared, gliding inches above the water before settling on the top of a leaning pylon.

The scene reminded him of Eugie's home and Maya's face appeared before him, looking as she had when they last spoke. He thought of the many ways he had let her down and again wondered what was wrong with him. Whenever he saw her all he wanted was to stay with her yet he had avoided calling her, avoided even thinking about her for weeks. How could both be true? He thought he must have some defect, some flaw that kept him at a distance from anyone that bothered to care. A smirk of self-loathing crossed his lips and then vanished as Hen paused, turning to him.

You alright with this, son? You don't look too glad to be here.

I was just thinking.

That thinking can find you some trouble if you do too much. You got to just live your life, Noll.

I know, Hen.

Looky here, this is some fine place Nip has got himself. A man could do alright here, fish every day if he wanted to. I'd never get tired of that.

My father dreamed of having a place like this. He'd take us down along the ship channel and talk about a place on the water he'd have one day. I imagined it just like this.

Nothing wrong with dreaming long as you remember a dream's just a dream.

I guess maybe he forgot that.

-Nip hobbled in his sideways gait toward the workshop, followed by Hen. A covered open-air work area stood further down the slope, its tin roof stretching over a long table scattered with tools, brushes and drip-covered cans of paint. Rows of wooden fish dangled from a wire suspended above the table. Noll turned from the horizon, climbing stairs set on the end of a broad wooden deck running the length of the shop, its unpainted rails weathered and rough against his palm. Driftwood planks, some still edged with dried and shriveled seaweed covered the wall fronting the shop. Noll stepped through the open door to find books covering every bit of wall space, broken only by five broad windows, two on each side and another at the far end. A green army surplus cot sat in one corner, piled with magazines and papers. A ragged sofa stood opposite.

You read all these books, Nip?

Hell no, it would take me five lifetimes to read all these books even if I could still read.

You didn't read any?

Why sure I did Hen, a few dozen or so I reckon.

But you want me to read you some of them now?

No, we don't want to be handling these books. They've got to stay in good shape if they're going to be worth much. You're looking at my retirement, Hen. I have some old paperbacks at the house we'll use.

I never thought about the outside of a book as long as it held a good story.

Hen, a collector doesn't care as much what's in a book as in what it's worth. We look at a book the way some people look at rare stamps or old coins. If it's a first edition or limited printing or some such rarity, I don't give a hoot what the story's about.

But the worth of a book is in the ideas, the story.

201

Not to a collector it's not. It's an antique not a book, an antique that could be worth a bundle. That's the thrill of it. Collecting is like hunting for buried treasure except instead of the bottom of the ocean or underground, you're searching out of the way auctions, bookshops or estate sales, maybe even a flea market. Think of it, Hen. A first edition Hemingway might be waiting for me at the garage sale down the street.

I can't say I understand it Nip but I can see it gets your blood going.

That's the truth and I've handed you men an earful too. Don't tell the Jacks, they give me grief enough about my books already. Speaking of the brothers, I believe I hear their twin outboards headed this way. They always come by boat.

They going to be alright knowing we're here, Nip?

You mean will they turn you in?

That's what I'm asking.

I never know what to expect out of those two, Hen.

I thought they were Eugie's friends.

Not exactly, Noll. Eugie called them because it's the only way to get word to me. I got rid of my phone. Best thing I ever did.

You got some idea what we should do?

I do. When they get here we see what's what and if they're willing to help.

What happens if they're not willing?

We talk over a price. They call it work but those boys will do just about anything for a dollar.

What sorts of things?

You don't want to know. They try to tell me but I won't listen. I think you've just got to take your chances with them.

Then that's what we'll do.

Twenty-three

Noll followed Hen out the door of the workshop and onto the broad deck as a boat appeared beyond a distant point of land and raced across the inlet in a wide arc before slowing all at once and gliding to the end of the pier. The roar of the twin outboard engines still hung in the air for a moment, mixing with a blue cloud of exhaust that hovered for a moment before vanishing in a gust of wind before the engines sputtered and died. Two figures hustled around the dock in a blur of activity and then turned to make their way up the pier at a brisk walk. Empty shirt sleeves dangled at their sides, jostling in the shifting breeze. As they stepped off the pier, one seemed a mirror image of the other.

The men started up the hill and then paused, looking from Nip to Hen and back. One scratched his red beard while the other adjusted his dingy cap, shifting from foot to foot, squinting and muttering in low tones. After another moment of fidgeting they continued toward the shop, their creased faces showing little emotion. One took a bandana from his pocket, wiping the sweat from his forehead and the back of his neck before replacing it. Nip stepped to the rail.

Dill, you sweat more than any man I know, even more than your twin brother. But then again, that's not saying much. You boys might swamp that boat of yours someday if you're not careful.

He even wakes up in a sweat.

There you go again, Bert making up stories.

Dill, you know it's true. I've seen you drip right into your oatmeal.

That's only because you're harebrained enough to cook oatmeal in the middle of the summer, Bert. A man can't eat oatmeal when it's a hundred degrees out.

I happen to like oatmeal in any weather. Besides, it's good for your health.

My health is just fine as long as I have a cold beer in my hand.

Well Dill, there you go. Beer is good for you too.

Speaking of cold beer, are you fellers just going to stand there all day? Let's load up my fishes and get on to Bubba's.

We didn't know you had company or whatever they are.

These are my guests if that's what you mean, Bert. The folks Eugie called about.

These two are who Eugie called us on?

Who did you think they were?

We thought maybe you got yourself in some sort of fix, Nip. That's what we thought just now, isn't it Bert?

That's what we thought Dill, it sure is. We looked up here and said to ourselves Nippy's got trouble.

Trouble? What kind of trouble?

We thought bad trouble, like you were being robbed or something. That's what we figured, isn't it Bert?

That's what we figured, Dill. We thought maybe one of those drug dealers from Mexico had showed up wanting a boat ride to the border.

Or maybe some criminal types came along looking for a boat to steal is what we thought, Bert.

We did have a lot of ideas when we looked up the hill and saw a…uh…a…not the type of person we'd expect to see. It's the unexpected that gets your mind to going, isn't Dill?

You got that right, Bert. I never did expect to find a…uh…unexpected man at your house Nippy, not in this part of the world. You know how people around here are when it comes to a…uh, unexpected people.

You said it there, Dill. When we spotted a…uh…you know, unexpected man right there on your front porch it was a big surprise, Nip. We got stopped right in our tracks at the sight of him alright. We didn't know what to think but it did worry us a bit. I mean, how many of them...uh...unexpecteds do we see around here?

So, you saw a black man and thought I was being robbed? You thought that because he's black he must be up to no good? Is that what you're saying?

Now don't get on your high horse, Nip. We just wanted to make sure nothing was wrong. You're our friend and we needed to know you were alright. We didn't mean anything by it, did we Bert?

That's right, Dill. You know as well as I do we don't see many, uh...you know...up this way, Nip. The county isn't exactly known for being friendly to their types. Don't forget, it wasn't that long ago those boys dragged one of them behind a truck and killed him.

And everybody knows the Koffee Kup Kafe was a big KKK hangout. That wasn't too long ago either, Nip. What Bert is trying to say is that we were just surprised, is all. We meant no offence. Why don't you introduce us, Nip?

Alright Dill, this young feller here is Noll Spencer and his partner is called Hen Feathers.

-The men took off their hats at the same instant, nodding gravely.

I'm Dill Jacks and this is my twin brother, Bert. Our daddy, Dilbert, always wanted a junior but he didn't know what to do when he had twin sons. Isn't that right, Bert?

That's the story, Dill. So, he decided to name us both Dilbert. I'm Dilbert A and he's Dilbert B. Our daddy didn't have much of an imagination when it came to names.

No Bert, he wasn't of the creative persuasion. It's fair to say our daddy was not at all an open-minded man of the world like our friend, Nippy.

From what I hear he was a hard-core bigot with a hair trigger temper.

205

Well Nip, it's true he was a man of strong conviction with a temper to match. He never hesitated to act if he felt the need. In fact, I expect he would have shot your friend Hen the minute he saw him.

I'm glad to know you two don't take after him.

It's true Hen. Our daddy was a hard man. The only time I saw him cry was when we lost our arms to that damn power line.

That was the one and only time, Bert. But he gave us the determination to do what we wanted to anyway. When nobody would hire us, we didn't give up.

That's right, Dill. We even offered to work for one salary. We thought that would do the trick, seeing as how we have two good arms between us. We couldn't even get an interview. That's when we decided to start the guide business.

The best decision we ever made.

Never a truer word was said, Dill. We decided the right hand should know what the left hand is doing, so to speak, and we decided to go into business together.

Ever since then we've been able to do whatever we want, when we want.

And it's cheaper too.

It's cheaper?

Sure it is, young feller. We only have to buy one pair of gloves for the both of us.

You boys going to gab all day when there's cold beer waiting? Let's get the boat loaded and go.

Alright Nippy, we're just trying to act friendly. What do you think Dill, should we give him a hand?

I think we ought to give him two, Bert.

Now that I think on it, I believe I'm dry as lizard spit.

Bert, lizards can't spit.

Sure they can, Dill. How else could they whistle?

I don't know why I put up with you, Bert.

The inlet opened before Noll in hues of green layered with marsh grass and mangrove that reached finger-like into the glistening bay, its outer reaches dotted with white cap and swell. A brisk wind whistled past the metal rails, setting guy wires humming above the roar of twin outboards. The wind-sheltered water, rippled, serpentine, tapped the hull in near-rhythm as they sped between islands, skimming over clear-water shallows thick with sea grass. Schools of cow-nosed rays scattered before the boat liked overstuffed birds.

Noll again recalled his father's love of the coast, a quality he had long forgotten until now. Strange the memories we choose to keep and those we forget, he thought. How would he have changed if he had reached his dream? Noll tried to imagine his father waist-deep in the inlet, fishing rod in hand, the morning sun just breaking the horizon. But the image hovered out of reach as the boat banked into a sharp turn, pulling him from his thoughts. In the distance a pastel-hued building rose above a small sand island, a broad wooden deck stretching from end to end and scattered with palm-covered tables. Water-stained stairs on one side of the building led to a floating dock crowded with boats. Across the railing hung a hand-painted sign reading "Bubba's Love Shack".

Noll followed Hen, the Jack brothers and Nip up the stairs and into an open air restaurant scattered with rough-hewn wooden tables and rusted metal chairs. Men in rubber boots and overalls crowded a bar that stretched across the far wall. Nip pointed to a table and they sat. He nodded to toward the bar.

We got us a mess of oystermen at Bubba's today, huh boys?

You got that right, Nip. I believe that's Juppy Macworter over there with the shaved head. He looks like some sort of axe murderer without hair.

If I'd known he was here I would've gone somewhere else.

You and me both, Nip. He's a dangerous young man. I hear he got religion but not the kind you've ever heard of.

Is that right, Dill? I'd be surprised if any religion would make him friendly to the likes of Hen.

You're right about that, Bert. He's looking over here right now and none too friendly either.

-A young man with an angular jaw approached the table, a smirk on his face.

Afternoon, Nip. Some fine crew you got there.

I don't believe it is afternoon, Jup but I can see you've had a few already.

I work hard, I play hard.

That's original, Jup. You think that up yourself?

What's wrong with you Nip? What are you doing hanging around the rejects? Don't you have any real friends?

I know quality people when I meet them. That's why I steer clear of you.

-The young man glared at Hen.

What are you doing bringing one of their kind in here, Nip? This is a whites-only bar.

A whites-only bar owned by a black man?

Bubba don't count. He's not like the rest. He owns a business and knows how to keep people like me happy.

You mean you think he knows his place. Well, you're wrong about that.

I mean he knows we let him be here because he sells cheap beer and doesn't backtalk. You could learn something from him.

-Nip stood to face the man.

And you plan to teach me?

-Hen rose and held up a gnarled hand.

Looky here, it's me you mean to be talking to. Go ahead and say what you have to say.

You don't have any right to talk to me, old man. Go back to Africa or wherever you come from.

I can see you're one angry young man but every time you open your mouth you show your ignorance too.

Who you calling ignorant?

I can trace my family in this country all the way to the American Revolution.

So what?

How long has your family been in this country?

How in the hell should I know?

But you got to know. Looky here, a man needs to understand where he comes from. A man's past tells him who he is. Are you smart enough to see that?

I'm plenty smart. Are you saying otherwise?

But you don't know where your family comes from?

They never said and I didn't ask.

Not even your father and mother?

I never knew my dad and my mother was a drunk.

So, you don't know your past?

I already said so. What's your point?

Would you say ignorance is lack of knowledge?

Sure, why the hell not?

And you don't know your heritage.

Don't waste my time old man.

But you don't know your past?

How many times do I have to say it?

Then you just admitted your ignorance, ignorance of your own past.

Don't put words in my mouth. You think you're real smart but we'll teach you coloreds what's right, you'll see. Maybe I'll start right now.

-A man appeared out of nowhere, his pockmarked face the color of motor oil.

Juppy, you get on out of here. I told you already you've had enough and need to leave. Now go on and get.

You can't talk to me like that, Bubba.

209

I can and I will. I own this place outright and I serve who I want, when I want.

You think just because them rich folks keep you in business you can treat us workingmen any old way. You'll find out you can't, just you wait.

Workingmen are welcome as long as they act right but I won't have anybody, rich or poor, cause trouble around here. Now take your skinhead self out that door.

-The young man stomped off, followed by several other oystermen.

I need to start digging my own oysters again so I don't have to deal with their types. Young men are nothing but trouble.

-He turned to Noll.

You're not going to cause any trouble for this man here, now are you young feller?

No sir. Hen is my friend.

-He squinted at Hen.

You're him. You're the black man they're looking for aren't you?

Who's looking, Bubba?

The law's got the game warden checking around, Nip. He came by early and I could tell he'd be back. You got to get yourself out of here.

Kenny Sewell couldn't find his own mother, much less someone he's never seen.

Kenny comes across a little slow but I wouldn't count on it. And you might find yourself some trouble if you stay here. He likes to time his stopping by with lunch so I expect him along any time.

Where can we go, Nip?

Well, I don't know.

There's got to be someplace.

We'll take you and Hen back to my place, Noll. Bubba, you know the area better than anyone. Do you figure that's safe enough?

I can't say as I do, Nip. Kenny said his job is to check all the homes on the inlet. He's slow but he can manage that. And knowing Kenny, he'll keep on checking until they tell him to stop.

Where then?

How about my hunting cabin out in the bay, Nip? Kenny won't think to look there.

I know the place. It just might do.

It's got to. I believe I hear his boat now.

Bubba, your ears must be gold-plated. I don't hear a thing.

My mama said I could hear a flea on a dog, Dill.

I guess she was right.

You boys best be getting on then.

Twenty-four

Noll crouched on his heels, his back against the side of the boat, trying to keep dry as jets of spray trailed across the bow and slammed into the windshield before scattering behind them in rainbow-hued sheets. Hen sat opposite, his eyes closed while Bubba's Love Shack diminished into the haze and then vanished behind a wall of spray. Leaden clouds raced overhead. Hen coughed into his fist, deep, guttural, bending him double. As he turned and spit over the side, Noll leaned in for a closer look. He seemed even thinner than usual, and his cough worse than when they had left Eugie's.

The boat slowed all at once and Noll peeked above the railing as they approached a small square structure perched high above the water, painted olive green and black. On the near side stairs, led from a floating dock occupied by a single overturned dinghy to a landing and weathered door secured with a pad lock. Screened windows shuttered from the inside covered the other three sides. The corrugated tin roof rattled in the steady breeze.

Bert angled the boat alongside the dock as Dill bent to open one locker after the other, pulling out nylon bags, jugs of water and two small ice chests. He grabbed an electric lantern and a flashlight from an overhead bin before hopping onto the dock and securing the boat. Bert cut the engines and tossed the gear to him, the two brothers working without a word.

You boys don't say much when you're at work.
Well Nip, why talk when you have nothing to say?
I've never known you not to have something to carry on about, Dill.
I got plenty to say but I have to keep an eye on Bert. He banged up the boat last time he was behind the wheel.

212

That was Walter Lindig's fault. He left a wake when he passed the size of a tsunami.

You used to could handle rough water, Bert. You've lost your edge.

The only thing I've lost is my toleration for your mouth.

Alright you two, we need to be quick in case Kenny gets a mind to follow us.

Right you are, Nip.

-Nip climbed the stairs and unlocked the door, followed by Hen, Noll and the brothers. Two metal cots and a table sat across from a gas stove and sink that emptied straight into the bay. A cloth curtain across one corner hid the bathroom. Nip swept an arm across the room.

There's a rainwater tank outside you can use for dishes and such. You can even take a shower if you want to.

Bert and I better get moving. A rich couple has hired us tonight. These supplies ought to do you for a while. There's even a bottle of whiskey in one of those bags.

I'll be by in the morning to check on you. I know I don't have to tell you lay low if any boats come in sight. Otherwise, enjoy the peace and quiet. I used to come out here with Bubba after his third wife left and we'd drink a whole bottle of Scotch between us. Other than the hangover, I remember those times as some of the best.

Looky here, Nip. I don't know how to thank you and the brothers here for all you're done. You don't have to help a wanted man. I appreciate it.

Eugie explained the situation. The boys and me, we can see you're a good man, Hen.

That's right, Nip. Besides, Hen, I was a sheriff once and I know how fickle the law can be.

Bert, you were a lawman?

-Bert shook Hen's hand.

213

They called this the long arm of the law.

Aw Bert, I thought I was through hearing that one and here you are trotting it out again.

It's too good to put up forever just because you've heard it once or twice before, Dill.

Once or twice times a hundred is more like it, Bert.

You two can argue on the way back. We should've already been gone by now. Your boat is too easy to spot out here on the open bay.

Noll stood next to Hen and watched the boat disappear over the horizon, spray from the engines tailing high into the air. Clouds streamed across the sky in ragged lines, formed and reformed without pattern, captured by the shifting wind. In the distance, whitecaps dotting the horizon flecked the rough water with glints of sun, vanishing almost before seen. A frigate bird floated overhead, dark, cross-like and a sense of dread passed through Noll like a wave, unexpected, unknowable. Hen coughed hard and wiped his mouth with the back of his hand.

I got to find me a chair. All this moving around has gone and tired me out. Besides, we best stay out of sight.

Are you feeling alright, Hen? You don't look too good.

I just need to rest a little, is all. Then again, I might ought to have some whisky, just to keep my health up, you know.

Sure, just to keep your health up. I've heard that one before.

Looky here Noll, if we got to be stuck out here in the middle of the ocean without one good book between us we might as well make the best of it. Now find that bottle and have a seat over here.

-Noll located the bottle and pulled two jars from a shelf, filling each and setting them on the table. Hen

drained the glass and then doubled over in a fit of
coughing. After a moment, he sat upright and tapped his
fingers on the table.

Set the bottle over here too, boy. No man wants to
have to get up every time he needs a drink.

Alright, you don't have to get ornery.

I'm feeling responsible, is all.

Responsible for what?

For you, that's what.

But why, Hen?

You believe in fate, Noll?

I guess so.

I believe in it. Fate got you and me out here and
I'm sorry for it. I never did want to make trouble for you.

You didn't make trouble for me. I'm here because
I chose to be here.

You decided to help me but it's fate that got you
out here. I got to hope for some luck to go with this fate me
and you are under.

If you say so. Luck hasn't been much good to me.

That's true, son. With the wrong kind of luck, fate
can be a cruel friend. A man's got to appreciate what he
can, while he can, so pour me up another glass.

I don't believe in luck or fate. Things just happen.

That's one way to think about it. People turn to
luck or fate to make sense of what goes on in this life, the
hard times, the mistakes.

My grandmother would say fate has nothing to do
with it. She'd say it's up to God to decide.

If it is up to God he hasn't been much good to
either of us, has he?

I guess not but I'd never say so. It'd probably kill
her *and* my mom if I did.

Young man like you ever think about dying, about
your own dying?

I thought about it after we fished Felix out of the
river.

215

Ha! That was a close call alright. All I could think was what Lio would do to me if something happened to that boy.

And I thought about it again today.

You mean just now?

When we were outside I was reminded of the bad things that can happen, like people dying.

Now why would you be thinking that?

I saw a frigate bird.

You saw a what?

My dad told me that sailors once believed seabirds like albatross and frigate birds carry the soul of a dead sailor. That's why they followed a ship for days. He said it after we spotted one, not long before he died. I don't know why I remember it but I do.

That's not something you're likely to forget.

I try not to think about people dying.

You get to be my age and you'll have a hard time not thinking about it.

Seeing that bird reminded me of him.

I believe your father was a poet.

A poet?

He saw that bird as more than just a bird. It had a meaning. That's poetry.

I never thought of him that way.

-Hen coughed hard, a long moment passing before he could speak again.

Tell me about him, then. Tell me about your daddy.

I don't know if I can.

Just say what you remember, son.

I've thought about him a lot this past year, trying to find the truth of who he was.

What did you find, then?

I'm not sure, Hen. He seemed like he was always at war with himself, like a clock wound up so tight it couldn't unwind. He could be cruel, especially to my

216

mother. His anger would take over and go on and on, making you think it would never stop. But then he would come home with gifts, take us out to get ice cream or ride the Ferris wheel, make us forget the way it had been before, at least for awhile. He even sat by the bed and read an entire book to me one night when I was too sick to sleep. That night, all of it, was his way to apologize although he never said so in words. He was way too proud for that.

It's never easy for a man to admit he's wrong, Noll. Us men, we do a lot of talking without words. And there are some things we may never be able to say out loud. That's just the way we're made. You can see it in yourself if you stop long enough to look.

There are things I could've said. I wish I'd talked to him when I had the chance, Hen.

A man will always feel he could have said more, done more, when someone close passes on. Make him think of his own end too and the way he lived his life. That's where fate comes in again.

But we're not at the mercy of fate, are we?

You got yourself a point there, son. I was born black and you white. I never knew my daddy and you lost yours too soon. Fate is always at hand. But we have a say so too. When I was a young man like you I thought my life had been laid out for me word by word so I had no choice in how it would be or who I might be. I thought other people had the say so, the people in charge, not anybody I knew or would know.

But then one day I took a good look around me and saw there was more to it than that, that some people, even your own kind will keep you down or turn their back on you. But other folks, maybe the types of folks you think are against you will let you be, even help you be the man you are or the man you could be. The world and people in it are more than they seem and you have a say so in how you move through that world, even when fate is at her worst.

217

I'd like to believe that, Hen.

Believe it Noll, while you have your time on this earth. None of us ever knows when our end is due.

Why did you ask me about fate and dying, Hen? Why is it on your mind?

Hold on, son. What's that sound?

-Noll went to the row of windows, peering out from behind the wall. He pointed toward the floor with his hand.

Get down, Hen. It's Kenny Sewell, that game warden Bubba told us about. He's coming this way and will see you for sure with those windows behind you.

-Hen slipped to the floor and made his way to Noll. They watched as a white boat carrying several antennas and the green seal of the parks and wildlife department approached and then slowed, idling while it drifted in a broad arc. Behind the console a stout man in khaki, his ruddy face bright beneath a navy cap, craned his neck toward the cabin. He reached to the controls and began angling toward the dock.

He's coming up, Hen.

I can't be found, Noll. You got to understand son, I can't go jail.

We're stuck, there's nowhere to go.

I can't do it. I can't go to jail. If I had a gun right now I'd use it.

I'm glad you don't, then. I'll figure something out.

You better get to figuring. I can hear his boat bumping up against the dock right now.

I wish we had a way to lock that door.

Maybe he's as dumb as they say.

I wouldn't count on it.

Maybe when nobody answers the door he won't come inside.

I have an idea, Hen. Don't say a word, just follow me.

218

Noll unlatched a window screen on the far side of the cabin, pushing it out just far enough to squeeze through as footsteps started up the stairs. In an instant, he climbed out and stood on one of the piling supports that crisscrossed beneath the house. He reached back inside, helping Hen though the window. They scrambled down the diagonal supports, easing themselves into the dark water with as little noise as they could manage. Above them the door opened and then slammed shut.

Within moments, Noll's teeth began chattering. He cocked his head, listening as the footsteps moved from one end of the house to the other. Hen clung to a nearby creosote-soaked pier, staring at the floor as if he could make out the man inside. After several minutes the footsteps ceased and Noll puzzled over what the man could be up to. He knew they could stay hidden neck-deep in the chill water for only so long.

Just as he started to pull himself up onto a support beam, thunder rolled in the distance. He turned to find a dark line moving toward them across the gunmetal surface of the bay like a shadow. A moment later a blast of wind sent spray flying into their faces. Footsteps again sounded above them and the warden appeared above the dock, rushing down the stairs and quickly freeing the boat before hopping in. He was gone in an instant.

He and Hen watched the boat vanish over the horizon before swimming their way through the pilings to the dock. Noll scrambled onto the dry slats but Hen could do no more than lay his arms across the flooring so Noll bent, pulling him out and for a moment they lay unable to move. Then it began to rain. Thunder sounded again but closer and Noll put Hen's arm across his neck, half-carrying him up the stairs and through the door. He eased Hen into a chair, his face drawn and dull gray. Noll grabbed the whisky and was about to pour when he paused, holding the bottle up to the light.

The bastard drank our whiskey.

He's not too dumb to pass up a free drink.

He ate some of our food too. I guess he figured the fishermen using this cabin wouldn't notice. Here Hen, let me pour you a shot. It'll warm you up.

No son, I believe I got to get myself into bed. That water put a chill in me whiskey won't cure.

-Noll helped Hen out of his wet clothes, his bony form angular in the half-light, and onto the cot, drawing a blanket over him. He pulled off his wet clothes, tossing aside his worthless cell phone, pulled up a chair and sat. In less than a minute Hen was asleep. Noll sat in the darkened room sipping whisky, wondering what would become of them as rain traced patterns across the bay, the storm drifting toward the horizon like a lost ship.

Twenty-five

Maya stood in a doorway wearing a simple white dress edged in blue lace, one hand outstretched, fingers bent as if motioning him over. Music drifted in from another room, coming and going, at times barely audible above the hum of an unseen crowd. She took a step toward him but then stopped and stood motionless, studying his face. He sensed a hint of sadness in her eyes.

Noll, you look tired. Are you alright?
I think so.
I worry about you.
I'm alright, Maya.
Why did you give up, Noll?
Give up on what?
Why did you give up on us?
I didn't mean to, Maya. Things happened and fate got in the way. But I've worked it out.
Have you, Noll? Have you really?
I refuse to be at the mercy of fate, Maya. Hen says we have a say so in what happens to us. It may not be easy but we can decide how we handle what comes along.
But how long does it take, Noll? Sooner or later time runs out.
We still have time, don't we?
-A voice sounded from the beyond the doorway, calling for her, deep, guttural.
I have to go, Noll. Basil is waiting.
Basil is here?
Are you coming with me?
Where are you going?
Don't you know? Basil and I are getting married.
-The voice sounded again, a dog's growl, a rasping bark.

Noll awoke with a start, nearly falling out the creaking chair. He peered into the darkness, for a moment unsure of where he was, the vivid whiteness of Maya's dress blurring his thoughts. He blinked and surveyed the dim room, finding Hen before him stretched across the narrow cot, his face turned away, the blanket crumpled on the floor. The repetitive wheeze of Hen's breathing cut the thick air. He leaned over the edge of the cot to cough, the sound in his chest a deep gurgle, and then spit. Noll switched on the lantern and stepped to the other side of the bed, the circle of light falling on a bloody handkerchief. Noll knelt next to him.

Hen, what's happened? Is that blood?
The cancer has got me.
The what?
-Hen spoke between breaths, labored, rasping.
My granddaddy always believed he would die of the cancer and he did. They tell me my daddy did too so I knew the same would happen to me. The reaper, he's been aiming to get at me for a long time and now he's here.
I have to take you to a hospital, Hen.
Don't take me to a hospital, Noll. They'll find me for sure. I won't spend my last days in some jail.
I can't just stand by while you bleed to death.
Rather die bleeding than in jail.
I won't let them find you but I've got to get you out of here. Will you let me take you to Eugie?
No way to leave this place until Nip gets back.
There's a boat down on the dock. Can you make it there?
I almost can't hold my own head up but I'll do what I can.
-Noll dressed and then grabbed Hen's clothes, the blanket and lantern before looping his arm over his neck and pulling him upright. Moving in lockstep, they hobbled out the door and down the stairs where he sat Hen on the

last step. He lifted the dinghy and turned it into the water, relieved to find two oars and life jackets beneath. Securing the boat to the pier, he tossed the gear aboard before pulling Hen up again and settling him into the well of the boat, draped with the blanket. Noll climbed into the stern and pushed off into the darkness.

The dim lantern cast Noll and the looping oars into a shadow of flight, filling his exhausted mind with the image of a frigate bird in relentless pursuit. He shook his head, trying to maintain a straight course by tracking the boat's wake as far as light would allow. His arms ached with every move. The rhythmic pull of oar through water mixed with Hen's ragged gasps and he found himself hoping the mere motion might ease his labored breath. He paused, cocking his head for a moment to listen but panic again gripped his chest so he turned and leaned into the oars, feeling the boat glide through the still water.

He thought again of Maya and the strange dream that had startled him awake. Was he too late in realizing his feelings for her? What defect had kept him from telling her? The questions pulled at him like water on a drowning man as the oars dug into his palms, feeling as if they moved through wet sand instead of water, straining his joints, burning his muscles. Strange shapes moved through the outer light. Then the bluish form of a single flying fish sailed across the water behind him, outstretched fins fluttering in short bursts, then another, then two more. How could an ocean-going fish be here in this shallow bay, he puzzled? It seemed beyond possibility.

Noll shook his head, staring into the distance when to his astonishment a dinghy crossed their wake, the figure inside stooped and pale. Noll started to call out but hesitated as the boat began moving his way. A moment later, the man turned and looked up, his father's face staring back at him, ghost-like in the lantern light. He raised a limp hand and pointed into the darkness. Noll dropped the oars, peering at him, unable to speak as all he wished to say came back at him in a rush, catching in his throat.

An instant later, the image vanished as a brilliant beam of light flashed over Noll's shoulder, casting the entire scene in near daylight. He turned, squinting into the brightness, trying to wave an arm that refused to move. The spotlight passed across them in a wide arc and then disappeared. He held his breath but no engines rumbled closer, no boat approached, Hen's rough breathing instead the only sound. How could they have been missed?

He shook his head again and tried to think. His father and the flying fish had come out of his exhaustion, his worry, his lack of sleep. Help was nowhere near. But the spotlight had given him something, a glimpse of a shoreline a hundred yards beyond. He leaned into the oars, careful to keep the direction steady. Water sucked at the hull as he increased his pace. The smell of decaying plants mixed with salt surrounded the boat in a rush. A moment later, mangrove branches appeared alongside the boat.

Noll pulled in the oars and stepped out of the dinghy, the lapping water chill against his bare ankles. To his relief the sand stood firm beneath his feet. In the darkness before him, a snowy egret cackled and started out of the mangroves, its hoarse cries trailing off into the night. He held up the lantern. As far as he could see, thickets of mangroves made the beach unreachable. Placing the lantern near the gunwale, he took hold of the bow rope and began slogging along the edge of the thicket. Blue crab and pipefish scattered before the light, disappearing into olive green stands of sea grass.

A hundred yards up the coast, the mangroves thinned and then gave way to open water fronting a sandy shoreline. He pulled the boat onto the beach and into the short grass beyond, and then tried without success to rouse Hen. He decided it best to let him sleep. He grabbed the lantern, cursing himself for leaving the cabin without more

224

in the way of provisions, especially a flashlight before heading inland. Fighting through thickets of brush, he followed a narrow trail that wandered along the shoreline before turning away from the water. Mosquitoes buzzed about his face.

Dense undergrowth throwing back the lantern glow trapped him in a yellow pool of light, leaving him unable see beyond the dim circle. Palmetto frond and greenbrier tore at his clothes. He pushed through the increasing thicket, dead tree limbs cracking beneath his feet. Then a car horn sounded in the distance. He stopped to listen, hoping another blast might help him locate a direction but the echoes faded into the night. A light rain began to fall.

Turning his attention back to the trail, he held up the lantern to survey the area. The way ahead appeared impassable so he picked a spot and pushed into it, losing his grip on the lantern before he had taken a single step. It hit the ground and darkness surrounded him even as the fading filament still glowed at his feet. As he cursed and bent to retrieve the broken lantern, a flash of car lights splitting the underbrush caught his eye. He leaned hard into the thicket, bursting forward and through a wall of branches and falling onto the manicured lawn of a croquet court, the wickets before him shining with dew. He scrambled to his feet and headed for the only light he could see, a low-roofed guard house sitting adjacent to an iron gate.

As Noll approached the building a man stepped out the doorway, tall and broad, his mahogany-hued face scrunched into a frown, his thick neck spilling over a blue uniform stretched to the limit at every button. A walkie-talkie crackled at his side. He peered at Noll before speaking.

Where'd you come from?
The beach, but I need….

How'd you get on a gated property without coming through the gate?

In a boat. Listen, I have a...

This here is private property. What are you up to? I bet it's no good. Better tell me now or I'll call the police on you.

Damn it, I'll tell you if you'll give me a chance.

Alright now, no need to get all worked up. I'll listen.

I have a sick friend in a boat down at the beach. He needs to see a doctor right away. Will you help me?

I can call an ambulance.

No, he can't go to a hospital.

Why not?

He says he won't go.

I say if a man's sick he needs to see a doctor.

Can you call someone for me?

Who do you want me to call?

A man by the name of Nip Nepplelipper.

You a friend of Nippy?

Call him and tell him to come pick up Noll right away. Tell him it's an emergency.

I'd call him but Nippy gave up the phone a long time ago, said if somebody wants to talk to him they'll do it in person or not at all.

Right, I knew that. We need to get to my Aunt's Eugie's house.

Eugie is your aunt?

You know Eugie?

Everybody around here knows Eugie. I'd do anything for her. She saved my life once, so to speak, but that's another story. I'll take you myself.

You can leave?

The family that lives here is gone and won't be back for a while yet so I can take you but you got to tell me something first.

Make it quick. My friend is very sick.

226

Is your friend a black man?

Yes, and I need your help to get him up here to the road. He can barely walk.

He must be the one running from the law. Bubba said the word is he's a good man.

And now he's sick so we better get him help as soon as we can, right? Are you with me?

Then he's the man Bubba said?

He's the one.

Alright then, I'm Rollins Gage and I mean to help a brother in need. I'll get my truck and we'll bring him up here real quick.

They reached the boat and Noll took hold of Hen's shoulder, giving him a shake. Hen stirred, mumbling something unintelligible, his breath weak and rasping. Noll shook him again, still with no response. Reaching around Hen's chest, he tried to raise him but realized he could not without Hen's help. A wave of panic passed through him as he lowered Hen back to the floor of the boat.

As he stood, Rollins pushed him aside with the back of his hand, bending into the dinghy and lifting Hen like a bag of feed. An instant later he had moved well up the slope, striding along at a brisk pace. Noll hurried behind him. As Rollins lowered Hen into the cab, he turned to Noll.

Your friend here is trying to say something so you better get in there and listen. I'll get us moving. He's got himself a fever, a bad one.

-Noll climbed into the truck. Wrapped in the coarse blanket, Hen leaned against the seat, his head back, eyes closed, still clutching the blood-stained handkerchief. He spoke in a near-whisper.

Noll, you there?

I'm here, Hen.

Remember what I said, no hospital.

227

I remember.

Give me your word. Don't let them find me, Noll. They won't let me die in peace and that's all I want.

We're taking you to Eugie's. You'll be alright.

As long as you keep your word, you hear me?

I hear you, Hen.

-Hen slumped into the seat as if talking had taken what little energy he had left. Above the engine's roar Noll tracked the rasp of his breath with every mile, fearing it might stop at any moment. Maya's face came to him out of the darkness and he wished for her, that she could be there with them now, that she would say something, anything that would ease his fear. He turned and studied Hen's face in the dashboard light, his features gaunt, mask-like, before turning back to the empty, rain-soaked night.

Twenty-six

Though dawn touched the eastern sky, yellow light spilled from nearly every window of Eugie's house as if they were expected, as if Eugie had called a party in Hen's honor. Craning his neck to get a better view of the living room, Noll knocked on the door as Rollins helped Hen up the porch stairs. The house seemed empty. He again pounded on the heavy wooden door, waited and then tried the latch. The door opened with ease. He called out before stepping through and motioning Rollins by him, down the hallway and into the study. A cot stood in one corner. Noll called out again as Rollins eased a semi-conscious Hen onto the bed.

A moment later, footsteps sounded in the hall behind them and Noll turned to find Eugie peering around the doorway, the big pistol in her hand. A wave of relief crossed her face before she stepped into the room. She waved the gun through the air as she spoke.

Noll, what are you doing back here? And you brought Rollins with you. You gave me a fright coming in all quiet like that.

I know how you feel. Watching that big pistol wave through the air has got me more than a little nervous. Why not set it down real easy, Eugie?

Well, alright. To tell the truth, your mother and I have had a bit of brandy. But why are you here, Rollins? And where's Hen? The law didn't catch up with him, did they?

He's why we're here.

Who is that on the cot? Is that Hen? Step aside and let me see him.

-She moved to the cot, placing her hand on Hen's forehead without hesitation.

Hen, can you hear me? He's burning with fever, Noll. How long has he been like this?

I found him coughing up blood earlier tonight. He thinks he has cancer.

We need to get him to the hospital.

We can't do that.

Why not? He needs medical attention.

He doesn't want to die in jail, Eugie. He made me promise.

Alright then, I'll call a doctor. My friend Sam Learner will come see him. He didn't say anything about a doctor, did he?

No, I guess not.

Rollins how did you get roped into this?

The two of them washed up over where I do my guard work. Once I found out who Hen was and that Noll here is your nephew, I knew I had to help.

Well, I thank you Rollins. Will you have a drink with me?

I need to get back before the family gets home. They might understand the situation and they might not, seeing as how Hen is a black man.

Alright then, Rollins. You come see me some other time when you can stay. I'd better go call the doctor.

-Noll thanked Rollins and watched him walk out the door with Eugie before pulling a chair next to the cot and easing himself into it. Hen stirred and Noll leaned toward him.

Don't die on me Hen, please don't die. I don't know what I'd do. I didn't want you to get caught by the game warden but if I'd known it was going to make you so sick I never would have taken us into that cold water.

-Noll felt a hand on his shoulder and he turned as his mother pulled over a chair and sat.

I heard what happened, Noll. Mr. Gage said you rowed Hen halfway across the bay to get him help. He must be a good friend.

A real friend wouldn't have got him into this. A real friend would've had more sense.

You stuck by him, Noll. You got him here, that's what counts.

-A knock came from the hallway and Noll turned to see Eugie and a short woman with close-cropped silver hair standing in the doorway. The woman stepped to the cot and bent over Hen, studying his face before taking his wrist between her thumb and forefinger. She held out her other hand and stood still for a moment, an eye on her wristwatch, and then pulled a stethoscope from her coat pocket and held it to Hen's chest. Noll looked to Eugie.

This is my doctor friend, Sam Learner. I imagine you're wondering how she got here so fast. Well, she lives less than a mile away, that's how. She's an early riser too, so she was ready to go. Lucky for us, huh Noll?

-Noll turned to where the doctor continued her examination. Hen coughed weakly and mumbled something, his eyes closed. She spoke without turning.

I understand someone here thinks this man has lung cancer.

That's what he told me. He said his father and grandfather had lung cancer so he knew he'd get it too.

Sam, this is my nephew, Noll.

Well Noll, I can't find anything consistent with cancer, none of the usual signs.

You mean he's not dying?

He's very sick, Noll. He has pneumonia but I believe we've caught it soon enough.

Hen's going to live?

He's not out of the woods but he seems fit enough otherwise. I expect he'll respond to a good dose of antibiotics. We'll know by morning.

-She left the room, followed by Eugie.

You see Noll, without your help he might have died.

I don't want him or anyone else dying on me, mom. I'm not sure I could take it.

When we lose someone close to us it feels like the end of the world, as if we can't go on, but we do. Sooner or later we find a way. In any event, you don't have to worry about me if that's what you're thinking.

I wasn't but I'm glad to hear you say it.

The person that gave you and Gannie a scare is gone, Noll.

Are you sure?

Things can change, Noll. People can change. Something you might not even notice can make all the difference.

Or a person can, someone you might never expect.

More likely a person than anything, I'd say.

So, you're feeling okay, not bad but not too good either? You know what happens when you start feeling too good.

Try not to worry about me, Noll.

Then why are you and Eugie up before dawn with all the lights on?

Gannie and I just got back from our trip out west. We decided to drive back to save on a motel room, and we've been showing Eugie our photos. She insisted on seeing them right away. I wish you could've been with us, Noll. The mountains out there are so beautiful.

So now you're a photographer?

I don't know about that but the instructor wants to show my work at his gallery.

He wants to sell your photos?

It looks that way. Eugie was just giving me some pointers. Speaking of that, I should get back to the studio. I left Gannie to clean up everything. Do you want to come along? I know she'll want to see you.

I believe I'll stay here.

Like I said, he must be a good friend.

Sunlight slanted through the open window, spilling onto the floor in yellow filigree as Noll awoke and looked about the bedroom, the events of the night before coming back to him in pieces. The room held no sound. He sat up, searching Hen's outline beneath the blankets for any sign of life, panic passing through him in a wave. Afraid to move, afraid of what he might find, he cocked his head, listening, waiting. Then the soft sound of Hen's rhythmic breathing reached him, quiet, free of labor and he stood, taking a breath of his own, turning toward the window with relief. Glints of sunlight danced across the inlet, skittering onto the porch for a moment before vanishing. A cloud passed across the sun, bathing the scene in a bluish hue as Hen's voice sounded behind him.

Am I in heaven? Sure does looks like it, all blue and peaceful like.

You're in heaven but you're still alive.

I'm weak as a baby but I feel too good to be dead.

You keep on smoking and you will be.

Noll, is that you over there talking nonsense or am I dreaming?

I'm here and I meant what I said. You've got to quit.

Why quit when that cancer's going to get me anyway?

You don't have cancer, Hen. You have pneumonia and it looks like the antibiotics are doing the job.

That cancer won't get me after all?

Not yet. Besides, you're too ornery to die. Don't you know that?

This looks like Eugie's house I'm in.

We brought you here last night. Don't you remember?

I don't remember much. What time is it?

I thought it was morning but that clock over there says half past three.

-A knock came from beyond the door and Eugie stepped through.

233

You sleeping beauties want some lunch? Or maybe you want dinner, late as it is. I've never seen so much laziness. How're you feeling, Hen?

Noll here tells me I'm too ornery to die so I guess I'll be alright.

Doctor Sam didn't mention anything about orneriness but I tend to agree with Noll. She did say you must come from good stock because you've improve so much quicker than she thought you would.

I might could eat something after I wake up a little, Eugie.

Then will you join me for a cup of coffee, Hen?

Sure might perk me up.

I hope you don't mind if I have a little brandy with mine.

Noll raked the last of the Live oak leaves onto an already smoldering pile, the acrid smoke swirling about him before moving past the house and into the trees beyond. Salmon-hued clouds drifted overhead, their mirror image captured in the still waters of the inlet. He stopped to study a bank of fog hovering beyond the outer peninsula, surreal, ghostlike until movement near the house caught his eye, a flicker of light, blur of motion, rustle of footsteps. Puzzled, he started toward the sound but a car rounding the trees stopped him. He turned as the car pulled to a stop before the house and the sheriff climbed out. Noll glanced toward the porch, hoping Hen had seen him too, hoping he could find a place to hide. The sheriff eyed Noll for a moment before starting toward the house just as Eugie stepped through the front door.

Why, Sutter Tomkins, I haven't seen you since I don't know when.

Hello, Eugie. Don't believe I remember either.

And you probably don't remember you forgot to show up when my house got robbed. That deputy of yours made a hell of a mess. He got fingerprint dust all over my dresser and stained my carpet too.

No, I didn't know that.

What *do* you know, Sut? What brings an important man like you way out here on the inlet?

Got some questions for you, is all.

Well, what are they?

Don't you want to invite me inside to talk?

Well Sut, we have ourselves such a nice day I believe I'll do my talking out here on the porch. So, what do you need to ask?

I'm looking for a man, a black man. It's important that I talk to him as soon as possible.

Is that a question?

I'm asking if you know anything about this man.

What makes you think I would, Sut?

-He eyed Noll again before continuing.

I have it on word from some oystermen out in east bay that a young feller and a black man were seen at Bubba's place a few days back. I believe he's the one I'm looking for.

You've lost me, Sut. How does something that happened at Bubba's concern me way over here on the inlet?

The oystermen aren't exactly your upstanding sorts so I'm not sure how much to believe. On the other hand, they said the two men were with Nip Nepplelipper and the Jacks brothers. Now I know Nip and the brothers are friends of yours so that's why I'm here. I'm wondering if you know anything about this black man's whereabouts.

Well Sut, I'm trying to recall if I've heard anything that would interest you. It might help if I knew what you need to talk to this man about. Has he done something wrong?

Well, yes and no, Eugie. He did kill a man. It happened at the university in broad daylight.

So, you mean to throw him in the hoosegow?

Not exactly.

Not exactly how?

Well, he did shoot and kill a man in front of God and everybody so normally I'd expect him to be arrested but it's not that simple.

Sut, you sure know how to drag out a story. You haven't changed a bit since high school.

By chance, the university president was standing at his window when the shooting happened. He saw the whole thing, said it was clearly self-defense and testified to that effect to the district attorney and anyone else who'd listen.

Then why are you chasing after this man?

The president knows people, the mayor, the county judge, the district judge.

And…?

The man involved disappeared after the incident. We've been told to find him and let him know he won't be charged with the shooting. He'll likely have to answer for leaving the scene but is shouldn't add up to much. Like I said, the president knows people. And, he wants the man to know he can return to his job as soon as he's ready.

He's going to get his job back after what happened?

If he still wants it. The university looked into it and found that the man who got shot had abused his position for some years, pilfering materials, firing people for no reason, absconding funds, the whole bit.

That's quite a story, Sut. I wish I could help. Have you tried talking to Nip and the brothers?

They said the same as you, more or less.

Those oystermen of yours must've been mistaken.

That could be the case. Like I said, they aren't known for their reliability.

If I should hear anything, I'll let you know.

I'd just as soon let it go, Eugie. I have real problems to tend to, you know.

236

You take care, Sutter Tomkins.

-A moment later a rustle came from the nearest window and Noll cocked his head, keeping an eye on the sheriff's car as it disappeared behind the line of trees. A voice whispered through the screen.

Is he gone, Noll?

Hen, have you been there the whole time?

I heard him coming. Those police cruisers have a peculiar sound to them so I got to this window here. If I got to run I need to know where he is.

But you heard they're not after you anymore, right?

I heard but do I believe? Looky here, I don't need to keep talking through this here window if he's gone.

You can come on out now.

-Noll had just started up the porch stairs when a figure rounded the house, emerging from the deep shadow of late afternoon and walking towards him. Noll stopped and blinked, thinking his eyes were playing tricks in the half-light.

Ranse, what are you doing here?

Hen is here, I heard him.

How did you know he was here?

My mama said he might be so I came here first. She sent me to get him now the police don't want him.

You knew about that? How did you find out?

That good looking Mexican girl told mama.

She heard about it from Maya?

She came over to mama's house, told her there.

How did Maya know?

Heard it from her daddy. Then she told mama where we might could find you and Hen.

Did she say anything else, anything about me?

Maybe but I got no time for all this talk.

Try to think Ranse, it could be important.

She did say something but I can't remember what. Now that you've heard from the law, you know what I do. I got nothing more to say.

If you knew they weren't pressing charges why were you hiding?

I got other troubles with the law. Like I said, I got no time for talk. Where's Hen? We got to get moving.

-Hen stepped through the door and faced Ranse.

What other troubles you got, boy?

Now Hen, don't get on me about that. I just got some business dealings I got to work out.

What kind of business?

I just owe some people money, is all. I'll get it worked out.

Sounds like the same trouble you got into before. You stay away from those people or you'll get yourself hurt. You hear me, boy?

I hear you, Hen. Now let's get us a move on. I got people to see in town tonight.

You always got people to see. I don't like the sound of it.

I can't be late, Hen.

Looky here Ranse, you sure it was Lio that said the law is off me now?

Sure, I'm sure. Maybe have a little trouble left but not much. You heard the lawman say it. I heard the girl say it too.

What else she say?

Nothing much.

What else she say about Noll?

I can't remember.

I don't want to hear that. Come on and think, Ranse.

Oh yeah, something about her brother in the hospital. That's right. She wanted me to be sure to tell him that. Can we go now, Hen?

What happened to him, Ranse?

I don't know and I don't care. That girl's your friend Noll, not mine. Are you ready to go, Hen?

-Eugie stepped out onto the porch.

Hen, are you feeling well enough to leave?

I'll be alright, Eugie.

Are you sure? It's only been three days.

You've been sick, Hen?

I got me a little bug is all, Ranse.

You know how sick you were, Hen?

Eugie, you treated me awful good but I can't take anymore females fussing over me like I'm some invalid. Anyway, after three days inside that house I got the cabin fever. Ranse, you got nothing more Noll needs to hear?

That's all I know.

You sure about that, boy?

I'm sure, Hen.

We can go then.

Twenty-seven

Noll hurried down the hospital corridor, feeling beneath his feet the same polished floor, water-like, reflective yet now solid. He peered at the number over each door, searching for Felix's room, hoping to find him yet dreading it. Rounding a corner, he slowed as he recognized the room. He paused before the doorway unsure what to expect, imagining Felix but instead seeing his father prostrate, comatose. Trying to prepare himself he took a breath and then he stepped into a dim room, the blinds drawn, a single light flickering over the bed. He looked one way then the other, hoping to see Maya among the shadows but instead finding no sign of her. Across the room a figure lay prostrate, propped on several pillows, eyes closed, the bandaged face spotted with bruising.

For a moment Noll wondered if he had walked into the wrong room. He again looked about for someone to ask and then turned to leave as a faint voice sounded over his shoulder, a murmur mixed with a cry. He stopped to listen, turning back toward the bed. The figure motioned him over with a bandaged hand, slapping the bed frame with the other hand as Noll stood unmoving. The muffled voice sounded again as the man motioned him near with a quick jerk of his bandaged head. Noll stepped to the bed, leaning in to listen. The voice hissed through clenched teeth.

Noll, it's me, it's Felix. Can't you see it's me?
Felix, is that you? What's happened?
I got hurt.
I can see that. I expected you to be hooked up to a bunch of tubes not covered in bandages.
I was attacked by a group of thugs Noll, three or four of them.
The cancer hasn't returned?
No, don't even mention that word while I'm in here.

So, you're not going to die?

Oh Noll, that's what I love about you. Your face is like an open book. I can see you've been worrying about me again. Go ahead and admit it. You have, haven't you?

Of course Felix, what else am I going to do when I hear you're in the hospital?

But you care enough to worry, don't you see? I need someone who's on my side, Noll. I need to know the whole world isn't against me and people like me.

Why isn't someone here with you?

Maya was here. You just missed her.

I was hoping to see her.

I'm not so sure that would be good for you, Noll the Brave. I know you're strong but even you have your limits.

What are you talking about, Felix?

Forget about her, Noll.

I don't want to forget her.

You'll find someone else, you'll see.

I don't want to find someone else. Why are you talking like this?

She's getting married to that rat, Basil. The ceremony is less than a month from now.

She's really getting married, and in a month? I knew she was engaged but I didn't think it would last.

Let's don't talk about her. She's my sister and I love her but I don't like her very much right now. She's been so smart about decisions until this guy came along. I can't understand how she could be stupid enough to fall for such a loser. He'll break her heart Noll, I just know it. And the thought of him as a brother-in-law makes me ill, physically ill. Let's talk about something else. How about me? After all, I'm the one in the hospital.

You're right. Are you badly hurt, Felix?

I'll be okay eventually but my jaw is broken so it's hard to talk. You know how much I hate not being able to talk.

241

Yes I do, Felix.

Still, it isn't so terrible. The pain medication isn't bad. And I get all the smoothies I want. I'm practically a hippie already.

Who did this, Felix?

Some redneck gay-haters.

Did you report it to the police?

Yes, but they won't do much to find them. A gay person is a low priority.

You didn't recognize any of them?

I don't know if I should tell you, Noll. Leave it to the police.

You just said they won't do anything.

I don't want you to do something foolish.

It was someone I know, wasn't it?

I don't want to say.

Felix, you can't let them get away with this. Look what they did to you.

I just want to forget about it, Noll.

I know you do. But think about it, Felix. Why won't they go out and do it again to someone else?

You think that's possible?

Of course it is. Don't fool yourself that this was a one-time thing. A man gets a taste for cruelty, he'll do it again. Trust me, Felix. They feel too much power to just give it up.

You sound like you're speaking from experience.

I am.

You mean your father?

That's right. Now who did this to you?

I recognized one of them as your friend from the party, the one named Vince.

That figures. This is going to end right here.

What does that mean?

I'm going to make sure it never happens again.

What are you going to do?

Whatever it takes.

242

Noll, you love me don't you?

What?

I should know better than to use the L word with a macho man like you. Let me try that again. Noll, you care about me don't you?

Of course I do, Felix. That's why I'm here. That's why what they did makes me so angry.

Then promise me you won't get violent with anyone on my account.

Violence is what they deserve.

But Noll, don't you see that would make you just like them?

Someone needs to teach them a lesson.

Violence solves nothing. Promise me you won't lower yourself to their level. You're too good for that, Noll. Please promise me.

Alright Felix, no violence, only talk.

And you won't do anything foolish?

I usually try not to be a fool if I can help it.

Then I'll send you on your way, Noll the Brave, my knight-errant.

Noll retraced his steps along the empty hallway, passing a distraught woman hovering outside a closed door. He again imagined his father as he had seen him last, his face ashen, the sound of his ragged breath mixing with his mother's quiet sobs. Quickening his step, he tried to focus on what he would say to Vince and as he rounded a corner, Maya appeared before him. Startled, he took a step back, staring at her without a word. She seemed more beautiful than ever. Before he had a chance to speak, Basil stepped beside her.

Is this Ginger's old boyfriend I see in front of me? Yes, it must be. Are you following me, Noll Spencer?

I'd say you're following me, Basil, first to Ginger and then to Maya.

I follow no one. I play second fiddle to no one.

You mean you play the field.

It is true I know the pleasure of women, something of which you have no appreciation. I have Maya because I know this.

Don't talk about me like I'm not here, Basil.

Listen to him, Maya. He thinks he owns you.

Just ignore him, Noll.

He'll only get worse, Maya. I've seen it before.

You are only jealous of what I have and you do not have.

Keep talking about her that way and I'll give you something I *do* have.

Noll, stop it! Basil, go wait for me in Felix's room.

-Basil disappeared around the corner.

Have you seen Felix?

I just left him.

I'm glad you came, Noll.

I got here as soon as I could.

I'm so angry at what's happened to him. How can people be so cruel?

I don't know but I'm going to make sure it doesn't happen again.

How are you going to do that?

Never mind. Are you really going to marry to Basil?

Felix told you about the wedding?

He mentioned it.

With a disgusted tone, no doubt.

I didn't mind.

You'll be there won't you?

I might do something I'd regret.

Don't be angry with me, Noll.

I need to get moving.

We can still be friends, can't we?

I wouldn't know how, Maya.

244

The street outside the house Vince shared with two other students was empty as Noll pulled his jeep to the curb. He figured if Vince was there he would likely be alone. Fronted by a narrow screened porch, the off-white frame house had the dingy look of a poorly maintained rental. Overgrown shrubs crowded the doorway. Noll took a breath before rapping the door with his fist. A moment later the door opened to a grinning Vince. He stepped onto the porch.

The working man has come to pay me a visit. Where's your blue shirt, Noll?

I'm off work today, Vince.

Then where's Ginger? If you're off work you should be hanging out with her.

Ginger and I split up a long time back.

Oh right, I did hear about that. You left her for some Mexican chica is what I heard.

Maya's not Mexican, not that it would matter to you.

You've been spending too much time with those ditch diggers if you don't think it matters. Besides, all those bean-eaters look alike to me.

How did you get to be so ignorant, Vince?

Why are you here, Noll?

You remember Maya's brother, the one you taunted at the party?

-Vince took a step back.

Why are you bringing him up?

His name is Felix and he was assaulted the night before last. He's in the hospital, Vince. You and your friends put him there.

Why would you think I had anything to do with something like that?

He recognized you, Vince. All white people don't look alike to him.

Why do you care, Noll? He's just a little fag.

245

-Before Noll realized what he had done, he had Vince against the wall, his hand around his throat.

He's a better man than you'll ever be, you bastard.

Noll, I didn't touch him. I swear I didn't. If I'd known what they were going to do I never would've gone along.

Who were they, Vince? I want names.

Noll, you're choking me. I'd never seen them before last night.

Don't lie to me, Vince.

I'm telling the truth. I swear it.

Tell me what happened.

A few people were sitting at the bar and these three guys started buying everyone drinks. They said they were from out of town and seemed friendly enough, even to him.

You mean Felix?

They were especially friendly to him. I was thinking about leaving when they invited us to a party. They invited Felix too. I was surprised they'd invite a…him when they knew he was…you know.

How did they know he was gay?

How would I know?

You told them, didn't you?

I didn't mean anything by it, Noll. I was only funning around.

You mean making fun of.

So you and Felix left with them.

They turned down an alley so I followed along thinking it was a shortcut to the party. The next thing I knew they had him on the ground, kicking him.

You mean they had Felix down, Vince. He's a real person and he has a name. Say it Vince, say his name.

They had Felix on the ground. The sound was sickening. I thought they were going to kill him so I ran the other way.

That was brave of you, Vince. He could've died in that alley.

I was scared, Noll. I didn't know what to do. You've got to believe me.

-Noll released his grip, stepping back.

If you ever see them again you'll tell me right away.

I will, Noll.

Give me your word.

I swear I'll call you immediately. I promise.

The narrow blacktop stretched before him, rimmed with Live oaks, the sky above clear, crystalline, the air swirling about him scented with smoke. Between the trees, blond grasses of early fall vibrated before a steady breeze that scattered leaves along the roadway in diagonal paths. Noll studied the scene through his windshield, crisp, well-defined, carrying a surprising clarity, as if a long-familiar haze had lifted to show the world as it is, detailed, intact, unadulterated by prejudice or expectation. He again thought of Maya, letting the dull ache of losing her move through him as it truly felt. The sadness lingered for a moment before passing into the broad light of afternoon.

All at once the trees fell away, the scene opening to a broad horizon, featureless, level, the reaching tips of salt grass and sea oats moving before the wind in rippled strokes. Behind him, scrub oaks bent by the constant breeze seemed frozen in the act of falling. Pink granite riprap marking the ship channel appeared to his left, the line of massive blocks stretching into the Gulf before disappearing into a cloud of sea spray. A dense bank of fog hovered beyond, thick, impenetrable. Noll cut the engine, stepping onto the damp sand and climbing the rose-hued stones that edged the channel, salt air settling on the back of his tongue, sharp, alive, a furtive breeze pulling at his shirt.

Fingers of fog streamed along the channel's far side, spilling over the opposite jetty and filling the space between with surprising speed. A moment later, the

247

emerald green of the channel vanished behind a dense cloud that raced before him in shades of white, undulating, curtain-like. He had never before seen fog move in such a way. A tugboat's deep rumble echoed along the stonework before fading, the passing ship near but unseen. Foghorns sounded through the thick air, muted, plaintive, like one lover calling for the other.

Thinking of Maya, he pulled his collar against the chill and studied the strange beauty around him, wishing that she stood beside him, that he could share it with her. How he could have let her go? He knew the answer. Shaking his head at his own folly he turned to leave, his part in losing her all too clear, his silence, his neglect, his eyes no longer blinded by pride.

Twenty-eight

Wisps of fog hid among mangroves, clinging to marsh grass and casting oak mott in washed out shades of gray and green, the main bank still hovering offshore, opaque, wall-like, reminding him of the past week as he rounded the line of trees separating Eugie's house from the road. Sunlight slanting through the trees lined the lawn in diagonal streaks, glinting off wet patches of grass in a splatters of gold. Sitting on the porch steps with a cup of coffee cradled in her palm, his mother studied him, her look expectant as he stepped from the jeep and made his way toward the house. Pausing, he again surveyed the inlet, the water broken, the sky now clear before a quickening breeze. Taking a deep breath, he turned to face her.

You have something to tell me, don't you?

I've sold the house, Noll.

We don't have a house. It burned.

You're right. I've sold the lot.

That's a big decision, mom. Are you sure you want to sell it?

It's done. I signed the papers yesterday.

What about Gannie's cabin?

The new owners are bulldozing everything. They're building one of those huge houses that cover the entire property.

Is this is a good idea, mom? You know how you can get with your big ideas.

It's time you got a place of your own, Noll. You've lived with your mother for too long.

What will you do? Where will you live?

The new owners have plenty of money so I got a good price.

But you still need a place to live unless you're planning to stay here.

Eugie has been so good to us but an artist needs her solitude. Besides, I have a new plan.

I don't like the sound of that. We both remember what happened when you thought you'd be the next great chef. You haven't already spent the money from the house, have you?

Noll, you're too young to be such a worrier. Let me tell you about it before you get yourself all worked up.

What new thing have you gotten into, then? How much will it cost?

That's just the point. It won't cost anything. In fact, I'll get paid.

You got a job?

No, I got a full scholarship to attend art school in Santa Fe.

You got a scholarship?

The workshop instructor I met last month recommended me but I think Eugie had something to do with it. She wouldn't say so but I know she made some calls. I like to think I earned my way in.

But would the school give you a scholarship if they didn't think you had talent?

I suppose not. They're even giving me a place to live.

What will Gannie do?

That's the best part. She's coming too. She says she's always wanted to see New Mexico, and we can share expenses.

It's a surprise but I'm glad for you both.

I told you I felt something had changed when we lost the house and now I feel it even stronger. Things can get better, Noll. You have to believe they can.

I'd like to believe it.

Will you be alright? Will you be able to find a place and get along without us here?

I'll figure something out.

And you still have a job?

I'd be back there already but the doctor said Hen needs a few more days of rest so I've decided to wait and return when he does.

What about your girlfriend, Maya is it? She was here with a Frenchman but I wasn't sure if they were friends or something more. I like her, Noll. Are you two still dating?

They're getting married, mom.

She's going to marry that guy? I like her but he got on my nerves.

That's the plan.

Oh Noll, I'm sorry. What happened? Did she dump you for him?

No, I was the problem.

-A car rounded the line of trees, coming to a stop next to the jeep before Adela climbed out.

Noll, I'm glad you're here. I've come to borrow some art supplies from Eugie but I need to talk to you.

You're an artist too?

Well, sort of. I had a stained glass business back in Mexico and now I have some work here thanks to Cyrus.

How do you know Cyrus?

He helped Humberto find an apartment near the Last Chance Bar so he could walk to work. That's how we met. A church he's doing some sculpture for has asked me to repair a few windows, and an old mansion that's now a museum has asked for a bid to replace a large stained glass panel. A private chapel has also contacted me, all thanks to Cyrus. I need to provide a sketch of a chapel window so I asked Eugie if I could borrow some supplies until I get paid.

You said you needed to talk to me?

I want to ask a favor.

What is it?

I want you to take Maya's passport to her. I borrowed it to make a quick run across the border. I lost mine when I had to leave home and we look so alike they never know the difference. Will you take it? I know where she is.

I'm the last person she wants to see. I wasn't exactly friendly toward Basil the last time I saw her.

But Noll, that's the real reason I want you to go. You've got to talk her out of marrying him. It's all wrong. He's all wrong. I don't know why she can't see that.

Why would she listen to me?

She trusts you, Noll.

She has a funny way of showing it.

Now you have to trust me. I'm her sister, remember? Please go talk to her.

I'll talk but I can't promise she'll listen. Where is she?

She's cooking dinner for Hen.

She's doing what?

She said he's so thin it worries her so she wants to be sure he's eating right. A little Mexican home cooking should do the trick. You can find her there. You'd better leave right away. Remember, she listens to you.

Don't get your hopes up, Adela.

Noll pulled to the curb outside Hen's small house and cut the engine, trying to imagine what he might say to Maya or if she would even listen. A yellow glow from inside the house illuminated the front windows, casting the lawn into dim quadrangles of light and dark, the porch swing creaking in the evening breeze. He walked up the narrow drive and on past the porch, hoping to catch a glimpse of Maya in the kitchen window but finding Hen instead leaning over the sink, his voice a dull rumble through the windowpane. Noll ambled up the porch steps, pushing through the door without bothering to knock, stopping in the kitchen doorway. Hen looked up, wiping his hands on a threadbare dishtowel.

Looky here, Maya, we got ourselves some company. Come on in here, boy.

You must be feeling better, Hen. I could hear you talking even before I opened the door.

Anytime I got a pretty lady cooking dinner for me I got to be feeling good. You remember Maya, don't you?

You know I do, Hen.

Then act like it and be friendly while I go get some beers from the garage cooler.

-Hen disappeared out the back door.

Hello, Noll. I'm glad to see you.

I'm surprised to hear it.

Why would you be surprised?

I thought you'd still be angry about the way I treated Basil. I wondered about it all the way over here.

You knew I'd be here?

Adela told me. She asked me to bring you your passport.

Is that the only reason you're here?

Not exactly.

What then?

I've been thinking about you. I hoped I'd see you so we could talk.

So, you came here because you wanted to talk to me?

Sort of.

Out with it Noll, why are you here?

I *have* wanted to see you, to talk to you. But the truth is I'm here because Adela asked me to.

Why'd she do that?

She wants me to talk you out of getting married.

She wants what?

She thinks you're making a mistake.

Adela should mind her own business. I'm more interested in what you think, Noll.

About what?

I want to know about everything, Noll, about how you are, about what's on your mind but especially about me getting married.

You want to know what I think about that?

Don't you know?

Well, sure I do but I don't know if I should say.

Why not, are you afraid to speak your mind to me?

No, but I don't see that it's my business.

I think you're afraid to tell me, Noll. In fact, I think you're afraid of me.

That's absurd.

Then tell me what you think.

I'll tell you but you won't like it.

Then you think I'm making a mistake?

I don't trust him.

You barely know Basil.

I've seen enough.

How can you tell if he can be trusted when you've spent so little time around him?

I don't know, I can just tell.

So you can just tell? I think you're jealous.

You asked what I thought.

Fine, so now I know.

Fine.

Is that all you think?

What do you mean?

You look like you have something else you want to say. Well, do you?

Are you sure he's right for you, Maya?

I don't want to talk about him anymore!

Alright, I'll stop! Go ahead and get married. Make all the mistakes you want, it's your life. I'll stay out of it if that's what you want.

Don't be angry, Noll. I really want to hear what you think.

You don't sound like it.

But I do. I want to know how you are, what you like and don't like, what you dream of. Does that sound so hard?

You make it sound like I've never talked to you, Maya.

Noll, you're like a mirror. You only give me what I already know. I see something there but I can never get past the surface. Why is it so difficult for you to say what you feel?

I don't know. Am I that hard to be around?

No, but can't you try?

I do try but I can't ever seem to say the right thing. And I'm never sure if you'll like or hate what I have to say.

Don't you know that I won't judge you?

I don't know why it should matter now that you're getting married.

But it does matter, Noll.

Does it?

I wish I could...

-Hen pushed through the back door.

I apologize for being away so long but I had some young men to deal with. Basil is out back and wants to talk to you, Maya.

He's here?

Ranse found him peeking through the kitchen window like some pervert. Ranse is no better, hiding out like some fugitive. I believe he would've roughed Basil up if I hadn't walked out right then. Maya, you better go talk to him.

What was Ranse doing out there, Hen?

That boy got himself in trouble again just like I knew he would, Noll. He said he's been hiding out in my garage but he wouldn't tell me why. All I got out of him was that his mama spotted Vaditch outside the house again. Princella chased him off with that rifle of hers but I got to believe Vaditch left when he decided Ranse was not at home.

255

Vaditch said if he had to come back there would be trouble for Ranse.

I remember, son. Maya, I told Basil he's got to leave so you best go talk to him. If we wait too long Ranse might get after him again.

Noll, I wish…I wanted to say…oh, I can't talk now. I have to see to Basil.

-Maya vanished through the door.

What's wrong with you, boy? You got that down and out look if I've ever seen it. You argue with Maya?

Not really.

But it's about her. I can see it in your eyes. Go ahead and say what it is.

I don't want to talk about it. I should go.

You don't like that she's going to marry that Frenchman?

Of course I don't.

Well, I don't like the look of him. Can't trust a man that follows his girl around peeping in windows and such, can't trust him at all.

I told her but it didn't do any good.

Then tell her again.

I've said what I could, Hen. Besides, the wedding is in less than a week.

You might could still talk to her, son.

I know you mean well but I'm too late.

Are you sure about that?

I'm sure.

Well, she's got to live her life the way she sees fit. But so do you, Noll. Don't let what's happened between you and her keep you down.

I won't, Hen.

You got pick yourself up, get it right.

I'll try.

You got to live each day, boy. You hear what Hen is telling you?

I hear you.

256

Now that I know I don't have the cancer, I aim to do that. I believe I just might live to be a hundred. How do you like that?

Aren't you already a hundred?

Looky here, now a man deserves respect in his own house. But I'll let that pass so you can stay for dinner.

I'd better go, Hen. Before I do, I have a favor to ask.

You go ahead and ask away.

My mother sold the house so I don't have a place to live anymore. Can I stay here for a little while, just until I find a place?

You got to know you can, Noll. There's plenty of room in this old house.

I appreciate it, Hen.

You sure you don't want to stay for dinner, son?

I should go.

I understand. You got to get on with your life. Besides, I don't mind that pretty woman all to myself.

Twenty-nine

A fine mist drifted through blackened trees, their bare branches stretching against a sky without depth or feature, infinite, colorless as Noll drove the familiar street to Hen's house, his thoughts again turning to Maya. He searched their last conversation for a sign, a word, telltale inflection in her voice, any reason for hope though knowing well his self-deception, her wedding only days away. Before him leaves took flight in the gusting wind, skittering across the road before vanishing onto already-covered lawns. The house came into view, Hen waiting at the porch rail, upright, rigid. Noll knew something was wrong even before he pulled to the curb and climbed out of the jeep. Hen hobbled down the stairs.

> Get back in the jeep. We got to leave right away.
> What is it?
> Eugie's had a heart attack. She's asking for you.
> How bad is she?
> I don't know for sure but it doesn't sound good.

The sky had faded to charcoal gray, flat and without contrast except where circles of light marked an offshore oilrig lurking below the low-hung clouds. Nearby trees stood in delicate silhouette against the silver bay like black filigree. As Eugie's house came into view, a figure stepped through the doorway and Hen hopped out of the jeep, making his way across the lawn and up the porch steps. Noll hurried after him.

> Hello, Doctor Learner.
> Hen, I'm glad to see you doing so well. I wish it could be under better circumstances.
> How is she doctor?
> Please call me Sam, both of you. She's had a heart attack Noll, her third.

258

Did you say third? You mean she's had three heart attacks? She never said a thing about it. Does she need surgery?

I'm sorry, Noll but even if she would allow it surgery is not an option in her condition, especially at her age. I'm afraid it's only a matter of time. The walls of her heart are barely holding together.

There's nothing you can do?

I'll make sure she's comfortable but what's more important is that you're here with her. She's awake and she's been asking for you. That's why I called Hen.

-Hen placed a hand on Noll's shoulder.

Looky here Noll, I'll follow along but you tell me if you want me to leave. I'll understand.

-Noll walked the familiar hall, the wooden floor creaking beneath his feet as he passed through the bedroom doorway. Hen moved along the wall behind him. In the dim light Noll could just make out Eugie's form covered in blankets, her face drawn, ashen, white hair spreading across the pillow like a feathered fan. Her ragged breathing seemed to fill the room. Stepping to the bedside he bent forward, taking her hand in his. Her eyes flickered then opened and she studied him for a moment before speaking, her voice a near whisper.

Hen, are you here?

I'm here, Eugie.

Thank you for bringing him. Nobody else knows, do they?

Nobody I know of.

Good. Now listen to me, Noll. I have something to say and it's important you hear it.

I'm listening, Eugie.

I lied to you and I'm sorry for it.

What do you mean?

I've been sick for a long time and didn't tell you. I didn't want you or anyone else feeling sorry for me. I can't tolerate pity. Can you understand that?

259

I don't like being pitied either.

I thought that's what you'd say. We're alike in so many ways, Noll. Have you talked to Sam?

She was waiting for us on the porch.

Remember your promise, Noll. Make sure they don't put me on some machine. Sam's my friend but she's also a doctor and may feel obliged to do something I wouldn't want. I'm counting on you.

I understand, Eugie.

There's something even more important I need to tell you. See that envelope over there? You put that in your pocket and keep it safe.

What is it?

It's a deed of ownership for this house and all my property on the inlet. I've already signed it over to you. The envelope has everything you'll need.

But Eugie, this is your house. I can't take it from you.

Noll, listen to me. I've given you the property because I know you appreciate the magic of this place. I want to know someone I trust will take care of it.

I'll do whatever you want, Eugie.

Then that's what I want.

I wish I could do something for you.

You already have, Noll. You gave me a boost when I most needed one. You have to promise me one more thing.

What is it?

Find someone who listens to you Noll, someone who wants to know your dreams, your disappointments, someone who accepts you as you are. Now I won't preach anymore. Oh, there's something I almost forgot. I want my ashes buried under the old oak out front. Cyrus has carved a small stone to mark the spot. Can you make sure that happens?

I can do that, Eugie.

And stay with me, Noll. Stay with me for awhile, will you?

That's why I'm here, Eugie.

-She settled back into the pillow, her eyes closed, her breathing labored but easier now. Noll moved a chair between the bed and the window and sat, listening to the distant call of an owl mix with the muted rumble of Hen's voice. Charcoal studies from Eugie's youth peppered the adjacent walls, some showing black workers picking cotton, their heads wrapped in flowered cloths, their oversized hands scarred by rough work, their hard labor made somehow beautiful. He wondered for a moment what Hen would think and decided he would appreciate the honesty and beauty of the work.

-He tried to imagine the house without Eugie but the thought hovered just out of reach, the pain of her coming loss closing over him like a veil. Her solid presence in his life, a seeming certainty until then, suddenly felt fragile, about to fade at any moment. A breeze rustled the lace curtain next to him, lifting the corner of an unfinished drawing as if considering its merit before passing through the room and on.

Noll stood on the porch as the last of the guests made their way out the door and down the steps. Appearing in the doorway, nearly filling the space, Cyrus handed him a half-filled glass before raising his own. Farley and the other rugby players waited in the yard, half-drunk and stumbling through an Irish ballad. Cyrus wiped his red eyes with the back of his hand, leaning toward Noll.

Eugie was like the mother to me, to us many, Noll. This you should know. I hope the marker is good enough. It is the finest marble I find.

The marker is beautiful and I'm sure she would approve.

She was a fine woman, Noll. I weep to see her go.

261

Thanks for saying so, Cyrus.

We drink a toast to Eugie.

-Just as they raised their glasses, Felix stepped through the door.

Cyrus! Noll! Wait for me. Are we drinking a toast?

We drink a toast to our Eugie. You join us, Felix.

Okay, Cyrus. I knew her only by what I've been told but she sounds like a wonderful person. My sisters sure thought so. I know you'll miss her, Noll.

I already do, Felix. It's a toast to Eugie, then.

-They drained their glasses and Cyrus turned toward the stairs.

Cyrus, wait for me. Cyrus is my new friend, Noll. He's been telling me all about Eugie cheering for the team. I think I may just have to take up where she left off. He and the team think it's a grand idea.

I can't imagine any better, Felix. You'll do Eugie proud.

Oh Noll, you think so?

I do.

I'm off with the team then. Until next time, Noll.

Dusk spread across the eastern horizon as Noll sat on the porch stairs, looking across the broad lawn to where Eugie's marker glowed in the fading light like a tiny island in a sea of grass. Beyond, sunset-tinged clouds drifted above the water, their blurred shapes spreading across the bay in hues of orange and purple. In the nearby shallows a heron stood motionless, poised, waiting for an unsuspecting shad to pass within reach while a line of pelicans appeared in the distance, floating inches above the inlet before disappearing around the point. He again thought of Eugie and the way she could find magic in just this sort of evening. He half-expected to hear her walk through the door and remark on the scene. A moment later Hen stepped onto the porch, collapsing next to him.

262

I found us some Wild Turkey hidden in the cabinet above the refrigerator. I believe Eugie left it there just for me.

Is that so?

Sure enough is.

It sounds to me like you've had enough.

Looky here, the problem is not that Hen has had too much.

What is the problem then?

The problem is that Noll hasn't had enough, not near enough.

I haven't had enough then? Is that it?

Tell Hen he's got to know the truth.

Hen knows I could use a drink.

See what I'm saying Eugie? This boy can't see the truth until it slaps him in the face.

Who are you talking to?

You don't think Eugie is right here with us? I can feel her.

Hen, we buried her today.

It makes me no never mind about that, she's here and I feel her sure as I see you sitting right next to me.

How many of me do you see?

You know I'm right, Noll. Your mind always got to be working, fretting over this, worrying about that so you miss most everything that matters, most everything true.

I know what matters.

But you got to just let yourself live, Noll. Stop worrying and make your mistakes. Then you'll find out the man you're meant to be.

I wish I understood what you're going on about.

If you do what I say you'll see Eugie's here with you, and a finer woman you'll never know. You carry her with you each and every day.

I carry her memory.

Same thing. What would she say right now?

263

She'd tell me to appreciate the sunset, wind rustling the trees, salt air off the inlet. Then she'd tell me to have a drink.

That's what I'm talking about.

Thirty

His mind still foggy from the whisky, Noll stepped onto the porch and squinted into a morning sky with no hint of dawn. Gray clouds raced above the inlet in ragged lines. Beyond the bay a wall-like line of storms towered over the outer island, its features nearly lost behind a wind-whipped haze. Nearby palm trees swayed to and fro at random.

At the far end of the porch Hen slumped in a rope hammock, snoring into the wall as Noll stepped to the rail and set down his coffee. A twig snapped behind him and he turned, spotting Ranse crouched near the house, the top of his head poking just above the edge of the porch. Noll called to him in a whisper.

Ranse, what are you doing here?

I'm not here, Noll. Don't be talking to me.

But I can see you.

Just act like I'm not here.

But you are here.

Just do what I say, Noll.

I will if you'll tell me why you're here.

Who is that yelling?

I'm not yelling, Hen I'm talking to Ranse.

Where's Ranse? I don't see him.

He's hiding over there. Come on out Ranse.

I can't come out, Noll. Just do what I say and act like you don't see me.

Ranse, where are you? Looky here, Ranse what's got into you?

Quit calling my name, Hen. Can't you see I'm trying to hide?

What no good are you up to, boy? You best come on and tell it to me now.

What if he sees me?

Who're you talking about, Ranse? Stop your whispering and come on up here.

-Ranse crept around the porch and up the stairs, looking one way and then the other.

I'm here on business, Hen. You got to let me take care of my business.

You're on business? What kind of business?

I can't say.

Can't say or won't say?

Just let me get it done with, Hen and I'll leave.

Why here and not someplace else?

I saw when I came down here before this was a good place to meet up with a boat. I'm about to meet up with a boat right down there on that inlet. Since you know these folks I figured it'd be alright.

You figured wrong, Ranse. You got no business bringing your shady dealings here.

How do you know they're shady?

Tell me they're not then.

I don't exactly know what business it is.

How so, Ranse?

I just bring a big canvas bag someplace and somebody picks it up, or they bring a bag and I take it.

I heard that before. You got yourself mixed up in the drug trade again.

No, Hen I swear it.

How do you know?

I looked in a bag and all I found was money, a lot of money. The bags are all the same. They're filled with money but that's all.

Still sounds shady to me.

I need the work, Hen. What else am I going to do? Besides, how do you know this business is against the law? It could be for something good.

Who're you hiding from, then?

Mama says that Russian is back hanging around the house.

You mean Vaditch?

That's him.

What'd you do to cross him, Ranse?

He's got no reason to come after me. It must be a mistake, like the last time.

All that money in your hands and you don't take a dime of it?

Listen Hen, I got to go now. You just let me do my business and you won't see me again.

That's right. You don't come back here, Ranse. You hear what I'm saying to you? You go live with your aunt in Detroit like your mama told you to. She said they'll take you in until you get settled. You can start a new life there Ranse, a clean life away from all this bad you got yourself into.

I wish I could, Hen but…what's that sound? Somebody's coming.

-Ranse disappeared through the door just as a black sedan rounded the trees and pulled to a stop. Vaditch climbed out and surveyed the area before walking to the foot of the stairs.

We meet again, gentleman. I find this scene somewhat reminiscent of our first meeting. I am down here on the lawn and you are up there on the veranda.

What do you want, Vaditch?

The reason for my visit also resembles the first, Noll Spencer. I am again looking for Mr. Ranse Jenkins.

You know he lives in town. Why look here?

I have reason to believe he has come to this place on business.

Well, you can find someplace else to look. This is private property.

I am aware that you are now the owner and the reason for it. Accept my condolences, if you will.

I don't want anything except you to leave.

You'll pardon me if I just have a look around first. I seem to have misplaced my watch, a family heirloom that is irreplaceable. Surely you wouldn't begrudge my looking for it?

How could you have lost it when you just got here?

Recall that I came once before but you were not here so I found you at the café by the ferry landing. I must have lost it then. I won't take long.

-He turned, walking at a brisk pace past the oak before vanishing behind a thick wall of undergrowth. Noll followed Hen through the door and from room to room looking for Ranse, ending up in Eugie's bedroom.

I hope Ranse got smart and headed for Detroit. We best go back out on the porch to keep an eye out for Vaditch.

I'm going to get some insurance first, Hen.

-Noll opened the dresser drawer, pulling out Eugie's pistol.

You sure you want to carry that big gun around? They say don't carry a gun unless you mean to use it.

I'm sure.

Then at least put it under your shirt.

-They stepped through the door and onto the porch just as the pop of a handgun echoed across the inlet, followed by two more in close succession. Hen rushed down the steps without a word. Noll hurried after him, plunging into the underbrush beyond the oak, taking the shortest possible route before bursting onto the small beach where Eugie kept the johnboat. An empty shoreline greeted them.

We got too many footprints to make any sense of it.

Except that the boat is gone.

I hope Ranse took it and got clean away. I promised Lavonia to protect the boy but when I heard that gun I was sure I failed her.

There's no sign he got hurt.

We best get back to the house in case he shows up. Vaditch may still be around.

-As they climbed the porch stairs, footsteps sounded behind them. Noll pulled the gun from his coat and turned to where Vaditch stood in the middle of the lawn, a wry look on his face, a cigar between his teeth.

Your friend Mr. Jenkins is quite clever.

You mean he got away?

Not only did he escape, Mr. Spencer but he had his business partners arrange an ambush for me. As you can see by my presence here, they were less than successful.

Those were the shots we heard?

There were two men in a boat.

But looky here Vaditch, how do you know Ranse got away?

Notice that my car is missing, Mr. Feathers.

Ha! How do you like that, Noll? That's one bad habit I'm glad Ranse learned.

So, it's time for you to go, Vaditch.

My grandmother lived in a home like this, Mr. Spencer. May I call you Noll? It was at the edge of a small cove on the Baltic. On a clear day you could see Finland.

Why are you still here, Vaditch?

My father would bring me from our home in the city and we would spend a week every summer fishing, picking wild raspberries and sailing down the coast almost to Estonia.

What do you want?

Did you come here with your father, Noll?

No, never. I'll say it again. What do you want?

You must learn patience, Noll. With patience comes understanding.

What does my father have to do with anything?

Do you know what happened to him?

What? Why bring that up again?

Do you, Noll?

Of course I do. He was shot and killed. The killer was never caught.

But do you know the circumstances? Do you know that he died protecting his family?

What are you saying?

He believed you and your mother were in danger.

How can you know anything about what happened that day?

I was there.

You were there when he died? You killed my father?

I only said I was there. I saw what happened. I heard what he said.

Tell me.

That big pistol must be heavy. You can lower it, you know.

If I get tired it might go off so you'd better hurry. Tell me what happened, Vaditch.

The object was only to warn him, not to harm him. You see, your father had made some unfortunate decisions and involved himself in a dangerous business.

You mean he was doing business with the cartels?

Something like that. As I said, he believed you and your mother were in danger. He felt he must protect you. In the midst of our conversation he raised his gun, a very unfortunate action.

You did kill him.

Your father was young and impatient and he made a mistake, a mistake both unfortunate and unnecessary.

You should be in jail.

Perhaps, but I am about to leave this country for good.

Not if I stop you first.

Go ahead and pull the trigger, Noll. You would spare me the hellish life that awaits me across the border.

I should turn you over to the police.

I regret what happened to your father, Noll. I lost my father when I was young also. That's why I came here

270

and killed the men who had your girlfriend, to do what I could for him, for you. Because of that I must disappear.

Nothing you can do will change what happened to him.

That is an unfortunate truth.

Why did you tell me?

I'm going to leave now.

How? You have no car.

You might say I have a boat waiting.

Why should I let you go?

Shoot me if you like. You will do me a favor.

Don't listen to him, Noll. You're a better man than him and his kind.

I could do it Hen, I know I could.

Sure you could, son but then you'd be no better than him. You're a good man, Noll. Just let him go on.

-Vaditch turned and started toward the inlet. Lifting the big pistol with both hands, Noll followed him over the shaking barrel, feeling the worn grip, the trigger smooth beneath his finger, all hesitation gone. Then Hen's gnarled fingers came to rest on his shoulder, a light touch, almost imperceptible, and Noll lowered the pistol, setting it on the porch rail, watching Vaditch as he disappeared into the thicket.

Thirty-one

The inlet stood still, inert, mercurial, paused as if waiting for the inevitable change in wind, sky, the overdue arrival of fall. Evening shadows stretched toward the bay, fracturing the lawn into odd shapes, indiscriminant, chaotic. He wondered about Hen's abrupt departure the day before, after a call from Lavonia had rousted him from an afternoon nap. He was due to return to work in the morning so he guessed he would hear about it then. A moment later, the creaking rumble of Hen's truck echoed through the thicket before it rounded the tree line and pulled up to the house. Hen cut the engine and climbed out, a troubled look on his face. He ambled up the walkway, climbing the stairs and sitting next to Noll without a word.

You don't look so good. Is Lavonia alright? Was there news, something about Ranse?

The news on Ranse is good. He made it up to his aunt's place in Detroit just like we figured. If he keeps his head on straight he just might be alright.

Then is there something else? Did something bad happen?

I wouldn't say it's bad, exactly. In fact it's good for the most part.

Well, why don't you say what it is?

What I have to say isn't easy for me, son. I've been thinking all the way down here about how I'm going to tell you but I still can't get it right in my head.

Now you've got me worried, Hen. You're not sick again, are you?

No, the doctor said I'm healthy as a horse. I do believe I'm going to take after my great granny and live to a hundred and seven.

Then what is it? What's so hard to say?

I might as well just be out with it. I'm going away, Noll.

272

You're what?

Lavonia asked me to go to California with her.

You're going on vacation, now of all times?

We're going there to live.

You and Lavonia are getting married?

Oh, we might get around to it sooner or later but we're going to take our time, see how it goes. This is a big step for both of us.

But why go to California, Hen? Can't you stay here to do that?

Her step-father passed on, left her a house and avocado orchard. You'd be surprised what you can make dealing in avocados. The orchard will give us a nice retirement.

You're going to California to be a farmer?

Farming runs in our family, Noll. Don't you remember?

But Hen, I can't imagine you not being here.

I know this is big news for you, son. That's why I didn't know how to tell you. But Lavonia asked me to go with her. Think what that means, Noll. After all that's happened, she wants me to be with her.

Big news is an understatement.

You going to be alright?

I'm just surprised, is all.

She surprised me too, Noll. Lavonia and me, we're going to start a new life for ourselves. I never thought I'd see the day. Can you see what it means to me, son?

What's wrong with me? Of course I can see it, Hen. I'm glad for you.

You like avocados, don't you?

I'm not sure.

I'll send you a box soon as we pick the first batch. Then you can see.

You know how to farm avocados?

I got to study up some but when I was your age I had a truck farm outside of town. It'll come back to me. I'll let you know how it goes.

You won't forget about me, then?

-Hen reached out, touching Noll's shoulder, his hand weightless, ethereal.

Looky here Noll, I have to go now. But you and me, we got us a connection no distance can break. You got to remember that.

I'll remember, Hen. I won't ever forget.

***

Noll hurried into the chapel, finding a seat in the back row a moment before the wedding party moved into place. Azure sunlight streamed through the open windows as if the sky itself had descended to earth, spilling onto the pews and filling the narrow aisle where Maya stood, her hair swirling about her face in the gusting breeze, the silken strands dark against the white of her gown. The music stopped and to his surprise she turned to face him, a half-formed question on her lips, her eyebrows raised in a wordless accusation, the meaning all too clear. Why did he let her go? Why didn't he speak when he had the chance?

A tear drifted down her cheek in a crooked line and he looked away, his shame so mixed with anger he feared what he might do. A moment later a panicked murmur passed through the crowd. He looked again up to see Maya sway one way then the other before collapsing to the red carpet. He jumped into the aisle, fighting his way through the on-lookers, breaking past them and on to the altar. He reached out to touch her. She flinched and then turned to face him but instead of Maya he found Ginger, a sneer on her lips. He awoke in a sweat.

After dressing he made his way to the kitchen, filling the kettle and placing it on the stove, trying to rid his mind of the dream. Looking around the room, he thought through all that had happened in the past weeks, finding it hard to believe Eugie was gone, the house now his. After a few days back at work, it had almost seemed as if nothing had changed except for Hen's absence. Yet he could feel there was no returning to the life he'd once known. The future seemed a haze of possibility, all conflicting, all uncertain. His thoughts again turned to Maya. For a moment he let himself imagine her in the white gown, standing in the aisle, a sight he would never see outside his private thoughts. Feeling restless, he finished making coffee, poured a cup and wandered toward the front of the house.

The inlet sparkled as he stepped through the door and sat, trying to clear his thoughts, breathing in the warm air, filling his lungs, tasting the sea salt as it settled on the back of his tongue, organic, alive. Leaves falling from the massive oak fronting the house bounced through the black branches in dry clicks, flickering as they drifted toward the porch. A flock of ducks circled overhead, splashing to a stop in the shallows just as Maya's car rounded the tree line. She cut the engine, watching him through the window for a moment and then climbing out, her dark hair swirling in the breeze as it had in his dream, her face beautiful but somehow sad. He shook off a shiver and tried to smile.

Don't you have a wedding to go to?
I called it off.
You're not getting married?
I thought you'd have heard by now.
I've had a lot going on.
I know you have, Noll. I was so sad to hear about Eugie. I'm sorry I missed the funeral. She was such a wonderful person and did so much for us. Adela is just heartsick she wasn't here but we were in Mexico trying to find some of her belongings.
What happened?

275

We were detained at the border because she had used my passport. It took forever to sort out.

I meant why aren't you getting married?

Oh, that. I caught Basil in bed with your girlfriend.

You mean Ginger? She's not my girlfriend.

That's good because she moved to France with Basil.

Why am I not surprised?

Oh Noll, you were right about him all along. I feel so foolish, not to mention humiliated. There's no embarrassment like calling off a wedding at the last minute.

Sounds like a bad dream.

The worst of it is having everyone mad at me. They think it's my fault, like if I'd been a better fiancé none of this would've happened.

I'm not mad at you.

I just feel like such a failure, Noll.

We all make mistakes, Maya.

I guess so.

Not necessarily a really big one like that.

You're not helping.

On the other hand if you're going to humiliate yourself why not go all out?

Stop, Noll.

Don't be too hard on yourself, Maya. It'll all fade into the past before you know it.

I wish it was that easy.

I can't say I'm sorry for what's happened. I never liked Basil. But I am sorry for the hurt he's caused you.

Are you, Noll?

You deserve better, Maya.

Still, it's a lonely place to be.

I know it is but you'll get through it.

Do you think so?

You're a strong woman, Maya. Everyone knows that.

Maybe, but I still get lonely. Be my friend Noll, will you? I could use one right now.

I never stopped being your friend.

Don't you wish we could turn back the clock to how it was before?

Part of me does wish for that. But I don't see how with all that's happened. The world feels different now.

You seem different, Noll.

I feel different.

I wonder if there's a place for me in your new world.

I could ask the same question. You've changed too, Maya.

I suppose you're right. But it's hard starting over.

I won't argue with that.

I don't know where to begin.

We'll figure it out together, then.

Will we, Noll? Can we figure it out together?

Come walk the inlet with me, Maya.

A warm breeze drifted in off the water. The sound of tiny waves collapsing along the shoreline in graceful, zipper-like lines, mixed with the hiss of wind through marsh grass now stiff and gone to seed. Maya's hair floated about her profile in silken cords. He walked a step behind, watching as she pulled errant strands across her face, tucking them behind her ear without thought or care.

At that moment Noll fully understood how hard it had been for her to come there on her own, no one else to act as a buffer, no way to avoid any hurt whether intended or not. On that day of all days she had come to see him. The thought stopped him where he stood, gripping him with a perplexing mixture of shame and gratitude. Realizing he had fallen behind, she turned and stepped toward him, searching his face as she drew near, reaching out and taking his hand, looking into his eyes as if for the first time.